TAYLOR & ROSE
Secret Agents

SPIES IN ST. PETERSBURG

Also by Katherine Woodfine

Peril in Paris

TAYLOR & ROSE
Secret Agents

KATHERINE WOODFINE

Illustrated by Karl James Mountford

EGMONT

EGMONT

We bring stories to life

First published in Great Britain 2019
by Egmont UK Limited
The Yellow Building, 1 Nicholas Road, London W11 4AN

Text copyright © 2019 Katherine Woodfine
Illustrations copyright © 2019 Karl James Mountford

978 1 4052 8705 0
67187/001

A CIP catalogue record for this title is available
from the British Library

Typeset by Avon DataSet Ltd, Bidford on Avon, Warwickshire
Printed and bound in Great Britain by the CPI Group

For Louise, of course

PART I

'Staying in one place is all very well – but there's nothing quite like the feeling of excitement I get when I see Papa bringing out the maps and railway timetables. Before I know it, he'll have our trunks fetched, and then he'll say: "Pack your things, Alice! We shall soon be on the move again!"'

– From the diary of Alice Grayson

THE DAILY PICTURE

DEATH OF RUSSIAN PREMIER

VIOLENT REVOLUTIONARY GROUP SUSPECTED

It was reported today that the Russian Premier, Pyotr Stolypin, has died in Kiev. Premier Stolypin was shot by an assassin at Kiev's Imperial Theatre several nights ago, during a performance attended by Tsar Nicholas II.

The assassin is believed to have been part of a violent revolutionary group, working to assassinate important Russian statesmen; there is speculation that the group had also planned to target the Tsar himself in their attack.

Over one hundred and fifty arrests have been made in Kiev following the shooting, and tensions look set to continue in the city with (continued p.5)

ON TOUR WITH THE CIRCUS OF MARVELS!

MADEMOISELLE FLEURETTE

INTERNATIONAL NEWS

Montreal bank robbers still at large - police have 'no leads' our Foreign Affairs reporter Mr R. Gleeson has the full story (p.19)

Tensions mount between Italy and Turkey (p.21)

In the first instalment of a spectacular new series, our reporter Miss R. Russell extends a cordial invitation to you to join her on tour with the enchanting 'Circus of Marvels'. Miss Russell will be accompanying the 'world's greatest show' as they commence a Grand Tour, travelling from Europe to Russia, Japan, and on to the USA. She will share incredible tales from behind-the-scenes in the thrilling world of the circus, starring the likes of Mademoiselle Fleurette 'Queen of the Air' and famous equestrian performers The Fabulous Fanshawes (continued p.7)

AERIAL TOUR FINALE

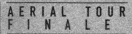

Champion pilot Charlton is guest star at Sir Chester Norton's London reception to celebrate the finale of the Grand Aerial Tour of Europe (p.3)

CHAPTER ONE

Mayfair, London, England

'Where will you be travelling this year, my dear?' asked the lady in pink satin ruffles. 'The Riviera, as usual?'

'Yes, and then to St Moritz for winter sports,' replied her friend in lace frills. 'What about you?'

'Oh, Charles is always so tiresome about wanting to attend shooting parties in the autumn,' sighed the lady in pink. 'Not at all my idea of fun! But I hope we shall go away in a month or two. I simply *long* for abroad!'

'London is so dull once the Season has ended,' agreed her companion, looking around the room with a disappointed air. 'Everything interesting seems to happen somewhere else.'

It was true that the summer Season, with its grand entertainments, was over. Yet this quieter autumn gathering was still magnificent by most people's standards. The long supper table was heaped with tempting delicacies, and silver bowls of fruit punch gleamed in the glittering light of the chandeliers. The ballroom was bathed in rich golden light, and outside the long windows, London was turning gold too. The leaves of the trees flamed yellow and orange, and a hundred little lights twinkled in the distance, as a soft blue twilight fell.

In the ballroom, a string quartet played an elegant waltz, and young ladies in white frocks danced gracefully with upright young gentlemen, whilst their mamas watched approvingly from the sidelines. At the edge of the dance floor, one of the sons of the house was being chivvied forward by his own mama.

'Good heavens, Rupert! What *is* the matter with you?' Lady Grenville pointed her fan in the direction of a young lady across the room. 'Look – there's Lady Cynthia, sitting all by herself! Can't you go and ask her in to supper with you?'

But Rupert shrugged her off. He had no interest in his mother's social gatherings, which he thought dull and old-fashioned. He didn't want to dance with the prim debutantes, or to chat with their earnest dancing partners. Most of all, he did *not* want to sit and have supper with the sneering Lady Cynthia, under the beady eye of her chaperone. Muttering something gruff, he strode off to the refreshment table, helping himself to another cup of punch before retreating to a corner where he stood alone, pulling at his too-tight collar.

From across the room, a girl stood and watched him.

4

Anyone who noticed her would probably think her just the same as the other young ladies present – a pretty girl of eighteen or so, who had no doubt made her 'debut' in society that summer. Yet a sharp-eyed observer might have noticed that there was something different about her. It was hard to pinpoint exactly what it was: perhaps her stylish white gown, perhaps her shining dark hair with the vivid spray of crimson roses pinned against it – or perhaps the bright gleam in her eyes, as she glanced around the room, as though she was seeing it more clearly than anyone else.

For a moment more, she watched Rupert fold his arms and sprawl back against the mantelpiece. Then she crossed the room towards him.

'These balls are so dreadfully dull – don't you think?'

Rupert turned in surprise. Wrapped up in his boredom, he hadn't noticed her approaching. Now, she stood just behind him, leaning against the wall as though she was as bored as he was himself. He looked up at her – for she was taller than he was – and his eyes widened. Well-brought-up young ladies did not normally go wandering about the ballroom, starting up conversations with young men to whom they had not been properly introduced.

'Oh yes . . . er . . . rather,' he stuttered in reply.

'I'd much rather go out on the town, wouldn't you?' She flipped her ostrich-feather fan open and began fanning herself lazily. 'Perhaps to the Café Royal. Now *that's* quite a place. You never know who is going to be there, or what is going to happen.'

'Oh *rather!*' said Rupert, more enthusiastically this time. He'd never actually been to the Café Royal himself, but he'd heard it was a wild and exciting sort of place – a thousand miles away from his mother's sedate ballroom.

The girl let out a sigh. 'If only we could escape! But I suppose we'll have to put up with all *this* instead.' She gestured dismissively towards the waltzing couples.

'Would you ... I mean ... do you think that you might like to ... ?' Rupert found himself asking, looking awkwardly from her to the dance floor, and then back again.

'To *dance?*' The girl laughed, as though he'd made a joke. 'Oh, good heavens, no, Mr Grenville! I don't care for that kind of dancing. If it was a ragtime tune, now that would be different. But I know – why don't you show me around the house instead?' She flashed him a dazzling smile. 'Perhaps we could find somewhere to sit and talk? That would be much better than a stuffy old waltz, wouldn't it?'

'Oh yes, *absolutely*,' Rupert replied fervently. He didn't think he'd ever seen this girl before, and he wanted very much to know her name, but somehow he felt embarrassed to ask the question – especially when she obviously knew who *he* was. Before he could say anything more, she had placed her hand on his arm, and they were going out of the ballroom and into the long hallway.

'Your father has a simply wonderful art collection,' she was saying. 'I'm tremendously interested in art – aren't you?'

'Oh *rather!*' said Rupert again, although the truth was he'd never given very much thought to his father's art collection, besides the fact that it was worth a terrific lot of money. Sir Edwin Grenville was a wealthy merchant banker, and buying art was just one of the things he did as a matter of course – like dining at his club, or playing golf with his business associates.

'Where does he keep the rest of his paintings? Perhaps you could show me?'

Rupert found himself blushing. Most of the debutantes he met were so polite and demure – it was hard to know how to respond to a girl who started conversations, and asked questions, and looked at him so directly with her large dark eyes. He opened the door to his father's study, explaining: 'Most of them are in here.'

The girl glanced quickly around, taking in the panelled walls hung with oil paintings in heavy gold frames. 'What a lot there are,' she observed. 'Where did your father get them all?'

'Oh, you know. Here and there,' said Rupert, trying to sound confident – though honestly, he was not entirely sure. 'Auctions and so on. He's travelled abroad a lot for his work, and he always seems to come back with something new. Actually, he said he'll take me with him on his next trip,' he couldn't resist adding, feeling a swell of pride at the thought.

'Oh, really? I'm fond of travelling myself. It's always thrilling to see new places and have adventures.'

Rupert felt rather surprised. 'I didn't think young ladies were allowed to do much of that sort of thing.'

'Didn't you?' She had turned to examine a painting more closely, now she turned back to him. 'It's not a bad selection. One or two nice pieces, I suppose,' she said, flipping her fan open once again.

'This isn't all of them, of course,' Rupert said hurriedly, keen not to disappoint. 'There are more paintings in the dining room – and some of the very special ones aren't on display.'

The girl's eyes brightened. 'Very special ones? Like what?' she asked.

'Well, he's got some Turner sketches,' said Rupert, remembering a name he knew.

But the girl wasn't impressed: 'Oh – *Turner*. I mean, they're wonderful of course, but I've seen dozens of them in galleries before.'

'Or there's a Benedetto Casselli,' Rupert added, knowing *that*, at least, was certain to be impressive. Still, he was unprepared for her awed reaction:

'A Benedetto Casselli? Not *really*? Now that's something! His work is terrifically rare.'

'It's a very important painting,' Rupert boasted.

'I say, how splendid. Will you show it to me?'

Rupert was struck by a sudden prickle of anxiety. He'd forgotten for a moment that the Casselli dragon painting was supposed to be a secret. His father kept it hidden away in his safe, rather than hanging on the wall with the rest – though he'd told Rupert and his older brother Oliver that it was the most valuable and important work in his entire collection. 'If anything should ever happen to me, you must make sure you take the utmost care of it,' he'd said in a very serious voice.

'I've never seen a Casselli painting before. They're supposed to be perfectly magnificent! It would be *such* a thrill to see it for myself,' the girl was saying.

Rupert frowned, battling with himself. He knew he'd said too much already, and he was about to try and explain that he couldn't show her – but the girl was still talking: 'And then – do you have a motor car? I've got rather a wicked idea! Why don't we slip away together, and drive into town to go to the Café Royal? We'd be able to have a bit of real fun that way – and I bet we could be back before anyone noticed we'd gone!'

All thoughts of the painting fled at once from Rupert's mind. 'I say ... could we really? That *would* be a lark!' As a matter of fact, he didn't have a motor car himself, but his brother did, and Rupert was pretty sure he could drive it just as well as Oliver. He could already imagine how marvellous it would be to roll into town in the fine new motor, and then pull up at the door of the glamorous Café Royal with a beautiful young lady at his side . . . He felt ready to charge out of the door at once, but the girl laid a restraining hand on his arm.

'Don't forget the painting,' she said. '*Do* just let me have a quick peep before we go.'

'All right,' said Rupert, unable to resist. 'But it's supposed to be a secret – so you won't tell anyone about it, will you?'

The girl looked even more excited by the prospect of a secret painting. 'Of *course* I won't tell a soul,' she said breathlessly. 'How perfectly thrilling!'

Feeling rather excited himself now, Rupert hurried over to the large mahogany cabinet in the corner which housed his father's big metal safe. Luckily he knew the combination, and a moment later he had removed the leather folder stamped with the shape of the twisting golden dragon, which he knew contained the painting. He laid it on the desk and lifted the cover with awkward fingers. Beside him, the girl gave a gasp of admiration.

The painting was small – not much bigger than a notebook – and obviously very old. She leaned forward, her hand tightening on his sleeve, as she gazed at the sinuous shape of the dragon, painted in a rich crimson. Its snaking form was shown against a background of a dark stormy sky, and piled at its feet were a heap of bones and what looked like a human skull.

Rupert had only seen the painting once before, and truth be told, he'd not been very keen on it – it was so small and dark, and so jolly sinister-looking – but it was clear the girl felt differently. For a moment or two, she said nothing and only stared.

'Do you like it?' asked Rupert at last.

'Oh, Mr Grenville,' she sighed. 'It's absolutely *marvellous!*'

'Do call me Rupert,' said Rupert at once, thinking how debonair that sounded.

'*Rupert*, then. Gosh – I've never seen anything like it! Thanks awfully for showing it to me.'

Rupert hurried the painting back into its folder, and away into the safe as quickly as he could. He most certainly did not want his father to know that he'd been showing his secret painting to one of their guests – though it had all been worth it to see the glow of admiration in her eyes. 'Shall we go, then?' he said, offering her his arm.

But just then the door of the study was flung noisily open. A young man came bowling into the room, followed by another young man and two laughing young ladies, who all flung themselves down into the big leather armchairs.

'Rupert, old chap! There you are. What are you doing back here? We've found your hiding place, old thing. Your mama's in a frightful tizz looking for you. She's dreadfully keen for you to dance with Lady Cynthia, you know. I say – who wants a brandy? You'll take one, won't you, Hugo?

And one for you of course, old fellow.'

Rupert found a glass was being thrust into his hand. He turned to smile apologetically at the girl – but then stopped in surprise. 'I say – wherever did she go?'

'Where did who go, old fellow? Cheers, everyone – bottoms up!'

But Rupert didn't join in the toast. He was still staring around him. To his astonishment, and intense disappointment, the beautiful young lady with red roses in her hair had vanished. He strode to the door, but outside the hallway was empty. It was as if she had never even been there. 'And dash it all,' he muttered. 'I still don't know her name!'

CHAPTER TWO

Secret Service Bureau HQ, London

Lilian Rose had quite a lot of unusual talents. She could perform a perfect double pirouette, sing various amusing comic songs whilst accompanying herself on the piano, and recite screeds of Shakespeare from memory. She was also not a bad burglar, when occasion required it – which in her line of work, it quite often did.

It had taken her just seconds to slip unnoticed out of Sir Edwin Grenville's study and into the darkened room opposite. Inside, she stood behind the door, peering through a crack as Rupert came out into the hall – looking all around him to see where she had got to – and then hurried off towards the ballroom.

She didn't have to wait very long before the others followed him. As soon as they had all gone, Lil opened the door, and slipped soundlessly across the hall. A moment later, she was back in the now-empty study. The mahogany cabinet was open, and she was expertly twirling the dial of the safe with her white-gloved fingertips. Really, poor old Rupert had made it far too easy for her – he hadn't even bothered to hide the combination.

Inside the safe, she found the leather folder stamped with the familiar symbol of the twisting gold dragon. She'd recognised it at once: after all, she'd seen a Casselli painting kept inside one just like it before, in circumstances she was not likely to forget. She grasped it and pulled it out – and then at last, the precious painting was in her hands.

Her skin prickled with the excitement and strangeness of it. She'd been hunting for *The Red Dragon* for a long time; it was hard to believe that the painting, which was supposed to have been destroyed centuries ago when a British ship was set upon by pirates, was really here, in this house in West London – and she had it at last! But she knew there was no time to hang about feeling pleased with herself. Quickly, she closed the safe and then the cabinet door: no sense in making it completely obvious that a burglary had taken place.

Silent in her satin slippers, she went back out into the long hallway. But before she could take another step, she realised that someone was approaching. Not Rupert but an older man with white hair and a bristling moustache, talking in a low voice to his companion, a middle-aged man in evening dress. Lil knew that the man with the white hair was Sir Edwin himself.

There was no time for her to get away, but Lil had done

this kind of thing far too many times to panic. By the time Sir Edwin and his friend reached the study door, they saw nothing but a young lady examining her reflection in a looking glass, her fluffy ostrich-feather fan cast down on a polished table at her side.

She turned, as if startled, and bowed her head politely – her cheeks pink, as though she was embarrassed to have been caught preening before the mirror. Sir Edwin gave her an indulgent smile and said 'Good evening', before disappearing with his friend into the study.

The second the door had closed behind them, Lil lifted the fan, revealing beneath it the painting in its folder.

Really, you never knew when a fan was going to come in handy, she reflected, as she swiftly picked up the folder and darted away down the hall.

She'd already planned her route out of the house, and now she went swiftly through the green baize door that led to the servants' quarters – knowing quite well that none of the grand party guests would follow her there. With the painting tucked under her arm, she went lightly down the stairs – past a busy kitchen full of steam and rattling saucepans, where Cook was yelling at someone about oysters, past the Butler's pantry, past a confused-looking boot boy – and then out of the servants' entrance and into the yard.

She'd stashed an old carpet bag amongst some bushes in the garden. Under cover of the shrubbery, she retrieved it, and a moment later the white evening gown was hidden beneath an ordinary brown coat, and the red roses by a plain brown felt hat. The painting was tucked inside the carpet bag, carefully cushioned by her fluffy fan. Now she was no debutante but an ordinary girl – perhaps a housemaid on her night off – walking briskly, but in no special hurry, down the street towards Park Lane where she could catch an omnibus.

Somewhere behind her, in the yard of Sir Edwin's mansion, she heard the sound of running footsteps. A voice yelled out; electric torches were flashed into the darkness of the garden. So they already knew the painting was gone? That was rather interesting. Had Rupert cottoned on and raised the alarm – or had Sir Edwin opened his safe and noticed his painting was missing?

Just the same, she forced herself to stroll on towards the bus stop without speeding up. She didn't even flinch when a motor car came roaring out of Sir Edwin's driveway, rushing past her at top speed. She knew that hurrying would only make her look suspicious – and besides, there was not the smallest chance that Sir Edwin, or Rupert, or any of the party guests would make a connection between the elegant young lady in white and the ordinary girl in the brown coat, waiting for the omnibus with a shabby carpet bag at her side.

The omnibus rumbled up, and Lil hopped aboard. 'Good evening,' she said cheerfully to the conductor, casting a last glimpse over her shoulder at the bright golden lights of Sir Edwin's mansion, before the omnibus carried her and the dragon painting safely away, into the London night.

Twelve hours later she was walking over the cobbles towards the headquarters of the Secret Service Bureau. Both the evening dress and the old brown coat had vanished, and she was dressed in her own clothes, but the carpet bag was still close at her side. A light rain was falling, but it was warm for September and Lil didn't bother with an umbrella. She whistled a tune as she walked, making a passing gentleman, with bowler hat and newspaper, throw her a disapproving frown.

Lil did not care a bit for anyone's disapproval. She was quite used to being thought unladylike. Besides, that morning, she felt more cheerful than she had since she'd returned from Paris three months ago. She'd spent ages tracking down *The Red Dragon* – and at last she'd found it. She'd discovered the painting; she'd removed it secretly from the Grenville house; and now she was on her way to deliver it to the Chief, who she knew would be jolly pleased with her. She hopped over a puddle and gave a beaming smile to a telegraph boy on a bicycle – who was so startled that he almost crashed into a lamp-post.

Her plan had worked awfully well, she reflected. She'd been spot on when she'd guessed that Rupert would be the best way of getting to the painting. She wondered whether he'd confessed to showing it to a mysterious young lady, whose name he didn't know. If so, she guessed he would be in rather hot water with his father this morning.

Poor old Rupert. He wasn't a bad sort, really. Doing this job was a peculiar thing sometimes: it did seem rotten, taking advantage of a fellow like that. Left to her own devices, Lil was really rather a straightforward sort of person. She'd have preferred to have marched up to Rupert, shaken his hand heartily and said: 'Hullo there, I hear you've got a rather important painting – I'm afraid I'm going to have to take it off your hands.' But of course, that sort of thing would not wash when you were working as an undercover spy.

It still felt odd thinking of herself as a *spy* at all. It seemed no time since she'd been in the classroom at school, scribbling notes to her chums or playing tricks on the mistresses instead of practising her ladylike deportment. Then a few dull months at home, followed by the blissful escape of running off to London to go on the stage. Although being an actress had been marvellous, of course, somehow it had never been all she'd dreamed. Perhaps it was because she always had to play such idiotic characters – weedy *ingénues* who wept or fainted away at the first sign of excitement. Or perhaps it was because the work she'd begun doing with Sophie had been so much more thrilling. Working with her best friend was tremendous fun, and detective work was always exciting. She'd soon discovered she loved undercover work: it was rather like acting, but without the footlights or greasepaint, the smoke and mirrors. She had to use all her charm, her instincts and her quick brain – and it satisfied her like nothing else.

Now, here she was: co-owner of Taylor & Rose, the detective agency she and Sophie had founded together. The agency had been in business just over two years, and their most important client was the Secret Service Bureau.

The Bureau was a top-secret government agency, responsible for intelligence work. Since Taylor & Rose had been hired by the Bureau, their lives – which had already been rather interesting – had become very interesting indeed. Earlier that year, Lil had been sent on an assignment to a royal castle, where she'd discovered a plot to kidnap the prince and princess of Arnovia, helped them escape, and then foiled a second kidnap attempt in Paris with Sophie's help. It had all been as exciting as the plot of a shilling shocker on a railway station bookstall.

Since she'd returned to London, things had been less thrilling – though still very busy. The Chief had put her to work investigating the dragon paintings by the artist Benedetto Casselli, which they now knew contained clues to the location of a mysterious hidden weapon. The shadowy secret society known as the *Fraternitas Draconum* were trying to find the weapon and use it to kick start a war in Europe – and they must do all they could to prevent them.

Lil knew that Sophie was just as intent on stopping the *Fraternitas* as she was. It had been Sophie who had encouraged them to form the Loyal Order of Lions, to oppose the *Fraternitas* and their schemes. The Order had no official leader, but if they had, it would certainly have been Sophie. Lil smiled to herself, thinking that whilst a small, politely spoken seventeen-year-old girl might not be most people's idea of a strong leader, Sophie would have surprised them. She was unshakeable in her determination to stop the *Fraternitas*.

Of course, that wasn't so surprising when you knew Sophie's history. Not only had the *Fraternitas* put her in mortal danger more than once, they had also been responsible for the deaths of Sophie's parents. It was because of them that she had been left all alone in the world.

Lil couldn't imagine what it would feel like to be so alone. She'd never experienced a loss like Sophie's. She'd spent her whole life surrounded by people: Mother and Father, of course, even if they never did know quite what to make of her; her bossy older brother Jack, who she loved and who infuriated her in equal measure; and dozens of friends. She'd always found it easy to make friends wherever she went – at school, in the theatre, and now even with a prince and princess. But she'd never had a friend who understood her like Sophie did.

It had been three months since she'd waved her off on

the airfield in Paris. Three months since she'd been back in London, without her. Three months of missing her – a horrid feeling, like a stomach ache. It seemed so wrong that she wasn't here: pacing up and down the office they shared, thinking out an assignment; leafing through the newspapers she read every day; or chatting over tea and cakes at Lyons Corner House, where they talked about everything from their latest cases, to the merits of a new hat.

But Lil knew Sophie was where she needed to be – following the trail of a stolen notebook, which contained vital information about the dragon paintings and the secret weapon. She'd be back in London soon enough, and they'd be together again. Until then, Lil would do everything she could to help with the investigation.

Inside the building, she told the concierge she was here to see 'Mr Clarke', and then ran up the stairs, through a door marked with a small card reading: CLARKE & SONS SHIPPING AGENTS. A few minutes later, she was in the Chief's office, laying the painting before him.

'Well! Miss Rose, you have outdone yourself!' exclaimed C, with a delighted chuckle. 'Sit down and make yourself comfortable while I admire it. My word – The Red Dragon at last. So full of malevolence – really, quite horrifying!'

Lil took the chair opposite his desk, glancing around her as she always did when she was in C's office. There were so many intriguing things to look at – the enormous gramophone in the corner, currently booming out a Glinka opera, the big map studded with pins and coloured flags, and the elaborate ink stand, filled with the bright green ink that the Chief always used.

'Carruthers!' C called out.

Almost at once, the office door banged open and C's secretary came in. Captain Carruthers was a tall thin young man, with horn-rimmed spectacles and a rather sour expression.

'Ah, Carruthers – you'll like this!' the Chief went on genially. 'Look what clever Miss Rose has delivered to us! Isn't she splendid? Now then – if you would take it, see it's wrapped properly, and put it into the safe? Very good – careful with it now, there's a good fellow!'

Carruthers threw Lil a glance that suggested he thought her anything but splendid, nodded to the Chief, picked up the painting and stalked back out of the room. As usual, C did not seem to notice his assistant's bad temper: he was busy rummaging amongst one of the tottering piles of paper on his desk. After a moment, he found the document he was looking for, and set it before him with a flourish.

C placed a large green-ink tick beside the words '*The Red Dragon*' and scribbled beside it '*found in the possession of Sir E. Grenville*'.

'So Sir Edwin must be a member of the *Fraternitas Draconum*,' said Lil.

'It would seem so,' said the Chief. 'What about the other fellow – the man you saw him with.

Was he anyone you recognised?'

Lil shook her head. 'I'm afraid not.' There hadn't been much to distinguish him – just a smart, middle-aged man with grey hair. 'But I did wonder if Sir Edwin was going to show him the painting. That might have been how he discovered it was missing so soon. Which would suggest that the other man is *Fraternitas* too, wouldn't it?'

'Very likely,' said the Chief, scribbling this down. 'This is most pleasing, Miss Rose. You've done an admirable job for us. Now, if you will see Captain Carruthers on your way out, I'd appreciate it if you could give him a description of the second man. Also the location of Grenville's safe, and the combination of course. You never know when that might come in handy! Then off you go and enjoy a well earned rest.'

A *rest*? 'Don't you need me to do anything else?' Lil asked, her eyes flicking to the other paintings on the Chief's list, marked '*under investigation*' or even more tantalisingly, '*unknown*'.

But the Chief just smiled blandly and said: 'Nothing for the moment, Miss Rose. You'll hear from us again as soon as we have a new assignment for you.'

Lil got to her feet, but before she left she had to ask the same question she always asked whenever she came to the Bureau – even though she knew she wasn't really supposed to. 'Have you heard anything from Sophie lately? Is she all right?'

BENEDETTO CASSELLI DRAGON SEQUENCE

SEPTEMBER 1911

1. THE WHITE DRAGON ✓
2. THE GREEN DRAGON ✓
3. THE RED DRAGON — *FOUND IN THE POSSESSION OF SIR E. GRENVILLE*
4. THE BLUE DRAGON ✓

DRAGON COURANT — *Stolen by FD from Col. Fairley, Alnwick. Current location under investigation*

DRAGON COMBATANT — *unknown*

DRAGON REGARDANT — *unknown*

The Chief gave her a kindly smile. 'Miss Taylor? Of course, my dear. Nothing to worry about on that score. Now then – run along. Good day!'

Lil left the Chief humming along to his music. She suspected he thought it was sentimental and a little silly, the way she asked about Sophie; and yet she always felt reassured to hear that all was well. She knew she shouldn't expect to get letters or messages from Sophie while she was travelling undercover – after all, she herself hadn't been allowed to send any when she'd been in Arnovia – but it was good to know she was all right and that her assignment was going according to plan.

Outside the Chief's office door, she found not Carruthers, but instead Captain Harry Forsyth – tall, bronzed and handsome. Forsyth was one of the top agents of the Secret Service Bureau, and it wasn't long since he and Lil had been on assignment together in Paris and Arnovia. Now he gave her a charming smile: 'Oh hello, old girl! Didn't realise it was you in there with the Chief. Ripping to see you, as always!'

'Hello, Forsyth,' said Lil cheerfully. 'Isn't Carruthers back yet?' For once, the secretary's desk was empty.

'Not in the least idea, I'm afraid. I s'pose he must have popped out on some errand or other. Well, I'd simply love to chat, but I mustn't keep the old man waiting!' He gave her a quick wink, then swaggered forward into C's office, without knocking. Inside, Lil heard the Chief say warmly:

'Ah, Forsyth! In you come – I've a great deal to acquaint you with!'

For a moment, Lil lingered by the door. She knew that the Chief took Forsyth into his confidence, sharing with him many details of the confidential operations of the Bureau. She and Sophie, on the other hand, were kept at arm's length, knowing nothing of the Bureau's bigger plans beyond their own assignments. It was frustrating when she knew that she was just as smart and dedicated as Forsyth – who as a matter of fact had spent most of their last assignment in Paris enjoying the city's night spots. Now, she wondered if she might catch a few words of their conversation, but she could hear nothing except the vague buzz of voices, and the hum of the gramophone. She gave up and wandered to the window: Carruthers would surely be back at any moment, and if he returned to find her listening at the Chief's door, she knew he would be simply unbearable about it.

She flopped down into Carruthers' chair to wait for him, glancing around at his typewriter, his notebooks, and the stubs of pencils that littered his desk. She helped herself to a biscuit from his tin, and then leaned back, putting her feet up on his desk in the style of Carruthers' usual pose. 'Oh, it's *you*,' she practised saying, in what she thought was rather a good imitation of his sardonic manner.

As she did so, she noticed something interesting. On the wall, just beside Carruthers' chair, there was a small air vent with a slatted metal cover – except three of the screws that should have held the cover in place were missing. Experimentally, she gave it a little push: at once the cover smoothly pivoted to the side. To her amazement, she realised that through the open vent, she could now hear, quite clearly, Forsyth and the Chief talking in the next room.

Well! Lil grinned as she settled back more comfortably in Carruthers' chair. How jolly intriguing! Perhaps like herself, Carruthers did not care to be excluded from important conversations and had found his own way to listen in.

The Chief was saying: 'I've had a message from our man in Hamburg. His report is ready.'

'That's the fellow known as Ace?' Forsyth asked. There was the flick of pages, as though he was looking at some paperwork. 'The one who sent all that information on shipbuilding that Admiral Stevens was so keen on?'

'That's the one. He's one of our most valuable overseas agents. But he's got some concerns about getting the report out of Germany. A couple of Ziegler's spies have been sniffing around.'

Lil listened intently, as she absent-mindedly crunched another of Carruthers' biscuits. She knew she shouldn't be eavesdropping, but she was fascinated. She'd had no idea the Bureau had agents stationed in the German Empire – although now she saw that if the German spymaster Ziegler had agents gathering intelligence in Britain, then of course the Chief would want his own agents doing the same in Germany.

'I can't risk losing Ace. You know that our top priority is to give the government advance warning when war breaks out – and I'm relying on Ace and his counterparts elsewhere in Germany for that information,' C was saying.

'But we don't know for certain that there will be a war, do we, sir?' asked Forsyth.

'Of course we don't know for certain. But there's no doubt that war is hanging over Europe like a shadow. It will only take the smallest action to inflame it – one spark to ignite the dynamite.' The Chief paused for a moment and sighed. 'The consequences of a modern European war would be unthinkable, so I hope very much that spark will never come. But if it does, we must be prepared, and for that, we will need Ace. I can't risk him being caught by Ziegler – and yet, Stevens does want that report . . .'

'Ought I to go out there, sir?' suggested Forsyth eagerly. 'We could arrange a handover. I could travel to Hamburg in disguise, collect the report and smuggle it out of the country.'

'I'm afraid your assignment here must take priority for now, Captain. But just the same, you're right – I believe I'll have to send someone to collect it.'

'What about Brooks? He's a sharp fellow.'

'No good – he's on assignment too. If only the Ministry

29

would see fit to increase our budget, so we could recruit some more agents. We are stretched in ten different directions at present!' He paused, and then said thoughtfully: 'No, I rather think I shall give this assignment to Miss Rose.'

'*Miss Rose!*' Forsyth's tone was incredulous. 'But sir – are you sure that's wise? I know she's a fine girl, but surely she isn't up to this kind of assignment?'

Lil almost choked on her biscuit. But through her rage, she was gratified to hear the Chief reply: 'Don't let the skirts and petticoats mislead you, Forsyth. Miss Rose is quite as competent as most of the young men I have on my books. What's more, there are obvious advantages to operating female agents – for one thing, they are far less likely to be suspected. Besides, this will be perfectly straightforward. All she'll have to do is collect the report and transport it safely back to London. She has a talent for undercover work, and we can easily concoct a good cover story for her. Yes – my mind is made up. Miss Rose shall go to Germany.'

Germany! For a moment, Lil was distracted – and rather excited. But her new assignment was forgotten at once when she heard Forsyth say: 'And what about Miss Taylor? Any news?'

'Nothing.'

'You're sure she made it to St Petersburg?'

'It would seem so. She successfully tracked the Count von Wilderstein there – and she was communicating regularly until she crossed the border. But since she arrived in Russia, we haven't heard a word from her. It's been well over a month now.' The Chief paused for a moment, and then went on: 'I'm afraid there can be no doubt about it, Forsyth. Miss Taylor has disappeared.'

CHAPTER THREE

Secret Service Bureau HQ, London

Lil's breath caught in her throat and she dropped the biscuit she was holding, not noticing the crumbs that scattered across Carruthers' desk.

Dimly, she heard Forsyth say: 'Oh, surely not, sir. Perhaps she's just being careful – maintaining her cover. After all, the Russian secret police are no joke.'

'That's precisely what concerns me,' the Chief replied. 'It's true that if the *Okhrana* are watching her, she may be keeping a low profile. But even with that in mind, she should have been in touch by now. There are arrangements in place for her to write privately by diplomatic bag, via the Embassy.' The Chief tapped his pen against the desk in time to the music. 'I must say, I don't like it. Von Wilderstein may be dangerous. And St Petersburg is volatile at present. With the assassination of the Russian minister, there's bound to be trouble stirred up.'

Lil's heart was pounding. Sophie had *disappeared* – in

Russia? The Chief had just told her that Sophie was fine – that there was nothing for her to worry about. But he had lied. He hadn't heard from Sophie for over a month – she was missing in St Petersburg, all the way on the other side of Europe.

'Of course, we don't want to ruffle the Russians' feathers,' she could hear him saying. 'The diplomatic situation is tricky. Officially we have no business sending spies into Russia. They are, after all, our allies. If she's been caught – well, I suspect the government will want to deny any association with her.'

'Will you send someone to look for her?' asked Forsyth.

'I've no agents I can spare to go all the way to St Petersburg at present. Besides, I have my orders – and the Ministry are very clear that Germany must remain our priority. They are interested in the *Fraternitas* and this weapon, of course – in fact, I may say, they are *very* interested. But it's not their most pressing concern. So I'm afraid Miss Taylor will have to fend for herself, for now at any rate. Don't let on to Miss Rose, Forsyth. I don't want her distracted from the Hamburg mission.'

'Of course not, sir,' said Forsyth, sounding as though nothing could be further from his mind than confiding in Lil.

As he spoke, Lil realised the other door was opening. At once she let the cover swing back into place, concealing the air vent – but it was already too late. Captain Carruthers was standing before her, his hands on his hips and a smirk on his face.

'Making yourself quite at home, I see? And listening in on private conversations too?'

'I was intrigued by your invention. Just seeing how it works,' Lil flashed back at once. 'Does the Chief know you've been eavesdropping on all his secret meetings?'

'Ha!' Carruthers scoffed. 'I'm his *secretary*. Do you really think he keeps anything from me?' He flung an arm out, gesturing to the row of locked filing cabinets. 'I see every letter, every telegram, every dossier. There isn't anything that happens in this office that I don't know about.' He looked at her rather smugly. Of course: he must know that Sophie was missing, Lil realised. Was there anyone at the Bureau who didn't already know, except for her?

Lil was not someone who lost her temper very often, but now she did. 'Well, I hope you have a jolly nice time with your letters and reports and your secret spy hole, and your *biscuits*,' she retorted. 'Tucked away nice and safe – while we're out in the field, doing the real work.'

Carruthers turned red, and she knew she had hit a nerve. He was envious of the Bureau agents who worked 'in the field' and resented having to stay behind to organise files and type the Chief's letters. Of course, it wasn't really his fault that he was a secretary instead of a field-agent; and whilst he might be a prickly sort of fellow, it wasn't exactly cricket to imply he was a coward. She expected him to say something spiteful in reply, but instead he just growled: 'Get out of my chair.'

He was even more bad-tempered than usual as he took down the description of the grey-haired man, and the particulars of Sir Edwin's safe. But Lil did not pay him much attention: her mind was far away, racing with thoughts about Sophie and St Petersburg. Vague images of the Tsar, and snow, and Russian ballet, and Cossacks on horseback danced about in her head. She could not even begin to imagine Sophie into the picture. Could she really have fallen foul of the Russian secret police that the Chief had talked about? Or worse still, could she have been caught by the Count and the *Fraternitas Draconum*?

A wave of cold dread swept over her. She was barely aware of walking home: she didn't notice the turning leaves as she tramped through the square garden, nor the omnibuses hissing by on the wet road, nor the woman with the basket of flowers on the corner, who called out to her: 'A sprig of white heather, miss, for luck?' Instead she only heard the Chief's voice, over and over again, like one of his own gramophone records, stuck in a loop. *The diplomatic situation is a tricky one . . . If she's been caught . . . the government will want to deny any association with her . . . I've no agents I can spare to go to all the way to St Petersburg . . . Miss Taylor will have to fend for herself.*

It didn't take long to reach home. She'd given up her old lodging-house room when she'd gone to Arnovia and when she'd come back to London three months ago, Jack had suggested she should come and room with him in the big, shabby Bloomsbury townhouse he shared with some of his fellow art students. Lil and Jack now lived in a set of rooms on the first floor, and just above them were their friends, Leo and Tilly. The house was a friendly, come-and-go-as-you-like sort of place, which suited Lil down to the ground. There were always the sounds of feet on the stairs, laughter, and spontaneous celebrations when someone sold a painting or passed an examination. There was always someone around to chat – and Lil loved chatting.

But today she felt in no mood to talk to anyone. She needed to be by herself to think: she thumped straight up the stairs and into her own rooms, shutting the door behind her to drown out the cheerful voices of the others.

The sitting room she and Jack shared was, as always, extremely untidy. The wallpaper was peeling in places, and the bare floorboards were only partly covered by worn but gaily coloured mats. Two threadbare armchairs, loaded with paisley-print rugs and colourful cushions, were drawn close to the fireplace. The mantelpiece was a jumble of flowerpots, photographs and party invitations; a playbill for a new show at the Fortune Theatre; and a coloured card advertising an exhibition at the Royal Academy.

Lil took off her hat, and tossed it on to the table, which was scattered with books and papers, along with the remains of Jack's breakfast – or possibly his supper – a willow-patterned plate scattered with crumbs and an empty cup. Beside it were several tubes of paint and a jam jar of paintbrushes. Jack said the light in the sitting room was good, and often painted here: there were always pictures pinned up unframed, or canvases propped against the wall. Just now there was an easel by the window, showing a half-finished portrait of a girl reading a book. Jack was experimenting with a new semi-abstract style, so the girl had bright yellow hands and a smudgy blue face – but even so, Lil knew that she was meant to be Sophie. She gazed at it for a few seconds, and then flopped down in one of the armchairs, leaning her head back against the cushion. 'Oh, bother it all,' she muttered aloud.

Sophie had disappeared in St Petersburg. No one had heard from her for over a month. She had followed the Count von Wilderstein there – but what could he be doing in Russia? In Arnovia, the Count had always seemed a harmless fellow, more interested in tinkering with aeroplanes than anything else. But now Lil knew the truth: he'd conspired in a secret plot to kidnap the Crown Prince, so that he himself could become King, and he was working for the *Fraternitas*. That meant he must be extremely dangerous.

Miss Taylor must fend for herself, she heard the Chief say again. His voice boomed in her head – suddenly steely, not in the least bit kind. She had asked about Sophie and he had lied to her. *Nothing to worry about*, he had said. He'd told Forsyth not to tell her the truth, simply because he didn't want her 'distracted' from another mission. And how readily Forsyth had agreed!

In a rush, she thought of everything she and Sophie had done for the Bureau. A few hours ago, she'd felt full of pride in their work – now she only felt stupid. The Chief didn't really care about them: they were simply useful to him. *There are obvious advantages to operating female agents.* It was all very well while they were doing what he wanted – but if something went wrong, he would simply wash his hands of them. *Miss Taylor must fend for herself.*

Anger bubbled up inside her, and all at once, she was seized with a furious desire to march straight back to the Bureau, to fling open the Chief's door, to tell both him and Forsyth exactly what she thought of them. But she knew that rushing about yelling was not the way to go. She had to be clever about this, she told herself. She had to think as clearly and sharply as Sophie herself would do.

But even as she tried to think, she pictured Sophie – trapped in some far-off police cell, or captured by the Count – and her anger flared all over again. Furious tears rushed into her eyes, quite as if she was one of those idiotic *ingénues* she had always loathed. *Tears won't help anything,* she remembered her old headmistress instructing the girls. *They will only make your eyes red and puffy.* 'Don't cry, you absolute donkey,' she muttered to herself. 'Think!'

Just then, she heard a knock on the door. She looked up, surprised. Jack was out at art school – and anyway, he would never have knocked. The other occupants of the house were not much given to knocking either: it was the kind of place where people just barged in. She got up, wiping her eyes on her sleeve, and went to answer it. Standing just outside the door, holding a small bunch of flowers and grinning at her, was Joe.

For a moment she felt completely confused – and then all at once, she remembered. Of course – they'd made plans to go and see the matinee at the Alhambra, and have tea. She'd thought it was just a casual arrangement – two pals out for an afternoon – but now here Joe was, looking rather handsome in what she knew was his best suit, with his curly hair carefully smoothed.

'Oh gosh,' she said. 'I think you'd better come in.'

It didn't take long to pour out the story. Joe was a good listener: he didn't interrupt, sitting beside her as she talked, his eyes fixed seriously on her face. When she told him what the Chief had said about Sophie, he looked astonished – and then very worried indeed. She knew Joe was very fond of Sophie: in a funny way, the two of them were rather alike, both alone in the world without any family of their own. But now Sophie was *really* alone – far away from all her friends, missing on the other side of Europe.

'I'm so furious I don't know what to do,' she finished up. 'How can the Chief think of just *leaving* her there?

She could be in any kind of trouble!'

'I'll admit, it doesn't look good,' said Joe, thinking hard. 'But don't despair. We don't *know* something bad has happened. Perhaps her messages just haven't been getting through?'

'But what if something awful *has* happened to her?' They had no way of knowing, Lil realised – and that was the very worst thing of all.

Rather as though he wasn't sure what else to do, Joe put an arm around her shoulders. For a moment, she felt taken aback. Joe had never really hugged her before – she hadn't thought of him as the hugging kind. She knew he'd always been a bit sweet on her, but he'd never done anything *about* it – and besides, she'd never wanted anything more than just to be good chums. But now that Joe's arm was around her, and her head was against his shoulder; now that his hand had closed over hers – warm and rather rough – her heart began to beat a little faster.

'She'll be all right,' he said gently.

'We don't know that. We can't possibly be sure.'

'She's *Sophie*. She's tough.'

'But she's all alone. We have to do something to help – or at least try and find out what's happened!'

'Well, maybe you need to go back and talk to the Chief. Admit what you heard and tell him he's got to help you get in touch with her. There must be someone in St Petersburg who could help track her down – or you never know, perhaps he'd even let *you* go out there and look for her?'

But Lil just shook her head. After what he'd said, she was certain there was no way the Chief would agree to send her all the way to Russia to look for Sophie. Besides, she didn't feel she could ever trust him again, after he'd lied to her face like that. 'He won't. Not when he needs me to go to Germany to pick up his stupid report,' she muttered angrily.

'Well then, while you're in Hamburg, the rest of us will start investigating from here. There's got to be something we can do, some way we can find her . . .' Joe began.

Hamburg! Lil jumped suddenly upright. 'Joe – that's it! You're a genius!'

Joe looked astonished – and a little disappointed that Lil was no longer snuggled against his shoulder. 'What d'you mean?' he asked warily.

But Lil was already on her feet, rummaging through books until she unearthed her copy of *Cook's Continental Guide*. 'Look!' she exclaimed, thrusting it under his nose, her finger jabbing at a map showing Hamburg, in the north of the German Empire. 'I'm supposed to go to Hamburg. Well, Hamburg is halfway to St Petersburg – don't you see?' She stared at him in excitement. 'What if I agree to the Chief's mission, then use it as a cover for a secret mission of my own? I can *say* I'm going to Hamburg, but actually I'll travel on to St Petersburg – and I'll find Sophie myself.'

Joe frowned. 'But if you did that, then you'd be

41

disobeying your orders from the Chief, wouldn't you? And he's not just an ordinary client. These are orders from the government.'

Lil shrugged that off at once. 'I don't care about the Chief and his silly old orders. If I did what he wanted, I'd be leaving Sophie in the lurch – and I jolly well won't do that.'

'You could get yourself into an awful lot of trouble,' Joe protested. 'Not only yourself – but Taylor & Rose too.'

Lil paused for a moment, and then grabbed her hat decisively from the table. 'Without Sophie there *is* no Taylor & Rose,' she said crisply. 'Come on. Let's go and find the others. If I'm going to do this, I'm going to need everyone's help.'

CHAPTER FOUR

Secret Service Bureau HQ, London

Lil didn't feel quite so confident as she made her way back to the Bureau the following morning. She'd spent all of the previous afternoon at Taylor & Rose talking with the others, but to her surprise and disappointment they'd shared Joe's uncertainty about her plan.

'Of course we're all worried about Sophie,' said Tilly, Taylor & Rose's resident technical expert, in pragmatic tones. 'Terribly worried. But you can't just rush off. We have to think it through.'

'We don't know anything about what she's doing in St Petersburg, or where you could look for her,' added Mei, who worked as their receptionist. 'And it's a very big city, isn't it? How would you even begin to find her?'

'I'm a detective, aren't I?' Lil protested. 'I'd *investigate*.'

She'd been sure that Billy at least would be on her side: she knew how devoted he was to Sophie. But to her annoyance, he agreed with Tilly and Mei. 'It's awful to think of Sophie being missing – and I agree we've got to do whatever we can to find her. But Lil, just think: if you abandon the mission the Chief has planned for you, then you'll be going against the Bureau and putting us at odds with the government. Directly disobeying the Chief's orders like that – well, it just doesn't sound like a terribly good idea.'

'I don't have to *abandon the mission*,' argued Lil. 'I can still do what the Chief wants. I could collect the report on my way to St Petersburg – or on my way home, perhaps. I'll simply be *extending* the assignment, that's all. Anyway, does anyone have any better ideas? Because I'm not going to leave Sophie all by herself in Russia and this is the only way of trying to rescue her that I can come up with.'

In the end it had been Joe who had said: 'Well, I reckon we should at least look into it. Work out how Lil would get to St Petersburg from Hamburg and what's possible.'

They'd all agreed on that and had spent the rest of the afternoon poring over maps and the *Bradshaw's Railway Guide*. Then the telephone had rung, summoning Lil to see the Chief the next morning to receive her new assignment. And now she was here once more – hurrying past Carruthers at his desk, and through into C's office, her heart thumping in her chest. Inside, everything was exactly the same as usual – the gramophone playing, the rain pattering gently against the window – and yet it didn't *feel* the same at all.

'Ah, Miss Rose,' said the Chief. 'Come in and sit down. I have a new assignment for you.'

It took all of Lil's acting skills to keep her face calm and attentive as he laid out his plans, explaining that she would be travelling to Hamburg to collect a report from one of his agents there. 'You'll travel undercover of course, posing as a tourist visiting the city. The papers you'll need are being prepared. Once you arrive, you'll see a few sights for appearance's sake – old churches, a museum, that kind of thing – and then proceed to the agreed rendezvous point where you'll collect the report. Then you simply need to bring it back here. There will be the usual border checks, but we've prepared rather a clever little suitcase with a hidden compartment, which will easily get round *those*.'

'And what exactly is this report?' asked Lil, trying to keep her voice light.

'No need for you to worry about that,' said the Chief breezily. 'Just know that Admiral Stevens will be very grateful to get hold of it – very grateful indeed.' He paused for a moment, and his tone became more serious. 'However, there is one other thing that I wanted to speak to you about . . .'

Lil leaned forward eagerly. Was he going to tell her the truth about Sophie at last? Perhaps she had misjudged him – perhaps he did have a plan to help her, after all?

'The Hamburg assignment is a straightforward one, and I know you're perfectly capable of handling it alone.

However, I'd like to ask someone else to accompany you.'

Blow, thought Lil. Was he planning to send Forsyth with her again? If they were travelling together, it would spoil everything.

'Carruthers!' called out the Chief. A moment later, Carruthers appeared through the door, looking as sulky as ever.

'Now then, old fellow. I have exciting news! I've decided that you're to go on your first field assignment – what do you think of that? Miss Rose, Captain Carruthers is going to accompany you to Hamburg!' he announced, with the air of a magician pulling a white rabbit from a top hat.

Lil gaped at him '*He's* coming with me?' she said incredulously – even as Carruthers himself burst out, 'You mean to say that my first field assignment is going to be with *her*?'

'That's right. Now, Carruthers here hasn't had much chance to get field experience. That's through no fault of his own – he's always needed here. But it's really too bad to keep him shut up with all these dossiers forever. He must have the chance to see what it's like out in the field. That's what you've been wanting, isn't it, old chap? And this assignment should be just the ticket. So, Miss Rose, you'll be heading up the mission – and Captain, you'll be there to follow along and learn. See how it works, get a feel for the fieldwork side of things.'

Carruthers' face was a picture of disgust. Meanwhile,

Lil's heart had sunk to her boots. Having Forsyth with her would have been tricky enough – but with Carruthers shadowing her, no doubt furious at the very idea of learning from her, it would be almost impossible to follow through with her plan. However would she manage to break away to St Petersburg now? 'Er – wouldn't it be better for the Captain to learn from Forsyth, or one of the other agents?' she asked, rather desperately. 'You know . . . someone a bit more experienced?'

'Please don't underestimate yourself, Miss Rose,' said C sternly. 'Your work for the Bureau has been exemplary. There will be a great deal the Captain can learn from you – I know he will be most interested to see how you approach an undercover assignment. Won't you, Captain?' He gave Carruthers a sharp look.

'Yes, sir,' mumbled Carruthers.

'Now, I've arranged things so you'll be travelling as brother and sister.'

'*Brother and sister?*' repeated Carruthers, more appalled than ever.

'Yes – that will make things straightforward. No eyebrows raised about unmarried girls racketing about Europe with young men, or anything like that,' said the Chief briskly. 'Tickets have been booked for you on tomorrow's boat to Ostend, and from there you'll take the train to Cologne, and change for Hamburg. Accommodation is arranged at a small guest house. You'll visit two or three tourist spots, and then collect the report and bring it back here to me.' He sat back in his chair, obviously well pleased with his plan.

Carruthers was scarlet with indignation, but as ever, the Chief didn't seem to notice. 'I'm sure you'll want to go and talk it over,' he said amiably. 'Here's the details of the rendezvous point for you, Miss Rose. Commit them to memory and then burn the paper, if you please.' He slid a document across the desk towards her. 'I'll expect you both back here by the end of the week with the report,' he finished. 'Good hunting!'

Lil got to her feet. Her mind was in a whirl, but all the same, she managed to ask the most important question. She wanted to give the Chief one more chance to tell her the truth. 'I was wondering . . . I know that yesterday you said Sophie was fine, but have you heard anything from her lately? Any letters – or telegrams?' she prompted. 'It's been quite a while now that she's been away, hasn't it?'

'Hmmm?' The Chief looked up, already preoccupied by the paperwork on his desk. 'Oh yes, well these things can sometimes take a while, you know.'

He gave her an avuncular smile – but to Lil it was no longer reassuring. Instead, it seemed more like a mask, concealing an expression that was cold and blank. She followed Carruthers hurriedly out of the room.

'Well, isn't this just *brilliant*,' Carruthers was muttering under his breath, banging things about on his desk.

'For my first field assignment! Good lord!'

But Lil wasn't listening. One thing was very clear to her. Whatever the Chief's orders were, whatever the others thought, and even with Carruthers joining her on the assignment, there was not in the least chance she was going tamely to Hamburg and back again. She was going to St Petersburg to find Sophie – and that was that.

PART II

'Last week we arrived in Russia, and I scarcely know what to write about it. I have visited a dozen different countries, but I really think St Petersburg is the most extraordinary place I have ever seen. I feel as though I have stepped into a fairy tale.'

– From the diary of Alice Grayson

CHAPTER FIVE

A Very Long Way from Piccadilly Circus

At the same time that Lil was preparing to attend Sir Edwin's ball on the other side of Europe, in the warm kitchen of a tall, pink house beside a narrow canal, Vera Ivanovna Orlov was telling stories to her grandchildren.

'Once upon a time, there was a cross old Tsar, who lived in a palace surrounded by a beautiful orchard,' she began. 'Amongst all the trees in the orchard was one that was very special: a wonderful apple tree, which grew magical golden apples – the Tsar's pride and joy. But one night, the Firebird appeared. It swooped down from the sky and ate the golden apples from the Tsar's tree. The Tsar was furious: how dare a mere bird help itself to his golden apples? He summoned his three daughters, and commanded them to catch the Firebird, and see it punished for its insolence. But the youngest princess, who was also the cleverest –'

'Wait! You're telling it wrong, *Babushka!*' protested Luka, aged seven. 'The story is supposed to be about the

Tsar's three *sons*. And it's the youngest *prince* who is the cleverest.'

Vera tutted, from where she was stirring a steaming pan at the stove. 'Who's telling this story – me or you?' she demanded, pausing to rap the fingers of six-year-old Elena with her wooden spoon, before they could creep any closer to the contents of her mixing bowl. '*Me*. And *I* say it was daughters. So . . . *as I was saying*. The youngest princess, who was also the cleverest and the bravest . . .'

Sophie grinned to herself as she passed the kitchen, with its smells of smoke and spice. She caught the fragrance of honey and nutmeg and sniffed appreciatively, guessing that Vera was baking a batch of her famous biscuits. They'd eat them later, accompanied by lots of black tea from the samovar, served with spoonfuls of jam.

'*Do svidaniya!*' she called through the kitchen door, waving goodbye to Vera and the children, before she went out of the house, on to the Ulitsa Zelenaya.

Bells were chiming out across the city as she crossed a little bridge over the misty canal. She'd never known a city with as many bells as St Petersburg: the silvery chime of the little bells blending in harmony with the deep, resonant toll of the larger ones. The air felt chilly against her face after the snug warmth of the house, and her breath puffed out in little clouds. It might still be September, but the weather was already beginning to turn. By the end of October, Vera had told her, the temperature would fall below zero, and the canal would begin to freeze. Now, Sophie could already feel the cold swish of the wind blowing up from the river, and she pulled her coat more closely around her, as she turned on to the Nevsky.

The Nevsky Prospekt was St Petersburg's grandest street, lined with elegant buildings that gave it the air of a London avenue, or a Paris boulevard. At night it glittered with new electric lights: now, in the morning, it was alive with the rattle of tram cars, the clatter of horse's hooves and the fanfare of motor horns. In the distance Sophie could hear the faint smoky hum of the mills and shipyards and ironworks – but the Nevsky was far from their smog. Here were palaces like birthday cakes, in a rainbow of ice-cream-coloured stucco. Here were the windows of magnificent shops, with their displays of feathered hats and furred capes, sugar-dusted chocolates and candied cherries. French boutiques offered Parisian gowns and gloves; the Eliseyev Emporium exhibited bon bons and cakes elaborate enough for a Viennese coffee house; and at the Magasin Anglais, Russian aristocrats could purchase Pears soap, Scottish tweeds and lavender water imported from England. Everywhere signs read *English spoken* or *Ici on parle Français*.

There were always many languages to be heard on the Nevsky. Sophie's ears hummed with Russian and French, English and Polish, Yiddish and German. At this time of day, it seemed all of St Petersburg must be here: fashionable ladies and gentlemen, taking in the shops; green-capped students with books under their arms, hurrying to the public library; a swagger of young officers, jostling a clerk in a cheap overcoat into the gutter; a gaggle of sightseers, gawping at the bright window displays. There was plenty for tourists to see here: Sophie knew all the sights now. There was the grand Mikhailovsky Palace, whose sumptuous halls housed the Russian Museum, and there was the dramatic sweep of the Kazan Cathedral, with its rows of magnificent columns. There was the elegant Hotel Europa – the best hotel in St Petersburg – and just beyond it, an enchanting glimpse of the glittering fairy-tale domes of the Church of the Savior on Spilled Blood. There was the glass-roofed bazaar, designed to look like an exquisite Paris arcade, and twinkling in the distance, the golden spire of the Admiralty Tower.

It was splendid – and yet, Sophie knew that if the sightseers were to venture the full length of the long street, they would find it changed entirely. By the time they reached its opposite end, the magical grandeur would have melted away like a dream. The shops and palaces would be replaced by ramshackle tenements; the elegant people by ordinary working folk in old shawls and big aprons, or muddy sheepskins; an old man selling roasted pumpkin seeds from a brazier, and beggars huddling out of the cold.

Just like London, St Petersburg had two different faces – and during the six weeks she had been here, Sophie had made it her business to get to know them both. She knew most English people in the city stayed away from its darker corners, remaining safe in their own comfortable circle – socialising at the New English Club, shopping at the Magasin Anglais, and barely understanding a word of Russian. But Sophie wanted to know the real St Petersburg. She'd spent hours walking around the city streets until her feet ached; and had persuaded Vera's son, Mitya, to begin teaching her to speak Russian herself.

Today however, no Russian would be required. Sophie's destination was on the most splendid section of the Nevsky. Beneath the sign of the Imperial Eagle, gold letters spelled out in both English and French: *Rivière's Jewellery & Fine Goods*. Some of the sightseers had paused to admire the sumptuous façade, and to peep into the arched windows, through which it was possible to glimpse St Petersburg's elite, lingering over glass-fronted cabinets. Inside them, a treasure trove of exquisite objects glittered like a fairy hoard.

Rivière's was a maker of marvels and dreams. There were twinkling crystal flowers fit for an enchanted garden; tiny jewelled scent bottles, no bigger than Sophie's thumb; and little gold tea sets that the Tsar's daughters used for their tea parties. There were jewel boxes no bigger than a bird's egg, and diamond brooches that glittered like frost. There were miniature animals, carved from precious stones, which Nakamura said made him think of the Japanese sculptures called *netsuke* – a carnelian fox with eyes of rubies, a crystal rabbit, a jade frog with a single pearl in its mouth.

But what Rivière's was really famous for was its music boxes. Each year, Monsieur Rivière himself designed a new music box for the Tsar to give to his children at the New Year festivities. Each music box was extraordinary – from a silver-gilt castle, with jewelled flags flying, to a moving carousel, complete with golden horses. Keen to follow the Imperial family in everything, St Petersburg's wealthy flocked to Rivière's to purchase music boxes of their own. Sophie's favourites were all in the shape of birds – a green parrot in a gilded cage, a wonderful peacock with a jewelled tail, and a magnificent golden firebird, decorated with gleaming rubies. They reminded her very much of a music box which had been made here in this very shop: the Clockwork Sparrow.

In a strange way, she thought, as she made her way behind the shop towards the staff entrance, it was the Clockwork Sparrow that had brought her here. It had certainly helped her get this job at Riviere's: when she'd explained she had worked at Sinclair's, London's finest department store, for the famous Mr Edward Sinclair, himself a great collector of Rivière's objects, and when she had talked of his marvellous Clockwork Sparrow, she had been hired almost at once. Of course, it helped that she spoke French – the language of St Petersburg's aristocrats, who considered Russian the language of the peasants.

And being English was a distinct advantage too: for in Russia, her new colleague Irina had explained to her, any English person was automatically considered someone of importance – even a 'milord' or 'milady'.

Now, she pushed open the door and went through into the workshop at the back of the shop. No one even glanced up at her – except for Boris, one of the master jewellers, and Vera's husband – who gave her a quick, kindly smile from where he was already hard at work examining some technical drawings that were spread out on the workbench before him.

Sophie was quite used to that. In Rivière's workshop, there was always a feeling of intense concentration in the air. The only sounds to be heard were the scrape of a stool on the floor, the clink of a delicate jeweller's instrument, or the occasional brief mutter in any one of a dozen languages – for Rivière's artisans came from all over Europe. With protective smocks over their clothing, the jewellers bent low over their workbenches, holding tiny paintbrushes or magnifiers in their hands – whilst behind them, polished wooden shelves stretched from floor to ceiling, each filled with miniature objects, glinting with precious stones or bright with enamel designs.

Sophie slipped quietly past, towards the cloakroom. She found herself thinking, as she often did, of how strange it was that the Clockwork Sparrow had been made here in this very room. How peculiar it was that so much could have come from something so small – a tiny mechanical bird she could hold in the palm of her hand! For if the Clockwork Sparrow had never existed and been stolen, she might never have discovered her talent for detective work; Taylor & Rose might never have existed; she might never have known about the Baron and his secret society, the *Fraternitas Draconum*. And of course, if it were not for the *Fraternitas* she wouldn't be in St Petersburg at all.

She'd come here on the trail of a notebook which the *Fraternitas* had stolen: a most important notebook that contained research about the sinister society itself, but more significantly, information about a powerful secret weapon they had hidden away centuries ago. They had concealed clues to the weapon's location in Benedetto Casselli's dragon paintings, so that future members of the society could find it. The notebook contained information about how the clues in the paintings could be 'decoded' to locate the weapon: but if the *Fraternitas* were to get hold of it, Sophie knew they would use it to help spark off a terrible war in Europe. It was down to her to get the notebook – and prevent them.

Somewhere, she mused, as she went into the cloakroom to hang up her coat and tidy her hair, in some other world, there was no Clockwork Sparrow. In that world, there was a Sophie who had never come here, who didn't think at all about things like secret weapons, or wars, or shadowy societies. Perhaps that Sophie was still selling hats at

Sinclair's, gazing out of the window at Piccadilly Circus, and looking forward to going out to tea with Lil.

It was a cosy thought, yet at the same time it made her feel strangely uncomfortable. Her old life seemed small and restricted – a little box into which she would no longer be able to contain herself. Now, she was a thousand miles from London and Piccadilly Circus. And yet at the same time, Rivière's was oddly like Sinclair's, she mused, as she went through into the shop, where sales assistants in white gloves moved quietly to and fro. There was the same sumptuously thick carpet; the same richly polished wood and velvet; the same aroma of beeswax, and perfume, and luxury. The Russian countesses admiring jewels could so easily be London ladies, excited about a new Paris hat.

The shop manager gave her a quick nod, gesturing towards a group gathered around a display of diamond bracelets. Sophie went over to them at once: '*Bonjour, mesdames,*' she began. 'May I be of any help?'

But even as she showed them the bracelets, Sophie kept a sharp eye out. There was someone she was looking for amidst the silk top hats and frothy ostrich feathers – one person she wanted to see, more than anyone else.

He wasn't the kind of person anyone else would have paid any attention to. He looked like an ordinary old man, with an unkempt beard. He wore a shabby overcoat with the collar turned up, and his hat pulled low. He wasn't like the other gentlemen who came to Rivière's: the haughty young aristocrats; the Tsar's officers with their gleaming gold braid; the wealthy merchants in fur-lined coats. And yet he visited the shop almost every day. Once there, he would shuffle his way slowly around, before coming to rest, in silent contemplation, before a cabinet of enamelled opera glasses and jewelled lorgnettes. It was always the same display that held him transfixed – and as he looked at it, Sophie looked at him.

The beard, the hat and the collar did not fool her in the least. She knew that this was no ordinary, shabby, harmless old man. In fact, the man who was gazing at the opera glasses was the reason she was here in St Petersburg – and he was someone very dangerous indeed.

CHAPTER SIX

Rivière's, The Nevsky Prospekt, St Petersburg

'I don't understand why you waste time on him,' Irina muttered, as she and Sophie stood together behind the counter, some distance away from where the old man was peering at a gilded magnifying glass. 'He's never going to buy anything! He's obviously got no money – just look at the state of his overcoat!'

'I know,' said Sophie, with a shrug. 'I suppose I feel sorry for him.'

Irina tutted disapprovingly. '*Alice!* I know you haven't been here very long, but you have to understand! If you want to earn a commission, you can't start *feeling sorry* for people. You have to choose your customers with care.' She cast her eye around the shop. 'Look – see him, for example? That young fellow, with the gold trim on his coat. He's got money burning a hole in his pocket, I can tell. See how he wants to impress his lady friend? I recognise her – she's a dancer from the Mariinsky. *He's* the one you want to go for.'

She raised her eyes at Sophie, encouraging her, but Sophie just smiled. 'He's all yours,' she said sweetly.

Irina shrugged. 'Your loss. I bet you fifty kopeks I can get him to buy that gold *bonbonnière*.'

She strolled off in the direction of the young man, and Sophie grinned after her. She was fond of Irina, whose easy confidence sometimes reminded her a little of Lil. But the truth was, she wasn't concerned with earning a commission. The small attaché case, carefully hidden under her bed in her room at Vera's, contained more money than Irina would earn in a year, courtesy of the Secret Service Bureau.

Sophie wasn't here to earn money. She was here for the old man in the shabby overcoat.

'May I help you? Would you like to take a closer look at the opera glasses?'

He looked up and smiled at her, a little embarrassed. 'You must think I am mad,' he said, in fluent French – though Sophie could detect the traces of a German accent. 'Almost every day I come here, and every time you are kind enough to show these to me.'

'Not at all. It's my job,' said Sophie pleasantly, as she unlocked the cabinet with one of the small keys that hung on her belt. 'We have many customers who come back to look at their favourite items. There is one lady who likes to try on a particular diamond tiara every week!' she added, with a smile.

The old man smiled back, but his eyes were already fixed on the pearl and ruby opera glasses she was showing him. 'Fascinating,' he murmured, extending a careful fingertip to touch the gold filigree. 'Such perfect craftsmanship!'

'Is there anything else you would care to look at today, Herr Schmidt?'

Sophie knew that the man's name wasn't 'Herr Schmidt', any more than her own was 'Mademoiselle Alice Grayson'. She'd decided to use her mother's name as her *alias* – her false name – while she was travelling undercover. It seemed rather appropriate, as she knew her mother had visited St Petersburg as a young girl: she'd read all about it in the old diaries that she had inherited.

For a brief moment, she wondered why the man standing before her had chosen 'Herr Schmidt' as his own alias. Perhaps he simply thought that with such an ordinary German name, no one could possibly guess that he was no harmless old man, but in fact the Count Rudolf von Wilderstein – disgraced cousin of the King of Arnovia, and husband of the notorious Countess von Wilderstein, hiding under a false identity in St Petersburg.

When Sophie had left Paris in Captain Nakamura's aeroplane, she'd never expected she'd end up following the Count all the way to Russia. She'd hoped she would be able to catch up with him at the next stage of the air race, and seize back the stolen notebook he was carrying: the notebook containing the all-important information about the secret weapon. But catching up with the Count had not been as easy as she'd hoped. After the dramatic arrest of the Countess in Paris, he and his plane had disappeared from the race, as though they had vanished into thin air.

It had been Nakamura who had explained that it would not be possible for the Count to disappear altogether – not if he continued to travel by plane, at any rate. After all, there were not very many airfields where a pilot could stop to refuel, or to fix the endless problems which Sophie had learned affected aeroplanes at every stage of a journey. And so, at each stage of the air race, while Nakamura had traded stories with the other pilots, or made essential repairs to his plane, Sophie had talked to the mechanics to learn what she could of the Count's whereabouts. As the weeks passed and they made their way across Europe, telegrams had zigzagged back and forth to the Bureau in London, and with their help, she'd pieced together the Count's route. At first he'd roughly followed the path of the air race, taking advantage of the free passage across borders offered to the pilots. He'd travelled out of France to Belgium, and then to the Netherlands, where they'd almost caught up with him, missing him at the airfield by barely an hour. After that they'd lost him for a while, before getting a tip-off that he had landed at an airfield in Sweden.

'He must be in a great hurry,' Nakamura had said, as they studied the route that Sophie had pencilled on the map. 'He's barely stopped to rest for more than an hour at a time – and flying is tiring. I would think it dangerous to fly so long without a proper break.'

'I think he's trying to put as much distance as possible between himself and Arnovia,' Sophie had observed. 'He must know he's wanted by the authorities, for plotting against the King.'

'So what will we do now?' Nakamura had asked. 'There are only two more stops: Milan, and then Zurich. The air race will be finished in a few days. After that, would you like to go in pursuit of the Count and the notebook?'

Sophie had looked up at him, pleased and surprised. She'd assumed that Nakamura would go back to Japan as soon as the air race was over – but now here he was, proposing that they keep following the Count.

'I'd like that very much, if you really would be willing. But I just wish I knew for sure that he still *has* the notebook.' It was far too precious to be sent by post, but there was always the risk that the Count had handed it to some fellow on an airfield somewhere, who'd been entrusted with seeing it safely into the hands of the *Fraternitas*. 'If he hasn't, then all I've done will be for nothing.'

Nakamura had been looking down at the map, as though already working out their route. He'd glanced up and raised his eyebrows at Sophie. 'Well . . . there's only one way to find out,' he'd said simply.

And Nakamura had been right. She'd come so far already: there was no sense in giving up. By the time they'd arrived in Milan, her sources were reporting that the Count had left Sweden for St Petersburg, in Russia, where he'd made arrangements to store his plane – suggesting he planned to stay there for a little while at least. A telegram to the Chief had ensured papers were ready for them to collect in Zurich, which would eventually allow them to travel over the border to Russia.

Once they'd arrived in St Petersburg, Sophie had put her detective skills to work, eventually tracking down the Count's aeroplane, stored in a farm shed not far from the airfield. From there she'd worked hard to locate the man himself, who she learned had taken a room in one of the city's dingier hotels, under the name of 'Herr Schmidt'.

'I bet he's meeting someone from the *Fraternitas* here to hand over the notebook,' she'd said to Nakamura that evening, over a Russian dinner of unfamiliar, strangely fragranced dishes. 'He can't have given it to them yet.'

'How can you be sure?' Nakamura had asked.

'If he had, they'd have paid him well for it – and that hotel doesn't look like the sort of place that a member of a Royal family would stay, if they had money.'

For the next two days, she'd watched the Count's hotel but there had been no sign of him. She'd barely been able to bring herself to stay away for a few hours' sleep, she'd been so determined not to miss her chance. At last, her persistence had been rewarded: she'd glimpsed the Count slipping out of the hotel, and hurrying along the street. Was he going to meet his *Fraternitas* contact at last?

But no meeting had taken place. Instead, Sophie had

tracked him to a bank on the Nevsky, where after a short conversation with a clerk, he'd passed a small parcel wrapped in brown paper over the counter. Afterwards, she'd followed him to Wolff's, where he'd bought an Arnovian newspaper; to a café where he'd sat at a table in the darkest corner, and furtively eaten a large pastry, topped with chocolate and cream; and finally, strangest of all, to Rivière's, the city's most magnificent jeweller, where he'd lingered outside for a while, as if trying to pluck up the courage to venture in.

He'd spoken to no one but the cake-shop waitress and the bank clerk. He'd walked with his head down and his collar turned up against the wind. Sophie knew he'd been a military man, who had won medals for his bravery, but he hadn't looked brave, nor in the least like someone who until recently had hoped to rule a country. Instead, he'd looked only lonely, tired – and afraid.

'He's hiding,' she'd said to Nakamura. 'He's worried about being caught, even here.'

'What about the notebook?'

Sophie had leaned her chin in her hands. 'I'm pretty sure the notebook is what was inside that brown paper parcel. It looked to me as though he was putting it into a safe deposit box at the bank, which is rather interesting.'

'Why?' Nakamura had asked. 'I would think that was a very sensible thing to do.'

'Oh, of course. It's absolutely sensible. In a bank vault

it's safe – there's no risk of someone like me trying to steal it. But I don't believe he'd have put the notebook into the bank if he was expecting to hand it over to the *Fraternitas* immediately. He must be expecting to wait for at least a few days.' She couldn't help thinking that was rather strange. She knew how important the notebook was to the *Fraternitas*, and how much they wanted the information it contained. Why would they delay collecting it from the Count?

What's more, how was *she* to get hold of it now? If the Count had kept it in his hotel room, or even in his pocket, she'd have had a chance at stealing it. But locked away in a bank vault? That would be impossible. She'd have to wait for the Count to withdraw it from the bank to give it to his *Fraternitus* contact before she'd have her chance.

She'd kept a careful watch on the Count, but even after a week had passed he hadn't returned to withdraw the notebook. It had been time for a new strategy, so she had come to Rivière's.

Now, under the twinkle of the crystal chandelier, the Count was saying to her: 'You must get quite used to these treasures, being surrounded by them every day.'

'Oh, I don't believe I could ever get used to them!' Sophie replied. 'I have my own special favourites too.'

She'd intended to point to one of the bird music boxes, but a sudden instinct made her point instead towards a silver box with a delicate enamel painting of a London scene on its lid – the river and the spires of Westminster.

The Count turned to examine it. 'A lovely English scene. You are English, are you not, *mademoiselle?*'

Sophie felt triumphant. She'd been talking to the Count at Rivière's for several days – but this was the first time he'd asked her a question about herself. 'Yes, from London,' she replied casually. 'This reminds me of home, which seems very far away. You're far from home too, aren't you?'

She said it as lightly as she could, turning slightly away to close the door of the cabinet, so the Count could not see her face. She dared to add: 'From Arnovia, I think?'

Even though she wasn't looking at him, she felt the Count stiffen. There was a moment of tense silence, in which she locked the cabinet door and then turned to him with an expression of perfect innocence.

'You know Arnovia?' he asked, in a hoarse voice.

'Oh no, not really. I've never been there. But I met a couple of Arnovians once, and I remember what they sounded like.' No lie in that. She *had* met some Arnovians once, if you counted those brief moments on the airfield in Paris, when she and Lil had rescued Crown Prince Alex with Princess Anna's help. 'I believe it's a lovely place,' she added.

Relaxing now, the Count nodded. 'It is,' he agreed, wistfully. 'The mountains are beautiful. And Elffburg, the capital – it is a perfect little city. There's nowhere else like it.'

'You must miss it very much,' said Sophie. 'I know

I miss London.'

But the Count only nodded briefly, as if realising he'd stayed longer than he should have. 'I've taken up too much of your time, *mademoiselle*. Thank you for showing me the opera glasses.'

Sophie smiled in her friendliest manner. 'Come again. It's been a pleasure to talk with a fellow exile.'

The Count looked at her sharply. 'Exile?' he repeated.

Her face remained innocent as she replied: 'Yes – it almost feels like that, doesn't it, when you're far from home? Come again and tell me more about Arnovia. Perhaps I'll go there one day. I'd like to see Elffburg – and I hear they have the most wonderful cakes!'

The Count's face broke into an unexpected smile. 'Indeed they do! The cake shops here are not bad – but I have found only one *patisserie*, in the Summer Gardens, that does real Arnovian-style pastries.'

'I'll have to try it,' said Sophie.

The Count bowed a polite farewell, and shuffled away – past Irina, who was taking the gold *bonbonnière* to be wrapped for her customer.

Sophie watched him go, disappearing into the crowds on the Nevsky. It might not have seemed like much of an exchange, but for her it was important. It was a small but significant step towards completing her mission – and she was beginning to think that her plan for getting back the stolen notebook might just work.

CHAPTER SEVEN

The British Embassy, St Petersburg

It was half past six by the time Sophie left Rivière's, having helped Irina to carefully lock away all the jewels in the enormous safe for the night. At this time of day, the Nevsky was still full of the clatter of tram cars and the jingling of carriages, driven by grand coachmen in blue coats and peacock-feather hats – no doubt conveying their passengers to the Mariinsky Theatre for the evening's performance.

As she always did, Sophie called in at Wolff's to pick up a London newspaper – noticing as she did so that the assassination of Stolypin in Kiev had made the front pages, even there. But she didn't dawdle for long – not to look at the books in the window of the English bookshop, nor to admire the pretty green frock on display in a French boutique, nor even to examine the enormous brightly coloured poster for the Circus of Marvels which was soon to arrive in St Petersburg. She had to drop off her regular weekly report to the Chief.

She'd been writing to the Chief each week ever since she'd arrived in St Petersburg. She knew he would want to keep up to date with her progress and especially the whereabouts of the Count von Wilderstein. It didn't take long to walk over to the Palace Embankment, where rows of immense mansions, painted powder-blue or butter-yellow, stood overlooking the wide grey river. The British Embassy was at number 4: an elegant mint-green mansion with a long balcony and a row of flags. As usual, she bypassed the grand front door and slipped round to a discreet side entrance. A footman in white gloves accepted the envelope, marked CLARKE & SONS, with a grave bow.

As she came back on to the Palace Embankment, she glanced swiftly around her. The Chief had warned her to be on her guard in St Petersburg and had instructed her to be particularly careful with her communications back to the Bureau. But there was nothing unusual to be seen on the street, so Sophie turned more comfortably towards home, looking forward to telling Nakamura about her day – especially her conversation with the Count.

Nakamura was her closest friend in St Petersburg and the only person who knew Sophie's true identity. Sometimes it was hard to believe that they'd met little more than three months ago. They'd exchanged only a few polite pleasantries before Nakamura had invited her to climb aboard his plane in pursuit of the Count.

You got to know someone very quickly when you were travelling with them in an aeroplane across Europe. But becoming friends with Nakamura hadn't been at all like getting to know Billy, or Joe, or Mei – and certainly not in the least like making friends with Lil, who from the very first moment they'd met had been falling over herself to talk. Sophie smiled to herself, thinking of how Lil couldn't wait to tell you everything about herself, and to ask you a million questions. Nakamura, on the other hand, had barely asked her anything at all – though surely he must have been curious about why a young woman was so desperate to chase after an Arnovian pilot.

For the first few days of the journey, they'd hardly spoken: after all, you couldn't have much of a conversation when you were high in the sky in an aeroplane. The wind had rushed in Sophie's face, and roared in her ears, leaving her unable to do anything but stare out at the immense blue sky and the green land, spread beneath her like a counterpane. She'd always had a secret fear of heights, and the thought of soaring into the sky in Nakamura's flimsy-looking plane filled her with horror. Yet once the first terrifying moments were over, she'd begun to take an unexpected pleasure in the tranquillity of the open sky. It was very calm, high up in the air, and in spite of the wind and the thundering engine, she'd found her thoughts drifting with the clouds, in a way that was quite different to anything she'd known before.

Sometimes she'd find herself thinking of the Bureau and the *Fraternitas Draconum*. Sometimes she'd think of her assignment in Paris: a blur of images of a bloodstained carpet, a strange alchemical diagram in an old book, the dark streets of Montmartre by night. Sometimes she'd think about Lil, waving goodbye from the airfield; and then about the offices of Taylor & Rose; and the Loyal Order of Lions; and all the adventures they'd had together. But often she thought about very different things. Orchard House, her childhood home. The smell of wet grass, and furniture polish; piano practice every morning; Papa sitting beside her at bedtime, telling her one of his stories. The pages of her mother's diary, fluttering beneath her fingertips, the shape of her handwriting in faded blue ink, spelling out her name: *Alice Grayson*. Memories blended together, like a kind of dream.

Now and then, Nakamura would make a quick hand signal to her from the pilot's seat, to let her know they were going to descend. But mostly he didn't seem to notice she was there, his whole attention fixed on flying the plane. When he did bring them swooping to the ground, it was a strange feeling to rattle down to the busy hustle of the airfield, where mechanics in greasy overalls hurried to and fro, fellow pilots called out greetings, or race officials came forward to confirm their times.

At first the airfields had seemed strange to Sophie. But she soon grew accustomed to the hot smell of oil, the quips and jokes between the pilots, and the peculiar language of things like 'fuel supply' and 'rudder control'. There was always a café close by, where pilots and spectators could get hot coffee and sandwiches, and here Sophie would sit, busily checking maps and charts, and making notes.

In Paris, she'd posed as heiress Celia Blaxland, in stylish gowns and expensive jewels. Now she'd become someone else altogether – Alice Grayson, the name on the passport the Bureau had sent her. They'd told people she was Nakamura's navigator and secretary, which was accepted without question, though it was scarcely a conventional job for a young English girl. But airfields were free and easy places: there were as many eager young women excited by the possibilities of flight as there were young men. There were even a few female pilots: on their first stop, at Liège, Sophie had been lucky enough to meet one of the most famous, Elise Deroche, who the press had christened '*la femme oiseau*'. She'd been quick to take inspiration from the daring Frenchwoman, with a memory of what her detective mentor Ada Pickering had taught her: 'Never underestimate the importance of the right *clothes*, Sophie!' She'd copied Elise's smart flying costume, travelling in a trim sweater and a divided skirt or slacks – every inch the bold young *aviatrix*. One or two of the journalists covering the race had wanted to take her photograph, but she always refused politely, not wanting to blow her cover, and she was always quick to slip out of sight on the occasions she glimpsed *The Daily Picture*'s Roberta Russell at the airfield, knowing that Miss Russell was certain to recognise her.

As the days had passed, she and Nakamura had slowly got to know more about each other. As they waited for a storm to pass in Belgium, he'd told her a little about growing up in Tokyo, the youngest son of a wealthy noble family. As they sat at the airfield in Denmark, waiting for the mechanics to finish a repair to the plane, he talked about being sent away to school in England, when he was just a little boy. He taught her a number of things with immense patience: how to read a map and calculate their flying speed; how an engine worked; and even a few words of Japanese. In return, she found herself confiding in him about herself and about her work. The Secret Service Bureau was a strict secret of course, but Sophie did tell him about Taylor & Rose, and her current mission to find the Count and the stolen notebook.

'Are you really sure you want to come on with me to St Petersburg?' she'd asked him, when the final stage of the air race was over. They'd been sitting in the café at the airfield in Zurich, admiring the gleaming bronze medal he had been awarded by Sir Chester Norton himself, after winning third place.

Nakamura had nodded at once. 'I would like to see as much of the West as possible. Of course, I know England well – and something of France too. But it has been most interesting getting to know more of Europe on this tour, and now I am keen to see still more of it.'

Sophie had known just what he meant. The air race had brought the map of Europe from her old school room atlas vividly to life, and she too felt the same hunger to explore it. St Petersburg intrigued her especially – perhaps because she'd read about her mother's experiences of travelling there in her old diaries.

'St Petersburg interests me a great deal,' Nakamura had said, his thoughts chiming with her own. 'They have a new Aero Club there, and I've heard a lot about a young Scotsman, Mackenzie, who is designing new aeroplanes for the Tsar.'

Sophie hadn't been surprised to hear that it was primarily for aeroplanes that Nakamura was interested in St Petersburg. She'd seen for herself how passionate he was about aviation: he could talk for hours with the other pilots and was always intensely fascinated by any new designs or developments. He'd even begun working on a few sketches for some new aeroplane designs of his own. Yet even so, his willingness to travel to Russia surprised her. She'd already seen how people looked at him: even in the café, a table of Austrian mechanics had been nudging each other and turning round to stare, as if they could scarcely believe a Japanese person existed – never mind one calmly eating an *apfelstrudel*. But Nakamura was always calm: their curious glances had seemed to slide right off him, and he'd gone on eating, quite unconcerned. Sophie had asked him about it, and he'd shrugged and grinned. 'Oh, I got quite used to that at boarding school,' he'd said. Yet she'd guessed it might be worse in Russia: it was only a few years since Russia and Japan had been at war, ending in a humiliating defeat for the Tsar's forces. In St Petersburg, would Nakamura be viewed as the enemy?

Just the same, she'd been very glad indeed that Nakamura would be travelling with her. As she'd flipped through the fat dossier that had arrived from the Bureau, she'd begun to feel a little apprehensive about making the trip.

The Bureau had all manner of mysterious ways of sending her messages. Sometimes they would be delivered by shifty-looking errand boys on bicycles, other times handed over discreetly by a mechanic. Once or twice they had even arrived with uniformed officials, who would ceremonially present her with an envelope bearing a grand diplomatic seal. This envelope had been a particularly thick one, containing a stack of Russian *roubles*, identity papers, and the dossier, which she recognised at once as Carruthers' work – she'd know his black type and inky scribbles anywhere. It had been accompanied by a brief note from the Chief himself, penned in his distinctive green ink. She had almost heard the sound of his gramophone in the background as she'd read it:

July 1911

Enclosed is a briefing on ST Petersburg - together with papers that have been drawn up to enable you to cross the border. I would ask you to proceed with the greatest of caution once you are within the territory of the Russian Empire. Be aware of the possibility of political unrest, and avoid public gatherings if you can. Tsar Nicholas II and his wife Alexandra are not popular with the people - be alert to the activities of the Underground revolutionary groups within the city particularly amongst the students and workers.

In particular, beware the Okhrana. They are the Tsar's Secret Police though they do not operate quite like any police force you will have encountered before. They are Spies, who work undercover, infiltrating every quarter of the city, often deliberately stirring up trouble. The Okhrana are dangerous, so be on your guard. As a stranger in the city they may be watching you: Conceal your true identity at all times and keep communications with this office to a minimum. Your reports may be sent confidentially c/o the British ambassador Sir George Buchanan - deliver to the Embassy on the Palace Embankment, Marked CLARKE & SONS. They will do the rest.

Good hunting - C.

ST PETERSBURG

Capital of Imperial Russia

Situated on Neva River, key Russian port offering access to the Baltic Sea

Population: 1.5 million and growing rapidly

Languages spoken: Russian (official language), Polish, Latvian, Yiddish, German, French (spoken by the upper classes)

Currency: Rouble (100 kopeks = 1 rouble)

Calendar: Russia uses the Julian Calendar and is therefore approximately 12 days behind the Western European (Gregorian) Calendar.

Religion: Russian Orthodox Church

Industries: Metalwork, engineering, textiles. Over 200,000 factory workers reside in the city, living and working in poor conditions. Industrial strikes are common, and suppressed harshly by the authorities.

Current status: No SSB agents currently stationed in St Petersburg.

A week later, she and Nakamura had arrived in St Petersburg – this city of smoke and mist, canals and spires. It had been strange at first, but now she knew it well: its smells of river water and incense and warm bread; its rich colours – old gold and bottle green; its sounds of rattling trams, and hooves on cobblestones, and lapping water.

Now, as she strolled back along the quiet streets towards the pink house beside the canal, she felt comfortable here – hands tucked into her pockets for warmth, beginning to wonder what they'd be having for supper. It had been a satisfying day – she was finally making progress with the Count – and yet, there was something that still troubled her. She couldn't fathom why the precious notebook was lying in a bank vault and why the Count was wasting his time looking at jewels in Rivière's. Why hadn't the *Fraternitas* come to claim it yet? What could they be waiting for? Not for the first time, she began to wonder whether she had got it all wrong, whether they could have discovered she was watching the Count – and were somehow toying with her, playing a kind of game of their own . . .

It was an uncomfortable thought. Even as she considered it, she became aware of a sound on the street behind her. It was the regular pad of footsteps, coming closer – more than one set of footsteps too. As she began to walk a little faster, she heard the footsteps increase in pace.

All at once, she was on alert. Was someone following her? Could it be someone from the *Fraternitas*? She was perfectly capable of shaking off someone tailing her – amongst the bustle of the Nevsky, it would have been easy – but this was a quiet, dark street. She didn't want to lead them back to Vera's but where else could she go? She glanced quickly up into the darkened window of a house, hoping to catch a reflected glimpse of her pursuers, but as soon as she did, she stopped and grinned in relief.

'Alice!' called a familiar voice, and Mitya came hurrying up behind her. Vera's son was a tall, scruffy, bespectacled young man, wearing the green cap favoured by the students of St Petersburg University. 'You walk so fast. I could hardly catch up with you!'

Two of his student friends came up too. 'So you can outrun a policeman, Mitya – but you can't keep up with Alice here?' teased Nikolai, a cheerful young fellow with a thatch of curly hair.

'Outrun a policeman?' repeated Sophie in surprise. 'What *have* you all been doing?'

'Our duty,' announced Viktor, in a rather haughty voice. He was a slight, sharp-eyed young man who wore his hair close-cropped under his green cap. Sophie knew he was something of a leader amongst the students, and much admired by the others, although she'd never found him as friendly as Nikolai or Mitya's other friends.

Before she could ask what he meant, Mitya was hustling them all forward. 'Come on!' he urged. 'Mama will have supper on the table by now and I'm starving!'

CHAPTER EIGHT

The House on the Ulitsa Zelenaya, St Petersburg

As they hurried inside the pink house, Sophie breathed in the rich smell of garlic which told her that supper was ready. The house was a dark and cosy place, with creaky staircases, crooked ceilings, and tall shuttered windows that opened out over the greenish water of the canal that lay below. The walls were hung with pictures and icons; the armchairs were strewn with books and newspapers in a variety of languages; a tabby cat slept curled on the hearthrug; and there was always the smoky scent of the crackling fire.

Tonight, the others were already in the parlour, sitting around the big round table with its lace-edged tablecloth. As they made their way inside, the small room seemed crammed with people – talking, drinking and tucking into steaming-hot bowls of Vera's *borscht*, possibly all at the same time. When she'd first arrived in St Petersburg, Sophie had found the food odd, but she'd grown to love dishes like this one – a rich savoury soup, served with salted cucumbers, black bread and sour cream.

Now, Boris called out to her in welcome: 'Alice – come and sit here by me, before these greedy ones eat up all the supper!'

Discarding her coat and hat, she squeezed into the seat between him and Nakamura. It was because of Boris that she and Nakamura had come to be lodging here, in the tall pink house beside the canal. Unlikely as it might seem, the big, bearded man was one of Rivière's most gifted craftsmen. Looking at him now, with a spoon in one enormous, spade-like hand, and a hunk of black bread in the other, it was difficult to imagine the precision of his work at Rivière's. Yet Sophie had so often seen those same large hands carefully positioning a tiny pearl into place, or delicately adjusting a minute cog.

Vera pinched her cheek in welcome, and filled her bowl at once with *borscht*, before turning to wave her ladle furiously in the direction of Mitya and his friends.

'You stupid boys! What were you thinking, giving out those leaflets in a public place like that? You could have been arrested!'

'But Mama, we had to spread our message,' protested Mitya, taking his own seat. 'It's important. People have to know the truth!'

'That may be the case,' said Vera darkly. 'But you won't

spread your precious *message* very far if you're arrested and locked up in prison – or worse!'

'Ha! They couldn't possibly arrest us,' boasted Nikolai. 'We're too fast for those policemen. They didn't even catch a glimpse of us. We ran as quickly as hares – they could never have caught up!'

He laughed but Vera didn't look very amused. 'It's not a laughing matter,' she said sharply, as she handed him a bowl of *borscht*.

'But Mitya is right,' argued Viktor. 'Sometimes we have to take risks in order to show people the truth – to open their eyes. The workers are being exploited, and the Tsar has nothing but contempt for ordinary people. Look at the way he hides in his grand palace in the country, when his people have need of him! His policemen will arrest anyone who raises their voice to speak up for justice – or his soldiers will shoot them down like dogs in the street. It isn't right! We cannot simply stay silent. We must take action – something must change.'

'The Imperial system is outdated,' agreed Mitya. 'It's barbaric! We should have a parliament of our own, like other countries, so that the people can have a voice. Russia must become a Republic.'

'A Republic is all very well, but it would be nothing without a wise Tsar to govern it,' objected his father.

'A wise Tsar, perhaps,' argued Vera. 'But it must be said that our Tsar has not always shown the greatest of wisdom.'

'Hmph! It is the fault of that holy man, Rasputin, pouring poison in his ears,' rumbled Boris disapprovingly.

'That's right!' exclaimed Nikolai. 'You wouldn't believe some of the stories about him I heard in the tavern yesterday. Did you know that . . . ?'

But before he could say any more, Boris held up his hands. 'None of your tavern gossip here,' he said gently. 'This is a respectable house, and there are children and ladies present.'

Sophie was eating her *borscht*, listening with interest. She'd never known anywhere that politics was discussed so often, and with such fervour, as in this house. Even the London suffragettes she knew, who fought so tirelessly for women's right to the vote, were not like this. At Vera's, politics were debated morning, noon and night – over breakfast, dinner and supper. Everyone seemed to have a different view: Boris was a traditionalist, who believed Russia must have a Tsar. He even kept a photograph of the Tsar's children hanging in the hallway, taking especial pride in the part he had played in crafting music boxes for them at Rivière's. But Vera was more critical, and as for Mitya and his student friends, they were strongly in favour of abolishing the monarchy in favour of revolution and democracy. They believed that ordinary Russians should be able to vote for a people's government, and attended many meetings, reading circles and lectures with others who believed the same. Now, it seemed, some of their radical activities had led them to a narrow escape from the police.

Sophie knew that expressing these kinds of views in St Petersburg could be dangerous. Since the assassination of Stolypin, there were even more suspicious mutterings than usual about 'reds' and 'anarchists' stirring up trouble, and the police seemed to be everywhere in their dark uniforms. You could be watched, searched, arrested or even imprisoned for nothing more than a policeman's hunch that you might be a political agitator. Then there was the mysterious *Okhrana* – the Tsar's secret police, who were rumoured to infiltrate every corner of the city, listening for even the slightest whisper of *revolution*.

'If the Tsar isn't careful, he'll get what's coming to him,' said Viktor now, as he reached out for the dish of pickles. 'Just like Stolypin.'

Vera frowned. 'Whatever you may think of him, shooting the poor man like that in cold blood in a crowded theatre was a shocking thing to do!'

'Of course, violence is always regrettable – but sometimes it is necessary, if there is to be real change,' Viktor announced grandly.

Nikolai nodded, as if this was an idea he had heard many times before. But Mitya looked more doubtful, and Boris shook his head as he wiped the last of his *borscht* out of his bowl with a piece of bread. 'If you had seen the true consequences of violence, you wouldn't make such declarations,' he said heavily. 'The bombs, the assassinations, the blood in the street. If you had grown up witness to all that, as I did, you would not talk so easily of *violence*.'

Vera nodded in agreement. 'Quite right,' she said crisply. 'And before you start rolling your eyes at me like that, young Viktor, let me tell you, it is not only us older people who think so. *You* agree with me, don't you, Alice?'

Sophie looked up from her bowl. She found everyone was looking at her, and for a moment, she hesitated. It was not an easy question to answer. Of course, the murder of Stolypin was shocking and wrong – and of course she didn't believe such a violent act could ever be right. Yet her father had been a military man: he had believed in the heroism of the battlefield, and raised her on stories of valiant men, fighting for honour and justice. Surely he would have agreed with Viktor that sometimes violence *was* justified – if the stakes were high enough? And she'd felt that herself too, hadn't she? After all, she'd faced down the Baron with a gun in her hand – and she knew she would have shot him herself if she could.

But: 'Yes,' she said simply, after a moment. 'I agree with you. I don't believe violence is the answer.'

'Nor do I,' said Captain Nakamura.

Viktor looked from one to the other of them in annoyance. 'And yet no more than five years ago, *your* countrymen were waging violent war against ours,' he snapped back to Nakamura. 'What have you say to that?'

'That's enough,' said Vera at once. 'The war is long since over, and Captain Nakamura is our guest.'

'Besides, you can't lay the blame at Japan's door,' Mitya argued, pushing his spectacles up his nose and leaning forward over the table. 'Everyone knows that the war with Japan was waged by the Tsar and his generals, in an effort to distract attention from problems at home in Russia! They thought they would have an easy victory and win the public's approval, but the Japanese proved them wrong. Isn't that right, Captain Nakamura?'

'It is certainly one way to look at it,' said Nakamura in his usual measured tone, wiping his hands carefully on a napkin. 'And I also know that my government were willing to negotiate peace early in the war, but the Tsar would not consent to it. But war is rarely a simple business. There is always blame on both sides.'

Viktor opened his mouth as though he was about to say something else, but before he could speak, Boris intervened. 'Let's change the subject. That's quite enough politics for one evening – eh, Luka? Now, did you see that the Circus of Marvels is to come to St Petersburg? It looks like it will be quite a show.'

After supper, Mitya, Nikolai and Viktor went out to attend one of their political gatherings. 'Take care!' Vera instructed anxiously, as they left.

'Don't fuss, Mama,' said Mitya, giving her a quick absent-minded kiss, before winding his muffler around his throat and pulling on his green cap.

But Vera stayed where she was, looking after him, as he went out into the street and over the bridge with Viktor and Nikolai. She shook her head as though she disapproved, though in fact she shared many of Mitya's views. But Sophie understood her worried expression. Not everywhere in St Petersburg was like the pink house by the canal. Here, anyone could say what they thought: out there, you never knew who might be listening.

Vera turned and saw that Sophie was watching her sympathetically. 'Ah, Alice, *lapochka*! You are a good girl – you would never worry your poor old mama in such a way, would you?' she said, touching Sophie's cheek gently, as she passed by on her way back to the kitchen.

Sophie just smiled. She didn't know quite how to say that her own mama was long gone – and that she thought Mitya impossibly lucky to have a mother like Vera to worry about him.

Truth be told, she felt rather lucky herself, to have met Boris at Rivière's, and through him to find such a safe and friendly home in the city. Boris and Vera were relaxed and broad-minded: they had welcomed a Japanese man and a young English girl who were travelling together, without even turning a hair. Sophie had felt fond of them both at once. She liked the way Vera offered lodgings to so many waifs and strays, who were always given a warm and kindly welcome. At present, as well as their younger son, Mitya, their two grandchildren, Luka and Elena, and of course, Sophie and Nakamura, the pink house was home to Alina, a shy Ukrainian girl, and two busy medical students who came and went at all times of the day and night. Really, the only problem was that in such a busy house, there was little room to spare – and it was rather difficult to find anywhere to have a private conversation.

'Come down to the cellar,' Sophie said to Nakamura now. 'I want to tell you what happened today.'

'The Count?' asked Nakamura, in a low voice, and she nodded.

Fortunately, like many St Petersburg houses, Boris and Vera's home had a large cellar, and it was here that Sophie and Nakamura usually had their private conversations. Much of the cellar was used for storing wood and coal, but Vera allowed Nakamura to use one of the empty storerooms as a kind of study, where he could work on the designs for aeroplanes that currently occupied much of his time. It was rather a dingy place, with a dirty line around the wall which showed where the waters had reached in one of the city's many floods; but there was a big window high up in the wall overlooking the canal, an old armchair in a corner, and a wooden table where Nakamura could work. The cellar room next door was frequently used by Mitya and his student friends for their reading and discussion groups – and sometimes, Sophie suspected, for secret political meetings.

Now, Nakamura lit the lamp, and slid a pile of aeroplane plans out of the way, to make room for them both to sit down at the table. It didn't take Sophie long to tell him all about her conversation with the Count.

'Now that he's told me about the café he goes to, I can meet him there, as if by chance,' she finished excitedly. 'It will give me a proper opportunity to talk to him.'

'I still don't really understand *why* you want more opportunity to talk to him,' said Nakamura. 'Isn't the Count your enemy?'

'Of course – but this may be the best way for me to get the notebook. Perhaps the only way. If he had it in his hotel room, I could sneak in and steal it. Or if he kept it with him, I could pick his pocket. But in a bank vault, there's simply no way I can get to it.'

'But how will going to this café help you to get the notebook?' Nakamura frowned.

'I've been talking to the Count at Rivière's to try and get to know him. To befriend him. I know he's isolated here, and lonely,' Sophie explained. 'Now that he knows me a little, when I see him at the café, I can get him to talk to me. Perhaps even to trust me. And then – well, perhaps I can persuade him to give me the notebook of his own free will.'

Nakamura's face creased into a sudden smile. 'However would you get him to do that?' he asked, with a laugh.

Sophie's eyes gleamed. 'By making him believe I'm the person he's waiting for,' she said triumphantly. 'I'm going to make him think that *I* am an agent of the *Fraternitas Draconum*.'

CHAPTER NINE

The Summer Gardens, St Petersburg

Sophie didn't wait long before putting her plan into action. She didn't want to risk a real agent of the *Fraternitas* appearing on the scene. She'd become increasingly certain that this plan was the best – perhaps the only way she could get her hands on the notebook. And yet, as she walked through the leafy Summer Gardens the next afternoon, she found that her heart was bumping nervously. Although she might have talked confidently to Nakamura about her plan, the truth was she'd never done anything quite like this before.

More than ever, she found herself wishing that Lil was here, walking by her side beneath the trees, down the long avenue of glittering fountains. Lil always made her feel capable of anything. What was more, she'd have known exactly how to trick the Count into believing that they really were *Fraternitas* agents. With her gift for acting, Lil would have put on a wonderful performance: but Sophie knew she did not have the same skills of charming and convincing. If she got this wrong, all the weeks she'd spent working at Rivière's to befriend the Count would have been for nothing – and the notebook would be even further out of reach than before.

She'd had to fall back on her own way of doing things, thinking her plan through methodically. She'd prepared carefully, taking a sizeable sum of money from the attaché case hidden under her bed, and putting it into an envelope – wondering even as she did so if it was the right sort of amount that a real *Fraternitas* agent would give, in return for something as important as the notebook.

She wished she knew a little more about the organisation. When she'd been facing the Baron, she'd understood what mattered to him, and the way his mind worked. But now the Baron was dead and there was only the *Fraternitas* – shadowy and faceless. All she really had to go on was the meeting of its London branch she'd once spied on, which had taken place in the room above a gentleman's club: a gathering of wealthy men, sitting around a long, polished table, talking over the crimes they were carrying out as though they were quite ordinary business matters. She didn't know who its leaders were: all she knew was that they planned to start a war in Europe and that they would use the secret weapon to help them. *That* was why she had to do whatever she could to get hold of the notebook and prevent the weapon falling into their hands, she reminded herself, walking a little faster, her feet scrunching over the gravel, as she came towards the Count's favourite café.

By now she knew the Count's movements so well that it was easy to guess when he would be likely to visit. She'd made sure she arrived before him, and now she settled herself down at a table large enough for two. The menu offered all kinds of delectable treats – honey cake served with blackberries, cherry dumplings with sour cream, raspberry and almond cake, and even a chocolate and meringue confection which had the intriguing name of *Ruins of a Count's Castle* – strangely appropriate, Sophie thought. But she ordered only tea, plus two of the pastries described on the menu as *Specialities of Arnovia*. The waitress looked rather astonished by the size of her appetite but brought them over just the same – two large pastries, filled with cream, chocolate and nuts, and dusted with icing sugar. While she waited for the Count, she began to nibble one of them, savouring the sweet, rich flavours. It was warm and delicious, and the perfume of chocolate reminded her suddenly of faraway Sinclair's.

The jangle of the bell above the door made her glance upwards. She saw that the Count had entered the café and was already shuffling towards his usual table in the darkest corner.

'Hello!' she called out, waving to him cheerfully, in spite of her heart pounding in her chest.

The Count blinked at her in anxious astonishment for a

moment – but then recognition dawned. 'Good afternoon, *mademoiselle*,' he said, rather awkwardly.

'After you told me about the wonderful cakes here, I couldn't resist coming to try them for myself,' said Sophie, in her best conversational manner. 'And you were quite right – they're absolutely delicious!'

'I'm very pleased to hear it,' said the Count, with a little bow. She sensed he was about to move away, but before he could do so she gestured quickly to the seat opposite her. 'Won't you sit with me and help me to finish them? I'm afraid I've ordered far too much, and it would be a terrible shame to let them go to waste.'

The Count looked at the tempting pastries, and then at her innocent, smiling face. 'Well . . . er . . . yes, I suppose it would,' he acknowledged and just as she had hoped, he sat down at her table.

The waitress brought some more tea, giving them a curious glance as she did so, no doubt thinking that the smart young shopgirl and the hunched, shabby old man made a peculiar pair. But the Count didn't seem to notice her puzzled glance: he was too busy tucking into one of the pastries, which Sophie had pushed at once in his direction.

She began to talk, making a few general remarks, before cautiously turning the conversation towards Arnovia, and telling him how much she missed her own home. It was easy enough – after all, it was true that she felt horribly far away from London and her friends, and here in the café, she felt it more strongly than ever. Perhaps it was because this place made her think of tea and buns at Lyons Corner House with Lil. How Lil would have enjoyed tasting honeycake with blackberries, or raspberry and almond cake!

Gradually the Count began to talk a little more, answering her questions about Arnovia. He didn't give much away about himself, but it was obvious to Sophie that he was lonely. He told her that he missed his dog, and took out a crumpled photograph from his pocket – a picture of a dachshund in a garden, with a girl and a boy.

'Who are they?' asked Sophie, pointing to the children – knowing very well that they were Crown Prince Alex and Princess Anna.

'Oh, just some young relations,' he said, hurriedly pocketing the photograph again.

Sophie glanced curiously at the Count's face. For a fleeting moment, he wore an expression of deep and endless sadness – and in spite of everything, she felt a stir of pity for him. How could she reconcile the sad and lonely old man sitting opposite her in the café with the sinister villain that she knew had conspired with the *Fraternitas Draconum*, plotting to kidnap the children in the photograph? She shook herself. She must not get thrown off course. She must remember who he was – and what he was capable of.

The Count's plate was empty now – he was looking around, as though to catch the waitress's eye and ask for the bill.

'Thank you for your company, *mademoiselle*. It has been most pleasant talking to you,' he said.

Sophie knew it was now or never. She felt a wild flutter of nerves, but forced herself to sit still in her chair.

'Before you go, I must tell you that there is another reason I came here today,' she said in a low voice. Her heart was thumping fiercely, but she kept her expression cool and calm, fixing her eyes on the Count's face. 'I have something I want to show you.'

'Do you, my dear?' asked the Count, looking a little confused, as if he couldn't imagine what such a thing might be.

Sophie took a deep breath. Then she turned up the collar of her jacket and displayed – pinned carefully underneath it – a small gold brooch in the shape of a twisting dragon.

CHAPTER TEN

St Petersburg

The effect on the Count was electric. He stared at the dragon pin as though he couldn't believe what he was seeing. Sophie watched him intently, her heart in her mouth.

She'd been pleased with the idea of the pin. She'd asked Boris to make it for her, telling him it was a request from a customer – an eccentric fellow, who wished to remain anonymous, but who would pay generously in cash. She'd made sure it resembled as closely as possible the sinuous, curving shape of the dragon that was the symbol of the *Fraternitas Draconum*.

Now, the Count stared and stared at it. All the colour seemed to have drained from his face. 'No . . .' he murmured, in a low, stunned voice. 'You can't be one of them. It's not possible.'

'I'm here for the notebook,' said Sophie – trying to speak gently, but firmly. An agent of the *Fraternitas* would be firm, she felt sure.

'I knew this day would come,' the Count whispered, as pale and sickly as a ghost. 'I just never thought they'd send someone like *you*.'

There was a split-second pause, and then, moving faster than she had thought possible, the Count was on his feet – sending their tea glasses rattling, his chair crashing backwards on to the floor. He reached wildly for the door. He was making a run for it, Sophie realised in astonishment: but why? Had he misunderstood what she'd been trying to tell him? She was so close – she couldn't let him get away now. Tossing a few coins on to the table to cover the bill, she leaped up and gave chase.

Outside, the Summer Gardens were full of people taking their afternoon promenade. Sophie dodged two girls taking photographs of one another with a Box Brownie camera, darting after the Count as he ran full tilt, down the avenue of fountains. He swerved right, past a tall hedge, running desperately, but Sophie could see he was already tiring. She put on an extra burst of speed, to try and catch him up. 'Wait!' she called after him. 'Where are you going? What's the matter?'

But her words only seemed to frighten him further. He turned blindly right – and then left – and then came to a sudden stop. He'd hit a dead end: he was standing in a small enclosed garden, surrounded by tall hedges. He turned to face her, his eyes full of fear.

'What's the matter?' she asked him again.

The Count was breathless and wheezing. 'You can have the notebook if you want it. I'll get it for you,' he pleaded. 'Take it, but I beg of you – please don't hurt me.'

'*Hurt* you?' Sophie stared at him incredulously. 'But . . . why would I do that?'

The Count gave a pained little laugh, which turned into an unpleasant cough. 'Do you really want me to list the reasons?' he puffed out. 'Very well . . . Because the plan was a failure. Because I betrayed your masters. Because I didn't go to the rendezvous I was given. Instead I ran – and hid. But you must understand, I never meant to get involved in any of this. I know nothing about your organisation – nothing at all! It was all my wife's doing.'

Sophie gazed back at him in disbelief. All this time she'd believed the Count was here in St Petersburg, hiding from the Arnovian authorities, waiting for his *Fraternitas* contact to arrive and collect the notebook. But the truth was, he'd been hiding from the *Fraternitas* all along.

'I have no wish to start a war,' the Count gasped out frantically. 'I don't want any part of this. Take the notebook if you must, *mademoiselle* – whoever you really are – but I beg of you, have pity on an old man who has already lost almost everything he has.'

The Count was shaking. He was afraid of her – terribly afraid, she realised. And no wonder: if he really had disregarded the orders of the *Fraternitas* and run off with their precious notebook, it wasn't surprising he was frightened for his life.

'I'm not going to hurt you,' she said, but the Count didn't seem to hear. He'd buried his face in his hands.

For a moment, Sophie was at a loss. What she'd thought was a clever plan had backfired entirely. She thought quickly, seeing at once that there was nothing else for it. She'd have to do absolutely the last thing she'd planned – tell the Count the truth.

'I lied to you,' she said in a low voice. 'I'm not an agent of the *Fraternitas Draconum*. In fact, quite the opposite. I work for the British government. I came here to St Petersburg to track you down and to get hold of the notebook, in order to prevent the *Fraternitas* getting the information it contains. I thought you were on their side, and I wanted to trick you into thinking I was one of their agents. But I see now I was wrong.'

The Count lifted his head, his eyes wide. 'How can I believe that?' he demanded in a shaking voice.

'I can prove it to you. I've got papers – and there's someone who can vouch for me. Come with me, please, and I'll show you. I promise I won't give you away to the authorities – and perhaps I can help.' But still the Count did not move.

'You must believe me. I'm telling the truth this time,' Sophie went on. Her voice was stronger as she realised something. 'And I think you know it. Because if I was really from the *Fraternitas* . . .'

'If you were really from the *Fraternitas*, I would probably be dead already,' the Count finished hoarsely. 'Very well. I will come with you. In any case, I know I have no choice.'

They walked slowly, side by side, the short distance back to the pink house. It was a strange walk: the Count watching her with anxious suspicion in his face, still wheezing after his dash through the Summer Gardens; Sophie slowing her usual brisk pace so that he could keep up with her. When they arrived at the house, Sophie was relieved to find that Nakamura was at home. She led the Count quickly down to the cellar, where she knew they would be able to talk undisturbed.

'This is my friend, Captain Nakamura. He was one of the pilots who flew in the Grand Aerial Tour of Europe. He can vouch for my identity.'

But the Count's eyes had widened in recognition already. 'Not just any pilot – the winner of the Bronze Medal!' he exclaimed – almost forgetting what was happening for a moment, in his enthusiasm to shake Nakamura's hand. 'It is a great pleasure to meet you, sir.'

Nakamura looked confused but accepted the Count's hand politely just the same. He eyed Sophie uncertainly, as if to ask if this was all part of her plan to pose as a member of the *Fraternitas*. But Sophie shook her head. 'I've told the Count the truth,' she explained. She turned to the Count: 'My real name is Sophie Taylor – I work alongside another agent, Lilian Rose, who you know as Miss Carter. She was sent by the British government to act as governess to Crown Prince Alex and Princess Anna, to help protect them. That's how I know all about what happened in Arnovia and about the kidnap attempt in Paris. I was *there* on the airfield. I helped pull the Prince out of your plane. I watched you fly away and then I followed you, with Captain Nakamura.'

'It's true,' said Nakamura. 'She's followed you right across Europe to get this notebook and the information it contains. She has told me many times that she must stop it falling into the hands of the society.'

The Count was staring at Sophie intently, a spark of recognition crossing his face. 'You ran towards me, when I was in the plane,' he muttered. 'I pushed you away . . .'

'That's right.' Sophie nodded. 'I was trying to get the notebook. That's all I want. I know you're hiding from the authorities. I won't give you up to them – and I can give you money, if that's what you want. But you must give me the notebook.'

'It's not money I care about,' said the Count, taking the seat that Nakamura was offering him and wiping his brow with a handkerchief. 'Though goodness knows, I have little enough of it left. It's what's *inside* the notebook that matters – and making sure it never falls into the hands of those villains.'

'Do you mean the information about the weapon?' Sophie asked at once.

The Count nodded. 'I spent a long time studying the notebook. I wanted to know why it was so important to them. Much of it is in some sort of code, which for all my efforts, I cannot understand. But from what I could make out . . .' He shook his head again, and then fell silent, apparently running out of words.

'It explains about the secret weapon, doesn't it?' asked Sophie. Excitement surged through her like an electric current. 'And how to find it.'

The Count nodded again. 'Even from what little I could read, it's clear that this notebook contains all the information the *Fraternitas* would need to decipher the clues in the paintings and locate the weapon. What's more, the weapon itself has incredible power. It is greater and more terrible than anything we can imagine.'

His voice dropped lower. 'Europe is already teetering on the brink of a war unlike any we have seen before. I have seen many a battlefield in my time, but the thought of what lies ahead – it terrifies me. The Kaiser is hungry for power; he's jealous of the British Navy and eager to prove himself a mightier man than his old chancellor, Bismarck. The Tsar will not tolerate any threat to his Empire; and as for your own government, *mademoiselle* . . .' He paused, and Sophie had the sense he was choosing his words with care. 'Your own government will stop at nothing to protect Britain's power and prestige. If the *Fraternitas* were to intervene and sell this dangerous weapon to the highest bidder, the balance of power in Europe could be completely destroyed.'

Sophie stared at him. 'But you worked for the *Fraternitas*,' she said. 'You conspired with them to have Prince Alex kidnapped, to cause chaos in Arnovia, so you could claim the throne for yourself.'

The Count's expression was deeply uneasy. 'I know. It was my wife's plan and I went along with it. But I had no idea what was at stake. I didn't understand then who the *Fraternitas* were – and I had no idea that all this was part of their bigger plan to spark off a European war. I certainly never meant any harm to come to Alex. You don't know how I've lain awake, night after night, tormented by the bitterest regrets – and wondering what was to be done.

'More than once I almost threw the notebook in the fire, so that would be an end to it. But I don't know what other secrets the coded sections may contain and how important they may be. What's more, there's no way of knowing how close the *Fraternitas* may already be to finding the weapon. More and more I have come to believe that the only hope is to find the weapon before the *Fraternitas* or anyone else can claim it for themselves.'

'And does the notebook really tell you how to do that?' asked Sophie.

'The notebook outlines the specifications of a device which is needed to decode the dragon paintings,' the Count explained. 'I suppose you might call it a kind of spyglass. It's made with a series of different coloured lenses, which can be used to allow the viewer to clearly see details that have been cleverly concealed inside the paintings.'

Sophie frowned, trying to make sense of this. 'How does it work?'

The Count cleared his throat. 'Imagine you are looking at a sheet of white paper, with a message written on it in blue ink,' he began. 'Now, let us imagine that another message has been written on the same paper in red ink, on top of the message beneath it. If you were to look at this paper through a piece of red glass, what would happen then?'

Nakamura was listening intently. 'The white paper would appear red – and therefore the message in red will disappear.'

'Precisely. But what about the blue message?'

'You'd still be able to see it,' said Nakamura. 'The red message would be gone and you'd see the blue message underneath.'

'Yes. But now, what if you were to look at the same message through a piece of *blue* glass.'

'This time the blue ink would disappear, leaving only the red message,' said Sophie.

'Exactly so. I believe that it is using this same basic principle that secret messages have been concealed in the dragon paintings. The spyglass contains a series of different coloured lenses, which can be raised, lowered and adjusted in different combinations. This will allow the viewer to see the secret messages, which would be otherwise invisible to them.' He paused for breath, and then admitted: 'For a little while, I have been wondering whether it would be possible for me to have the device made, so I could obtain the secret messages and destroy the weapon myself.'

'So *that's* why you came to Rivière's so often!' exclaimed Sophie. 'And why you always wanted to look at the opera glasses. You thought they might be able to make the spyglass there.'

'Yes. The craftsmen at Rivière's are amongst the few who would be able to construct such a sophisticated and intricate device. But such a commission would be expensive and I have little money left. Besides, I have no way of finding the paintings. Yet something must be done.'

Sophie leaned forward across the table. 'Something *can* be done,' she said. 'If you give me the notebook, I'll take it back to the British government. We have some of the paintings already, and my colleagues are even now hunting for the rest. We'll be able to construct the device, examine the painting and locate the weapon – and prevent the *Fraternitas* from ever getting it!'

The Count gave her a long, thoughtful look. Then he said gently: 'But you must see that is impossible. If I give this information to the British government, they could use it to further their own power. To wage war on the German Empire, to strengthen their Naval might, or even to expand their territory in Africa or Asia. The British Empire is perhaps the richest and most powerful in the world. I don't believe they could resist the temptation to become more powerful still.'

For a moment, Sophie was silenced. She'd never considered such a thought before. But if they found the weapon, surely the Chief would not simply hand it over to the government to use against their own enemies? The Chief would feel as she did – that the weapon must be destroyed, before it could cause any harm.

'But that's not why I'm here. I'm here to stop the *Fraternitas*,' she explained. She hesitated for a moment, and then went on: 'My mother and father both gave their lives to oppose them. I don't know what more I can say to convince you, except that you have my word that I will see this weapon found and destroyed – not handed over to anyone else.'

The Count's eyes were keen in his haggard face. There was silence for a moment as he looked at her; she looked back at him; and Nakamura watched them both.

'Very well,' said the Count at last. 'I have always heard that an Englishman's word is his bond – I must hope that is true for an Englishwoman too. For if what you say is true, then you are the answer to my prayers. I will give you the notebook.'

A bright flame of joy seemed to spark inside her. 'Thank you. I promise I won't let you down.'

'We can go to the bank vault and collect it whenever

you wish. But you must keep it safe – and take it away from here quickly. There's no hiding from the *Fraternitas*. I am certain they know I am here. Putting the notebook into the bank was the only way I could think of ensuring its safety – and my own safety too.'

Sophie nodded, knowing at once what he meant. The *Fraternitas* had killed for the notebook already – they would certainly not hesitate to harm the Count to get hold of it.

'Can you tell me any more about the *Fraternitas*?' she asked him eagerly. 'How did you and the Countess come to be involved with them?'

The Count shrugged wearily. He looked older and smaller now that he had confessed his secrets. 'I can't tell you much. The plot was my wife's doing. I don't know how she encountered the *Fraternitas*, and I don't know the name of the fellow she dealt with. She always used a code name for him – "Gold" she called him. She would get letters and telegrams sometimes, which I suppose contained her orders. I buried my head in the sand – I didn't want to know what she was doing. I should never have agreed to the kidnap. I couldn't be sure no harm would come to the children, but what they were offering us was impossible to resist. My wife had always had grand ambitions, and now she saw me as a king and herself as a queen. I was naive – I really believed it was for the best, that I could make a difference . . .' His voice drifted and he shook his head sadly. 'Now, I suppose I shall never see Alex and Anna again.'

Sophie felt a sudden stab of sympathy for him. The Count had been weak and foolish, and there was no doubt he had made some terrible mistakes, but he was facing a dreadful punishment – forced to hide far from everything and everyone he cared for.

'I knew nothing of any notebook until my wife put it into my hand on the airfield. All I was told was that it contained vital information about an important weapon, and I needed to deliver it to a rendezvous point in Vienna. But then my wife was arrested – I was afraid and alone, with nothing but my plane. I didn't know what to do, but I knew I had to get away, find somewhere safe to hide. I hardly thought about the notebook at first, but when I examined it and learned a little of what it contained, I was more frightened than ever. The *Fraternitas* were on my tail: their agents nearly caught me twice, but I managed to get away. I hoped Russia would be safer, at least for a while, but I had no doubt they would find me eventually. They must have their agents here, as they do everywhere.'

'So what will you do now?' asked Sophie. 'Will you stay in St Petersburg?'

The Count shrugged. 'I haven't the least idea. I'm not sure which would be worse – being murdered in Russia by a *Fraternitas* agent or spending the rest of my life locked in an Arnovian prison, a traitor to my country. Though I daresay neither is worse than I deserve.

'I'd hoped to travel further East, but I don't have the money. I thought of selling my plane, but it's risky – it might draw the attention of the *Fraternitas*. So for now, yes, I believe I will stay here. Perhaps I may find some work and save a little, so I can travel onwards.'

'We may be able to help you there,' suggested Nakamura quietly. 'You know about aeroplanes – perhaps there may be some work at the Aero Club?'

The Count nodded, but he looked defeated. Sophie did not envy him the prospect of staying in St Petersburg, jumping at every noise and every shadow, watching and waiting for a *Fraternitas* agent to catch up with him. But what else could he do?

'Let's go to the bank now, before it closes,' she said, eager to have the notebook in her hands at last. 'And then why don't you stay here tonight? It may be safer for you. Vera, our landlady, has a spare room, and there's always plenty of supper to go around.'

'We could talk more about the Aero Club,' Nakamura suggested. 'And I'm working on some new aeroplane designs – I'd like to have your input, if you're interested?'

'Thank you,' said the Count, gruff but grateful. 'I believe I should like that.'

They set out to the bank shortly afterwards. The Count's face grew paler as they approached, and she saw that even Nakamura, who had insisted on accompanying them, was glancing sharply around as if anticipating trouble.

Inside, it only took a few short moments for the Count to withdraw the brown paper parcel from his safe deposit box. For a few moments, he hesitated, as if he couldn't quite bring himself to give it up – but then he took a deep breath and gently placed the parcel into Sophie's hands.

Her fingers closed around the rustling brown paper. Lifting a small corner of the wrappings, she glimpsed a notebook so very ordinary-looking that for a moment, she thought it must be a mistake. Just a battered old composition book, with a marbled cover. It looked more like a school exercise book than a secret document.

'We should go,' said the Count anxiously.

Outside, Nakamura hailed them a cab, and they made haste to scramble in, Sophie's hand wrapped tightly around the parcel in her pocket. She did not feel quite safe until they were back inside the pink house – the heavy front door closed firmly behind them.

That night, after the Count had been safely installed in one of Vera's spare bedrooms, Sophie stayed awake for a long time, looking at the notebook. She sat up in bed, leaning back against the pillows, carefully turning over the pages. It seemed so extraordinary that she had it in her hands at last – it gave her a rather strange, shivery feeling to examine its pages by the light of the flickering candle. They were scribbled all over with strange writing: although she knew something about cracking codes, like the Count, she found it mostly indecipherable. Yet there were fragments she could understand: here a scribbled note on the origins of the *Fraternitas Draconum*, written in English; there a translation from an old document in what looked like Latin. And then there was the diagram the Count had talked about – an intricate illustration of the spyglass:

She pored over it for hours, and it was very late when she at last slipped the notebook carefully under her pillow and blew out her candle. But even in the dark, she felt too excited to sleep. She'd done something that she had never even dreamed would be possible: she'd travelled across Europe by aeroplane, she'd found Count von Wilderstein, and now at last she had the secret notebook too.

There was such a lot to think about. Should she leave St Petersburg at once, and take the notebook straight back to the Bureau? Or should she perhaps stay and have the spyglass made at Rivière's? There wouldn't be many people that could craft such a device, but she knew Boris would be able to do it. At last she made up her mind: she would write to the Chief, explaining everything and asking him what she should do next. In the meantime, she'd go about her business as usual. She'd wrap the notebook up again and lock it securely in the big safe at Rivière's – which must certainly be one of the safest places in St Petersburg, perhaps even more secure than the bank.

She smiled in the dark. Whatever the Chief's instructions, she knew she'd soon be back in London with Lil and the others. Back at Sinclair's, in the wonderfully familiar offices of Taylor & Rose, and then all this would seem like an extraordinary dream. She'd been working undercover since Paris, trying on different names and different identities, but soon she could be herself once again. She'd be sad to say farewell to St Petersburg, and to Vera and Boris of course – but it would be such a relief to be Sophie Taylor once more, and to be back amongst the people and places she knew. She wrapped her hand carefully around the notebook under her pillow, and at last she fell asleep.

The next morning she was up at dawn, writing her letter to the Chief. But once it was safely delivered to the Embassy, she knew she would have to wait a while for his response. Even when they were sent via diplomatic bag, it took a while for messages to get through. Yet this time the Chief's answer came within a matter of days, in the form of a telegram. It was short and very simple:

ПОЧТОВЫЙ ОФИС ТЕЛЕГРАММА

расходы на оплату	префикс. Время сдано. Офис orgin и сервисная информация	
13/00		No 24
получeнное для		
No *165 06 -21* CA *5*		Ro *19. 00*

29.09.1911

TO: ALICE GRAYSON, RIVIERE'S, ST PETERSBURG, RUSSIA

FROM: CLARKE'S SHIPPING AGENTS, LONDON, ENGLAND

ORDER GRANDFATHER'S BIRTHDAY PRESENT AND BRING ASAP - CLARKE.

Sophie grinned. She knew exactly what the Chief meant. He'd given her the go ahead to have the spyglass made, and he wanted her to bring it back to London as soon as possible.

At Rivière's the next morning, she slipped through into the workshop to find Boris.

'I've got another commission for you,' she began, reaching in her pocket for the diagram, which she had carefully copied from the notebook. 'It's for that customer again, the one who ordered the dragon brooch. It's something a bit more unusual this time – it's rather urgent and it has to be a secret.'

PART III

'It was tremendously exciting when our train arrived at Virballen. As we approached, I could see the fence that marked the Russian border, decorated with flags and the sign of the Imperial Eagle.

The train stopped in the station, and we all had to get out and show our passports to a policeman. They checked our luggage too: two of Papa's books and my little pack of patience cards were confiscated by Customs, but we did not mind too much. Afterwards they marked each of our trunks with a white cross and gave us our passports back. There was a while to wait, and so Papa and I ate a very curious meal at the little eating place in the station, before we got onto another train – and then we were over the border into Russia at last!'

– From the diary of Alice Grayson

CHAPTER ELEVEN

London to Cologne

'Sure you've got everything?' asked Joe nervously, as they drew up outside the station.

Lil nodded, glancing down at the small suitcase the Bureau had given her for the Hamburg assignment. The secret compartment was intended for hiding the report she was due to collect, but she'd already put it to good use, concealing everything she would need for her journey to St Petersburg – maps, a railway timetable, and plenty of Russian *roubles*. She'd put a fur-trimmed hat and gloves inside too – she knew St Petersburg could be cold at this time of year, but she didn't want Carruthers asking awkward questions about why she was bringing such warm clothes for a few days in Hamburg.

Planning the journey to St Petersburg without giving anything away to the Bureau had not been easy. But Billy and Mei had been ingenious, coming up with clever ways to arrange everything that Lil would need. The only thing missing was the special visa she would require to cross the border into Russia. That had been a puzzle: after all, Lil could scarcely just go to the Russian Consulate to get one, like an ordinary traveller. The Bureau had eyes and ears everywhere and would be certain to find out. In the end, they'd had to come up with a very different – and more dangerous – scheme.

'Are you quite sure about this circus plan?' Joe asked now.

'Of course,' said Lil at once. 'We've been over it a dozen times. The Circus of Marvels is travelling from Europe to Russia. Their route has been set out in the papers, and we know they're due to leave Cologne for St Petersburg tonight.'

'And you think you'll be able to sneak on to their train?'

'Absolutely. It's simply enormous – sixty carriages! All I have to do is travel as far as Cologne, slip aboard their train and hide somewhere – and I'll be able to get across the border to Russia without needing a visa at all.'

Lil's eyes were sparking with excitement, but to Joe, the plan seemed full of risks. There were so many ways it could go wrong – and if it did Lil would be alone, without the Taylor & Rose team to help her. 'Lil . . .' he began.

She gave him a very stern look. 'It's no good trying to talk me out of it. I've absolutely made up my mind,' she declared.

'But you don't have to do this on your own. Couldn't I

come with you?'

Lil smiled at him but shook her head. 'You're needed here. You and Billy have to take care of Taylor & Rose.'

'But Billy could do that – with Mei and Tilly,' Joe argued. 'Come on, Lil. You know we make a good team. Anyway, I reckon it'd be interesting to go to Russia. That's where my old granddad came from, which I s'pose makes me part Russian too,' he added. It was a queer kind of thought. Joe had grown up on the streets of the East End and had hardly left London in all his life. The thought of travelling right across Europe made him as jumpy as a cat – though he'd do it in a heartbeat for Lil.

'Funny to think of him travelling all that way,' he went on. 'He told me once that he walked most of it. There were lots of Russians round where I grew up: Russian Jews mostly. It wasn't so good for them out there – that's why they left. Some of 'em were cabinet makers like Granddad – or clock makers . . .' he added, falling suddenly silent.

It had been a long time – a very long time indeed – since he'd thought about the old clock maker. That night seemed to belong to another life. In those days, he'd been running with an East End gang, the Baron's Boys. Jem had told him to finish off the clock maker – but he couldn't do it. He'd known then that he could never be one of them. He'd had to run for it: he'd slept on the streets for a bit, looking for places to hide. Then he'd found Sinclair's, and first Billy, then Sophie, then Lil.

They'd changed a lot since then – all of them. He'd been on the run without a penny, and now look at him, with a real job and a decent place to live. Billy had been just a lad, a dreamer, his head stuffed full of stories, but now he was smart enough to arrange a secret mission to Russia. As for Lil, she'd gone from the jolly girl he'd first met to a young woman who was intrepid enough to travel to the other side of Europe to help her friend. Looking at her, he felt a sudden rush of pride.

She was smiling back at him. 'I'd love you to come – of course I would. But Carruthers would think it was strange, and he might get suspicious.' She glanced up at the clock. 'Oh gosh – look at the time. I'd better hurry.'

The train was waiting on the platform but before Lil could climb aboard, Joe reached for her arm. 'Before you go –' he began.

'*Joe!* I told you already – you can't talk me out of this.'

He grinned at her, his eyes creasing up at the corners. 'I'm not going to try,' he said, with a laugh. 'I wouldn't dare! I'll admit I wasn't too sure at first, but then I realised something.' He took her hand and squeezed it. 'I've never known anyone like you, Lil – and I know that you wouldn't be *you* if you didn't do mad things like this.'

Lil stared up him. His hand was warm in hers and he was looking at her so admiringly that, all at once, she felt that she didn't want to get on the train at all. What she wanted most of all was to stay here, with Joe holding her hand and looking at her like that.

'All I was going to say was – be careful,' he said, in a rather husky voice. 'Because I . . . well, I mean, all of us – we care about what happens to you. We care a lot.'

Impulsively, Lil reached out and hugged him. It wasn't a quick squeeze, like the farewell hugs she'd given to Billy and Mei back at the office, but a real hug. She buried her face against the rough tweed of his jacket, breathing in the familiar scent of horses and hay. His arms tightened around her; she lifted her head, and for a brief moment their cheeks brushed together – and then dimly she heard the train conductor blow a whistle.

A head emerged suddenly from the train window beside them. 'What a lovely romantic scene,' observed the dry voice of Carruthers. 'Now, if you've *quite finished* dallying with your young man, I've heard it's generally considered wise to get on the train *before* it leaves the station.'

Joe released her at once. 'I s'pose I'd better be going,' Lil muttered.

'Come back safely,' said Joe.

She clambered aboard, and Joe handed the suitcase up to her, and closed the door behind her. She pushed down the window to give him one last wave. He smiled and gave her a quick wave back – and she stayed where she was, watching him standing on the station platform, hands in his pockets, growing smaller and smaller, as the train chugged slowly away.

*

The first part of the journey was uneventful – unless you counted Carruthers making various sarcastic remarks about 'courting' and 'sweethearts'.

'You do realise this is a very important mission,' he informed her pompously. 'You can't just have your young man hanging about whenever it takes your fancy.'

Lil ignored him, but she did feel rather pleased when they got on the boat for Ostend to find that the crossing would be a choppy one and a distinctly green Carruthers retreated to a cabin, refusing to admit to seasickness. It served him right, she thought.

She stood by herself on deck, watching the swirl of the grey sea. She never felt seasick, and besides, she liked the wild feeling of the wind, buffeting against her face and tangling in her hair. It was good to be by herself and have time to think over her plans once more – though somehow, her thoughts kept slipping back to Joe, on the station platform.

Concentrate, she told herself. From Ostend they'd take a train to Cologne, arriving at nightfall. They'd have a little while to wait for the connecting train to Hamburg in the early hours of the morning: this would be her chance to slip away and board the circus train, which was scheduled to set off from Cologne at midnight. Once the circus train left Cologne, it would take about a day to reach St Petersburg, or perhaps a little more. The trickiest moment would be crossing the border at Virballen, going from Germany into Russia. The border guards were notoriously strict, but surely even they wouldn't try to inspect every inch of a sixty-carriage train?

If Carruthers hadn't interrupted like that, might Joe have kissed her goodbye, she wondered suddenly. Had she wanted him to? Gazing down at the tossing waves, tipped with their frills of white foam, she admitted to herself that she had. When had that happened – and was it her that had changed, or was it partly Joe himself? He was certainly very different now from the awkward, uncertain fellow she'd first met – so much more sure of himself. And when he'd hugged her, she'd felt filled with a sort of warmth and lightness that she'd never experienced before. She'd known that he would always be there for her – no matter where she went or what wild plans she embarked on. If she was a boat on a stormy sea, he would be a lighthouse on a clifftop, she thought suddenly – always giving out a steadfast light.

She shook herself. What was she thinking, dreaming about Joe in such a silly way? She was supposed to be making plans, not thinking about *kissing boys*. Sophie would think she was being quite ridiculous!

Her thoughts were interrupted by the sound of a sharp *click* somewhere behind her. 'Very nice,' said a voice. 'Good pose. Serious.'

Lil spun round. A man holding a small camera was

standing behind her. He had evidently just snapped a picture of her looking out to sea.

'What *do* you think you're doing?' she demanded indignantly. 'You can't just go round taking photographs of people without even asking them if it's all right!'

'Sorry,' said the man cheerfully, not looking very sorry at all. 'Bad habit of mine. Taking pictures is my job – and you made such a good shot then that I couldn't resist.' He held out a hand. 'Charlie Walters, photographer. You know, I might be wrong, but I think I've taken your picture before. I've got a good memory for faces and yours is one that I wouldn't forget.' He studied her for a moment, and then snapped his fingers. 'Got it. You're Lilian Rose. I took some pictures of you once for a story about Sinclair's. Good ones too. You came to my studio and we were going to do some more portraits, though I don't think we ever did.'

Lil remembered at once. It had been soon after Sinclair's had first opened: they'd been on the trail of the Baron and the Clockwork Sparrow, and one of Charlie Walters' snaps had ended up being a vital clue. Now, the photographer grinned at her. 'Good to see you again, Miss Rose. What brings you here – where are you heading?'

'Oh . . . er . . . to Germany,' said Lil, a little awkwardly. She remembered that the photographer had been a pleasant fellow, but just now, she wished that he was a hundred miles away. She didn't want any more complications on this assignment.

'Germany, eh? Got friends out there? I'm headed to St Petersburg myself.'

'St Petersburg?' she repeated – surprised, and a little alarmed.

'I'm on a job for *The Daily Picture*. They're doing a whole series on the Circus of Marvels, and I'm going out to take some shots of the big show they're putting on in St Petersburg for all the Russian bigwigs. You know – counts and princes, all that sort of thing. Apparently the Tsar and his family might even be attending.'

'Sounds fun,' said Lil with polite interest – though inside her heart had sunk. The last thing she needed was someone hanging about who knew her from London and could blow her cover at any moment. She would have to give Charlie Walters a very wide berth indeed.

'It's not a bad gig. It's grand to have the chance to travel – and Roberta Russell, the journalist writing the piece, will be over there too. You know her? She's a fine girl and a good sport.'

Lil shook her head, and tried to look as if she'd never heard of Miss Russell in her life – though really she remembered her name very well indeed. She was the young journalist who'd been on the airfield in Paris, and whose reports on the dramatic kidnap attempt had been splashed all over the front pages.

'Well, looks like we're coming into port,' observed the photographer, staring out at the docks approaching.

'Better be off. Need to make sure all my equipment gets unloaded safely. Grand to see you again, Miss Rose – have a jolly time in Germany. And when we're both back in London, come and see me in my studio. I'd like to have a bash at those portraits, if you're game. I'll bet we could do some good ones!'

He set off to attend to his luggage, just as Carruthers emerged on deck, looking pleased to see Ostend rapidly approaching.

'Befriending more young men?' he said, coming over to lean on the rail beside her. 'Dear, dear – I hope you're not going to break your sweet young friend's heart . . .'

'Oh, *do* shut up,' said Lil.

The train journey from Ostend to Cologne took up the rest of the day. When they arrived into Cologne station that evening, their connecting train to Hamburg was already waiting on the platform – although it would be several hours before it left the station.

'Well, that's something,' said Carruthers, yawning and stretching. 'If we get on now, we'll have the chance to get a few extra hours shut-eye.'

'You go ahead,' said Lil. 'I think I'll go and see if the station buffet is still open.'

'I've already looked. It's closed,' said Carruthers, heaving a deep sigh. 'I *knew* we should have got some more things to eat at Ostend.'

'You were the one who said you weren't hungry!' protested Lil, seeing no alternative but to follow Carruthers on to the train, and into an empty compartment. To her relief, he really did seem to want to sleep, settling himself back in a comfortable corner seat, and pulling his hat down over his eyes.

Lil settled back too and waited. She heard the station clock strike eleven, and began to feel restless – but she forced herself to be patient, and to stay quite still listening to all the sounds of the station, until she was certain Carruthers was fast asleep. At last, hearing the sound of gentle snores, she cautiously rose, and went over to the carriage window.

Peering out, she saw the circus train at once on the opposite platform. It would have been hard to miss – it was even more enormous than she'd imagined. It was getting ready to depart: a team of station porters were loading a succession of big crates and boxes on board; smoke was beginning to unfurl from the tall black chimneys; and lamps illuminated vivid red and gold paintwork, spelling out in ornate gilt lettering, the words *Circus of Marvels*.

Casting another quick look at Carruthers to check he was still asleep, she quietly lifted her suitcase down from the luggage rack, padded softly across the compartment, and slid open the door. Looking all about her to make sure no passenger or train guard was nearby, she slipped out into the corridor, opened the carriage door, and a moment later she had jumped lightly down – not on to the brightly lit platform, but on to the shadowy tracks on the other side of the train.

She crept forward, being careful not to trip on the rails. Little pools of light were cast down from the train windows above, and she picked her way around them. She knew she must go cautiously – and yet, she had no time to lose if she was going to climb aboard and find a safe place to hide before midnight.

Close beside her, the train seemed bigger than ever, its enormous painted sides stretching above her. Carriages loomed over her, full of noises: the rumble of voices talking in a foreign language, a dog barking, the whinny of a horse. From somewhere came an extraordinary trumpeting sound – could that be the elephant? she wondered. Someone was laughing, and there was the faint hum of music – an accordion perhaps, and a violin? She went on, going faster, once or twice almost losing her footing, bracing herself at every moment for a yell or a flash of light that would mean she had been seen, sneaking along the tracks in the dark.

From what they'd learned about the circus train, Lil knew that towards the back there were a series of luggage vans in which the circus props and costumes were stored. She reached them only just in time – a porter on the platform called out '*Fertig!*' and then the doors were slammed shut.

For a minute she hung back in the sheltering shadows of the train, making sure that the porters had moved away. Then she slipped quickly up the steps at the back of one of the luggage cars. She put an ear to the door and listened carefully, but there was not a sound within.

Cautiously – very cautiously – she tried the door handle. It wasn't locked, and the door swung back to reveal a large dark carriage, empty but for dozens of carefully stacked crates, boxes and trunks.

Lil darted inside at once, closing the door softly behind her, letting out a breath of relief. She was aboard the train: now, all she had to do was to find a safe corner amongst all these boxes, where she could hide herself out of sight for the rest of the journey.

But before she could even begin to hunt for a place to hide, she heard a shrill creaking sound that made her turn ice-cold. Someone was opening the door to the carriage. Someone had followed her.

There was nothing she could do, not even a second to hide herself. A dazzling light flashed into her eyes, blinding her for a moment – and then a furious voice said:

'What *on earth* do you think you're doing?'

CHAPTER TWELVE

To St Petersburg

L il blinked in the brilliant light. Someone was standing in front of her, pointing an electric torch at her – and although she couldn't see their face, she recognised the angry voice at once.

'You *followed* me!' she burst out.

'Of course I did,' retorted Carruthers. 'You woke me up, crashing about in the dark. I could tell straight away you were up to something – but what are you doing? Trying to leave me behind and get to Hamburg on your own, I suppose – so you can get all the glory for yourself!'

'As if I'd do an idiotic thing like that!' Lil flung back. 'This train doesn't even go to Hamburg!'

'Then where in heaven's name *does* it go?'

There was no sense trying to conceal it now. Lil held her head high as she said briskly: 'To St Petersburg. It's the train belonging to the Circus of Marvels. It's going to Russia – and that's where I'm going too.'

'To *Russia?*' Carruthers squeaked, incredulous. 'But our assignment is in *Germany!*' He stared at her for a moment, as though he thought she was completely mad, and then realisation dawned across his face. '*Oh.* I know what this is about. This is about your friend, Miss Taylor, isn't it? You've got some crackpot scheme to hare off to St Petersburg to find her.'

'It's not a *crackpot scheme*,' Lil snapped. 'It's a very good plan – or at least it was until you started interfering.'

'Ha! You really think throwing aside your mission to hide aboard a circus train and go illegally into Russia is a *good* plan?' Carruthers gave a sardonic snort. 'It's the *worst* plan I've heard in all my life!'

'What else was I supposed to do? I know Sophie is missing. I know the Chief hasn't heard a word from her since she went over the border into Russia – not a letter, not a telegram, nothing. Anything could have happened to her! No one even told me that she was missing: The Chief – Forsyth – you – not one of you could care less. But *I'm* not going to abandon her on the other side of Europe. It's simply not decent to leave her alone and in danger, whatever *you* may think.'

Carruthers glared at her – but for a split second, Lil thought she caught a look on his face that was almost, but not quite, ashamed. Then he said: 'This is precisely why the Chief didn't tell you, you know. He must have known you'd do something hare-brained like this.'

'*Bother* the Chief,' said Lil, folding her arms. 'And bother you too. Why don't you go to Hamburg and get the report? There's no reason you can't do it on your own. You'll get to have your big field assignment – and you'll get all the credit. You can go home and tell the Chief whatever you like about me. But *I'm* going to St Petersburg, whether you like it or not.'

Carruthers blew out a frustrated breath. 'Have you got any idea how ridiculous you sound? You're behaving like an idiotic schoolgirl!' He shook his head in silent disbelief. 'You work for the *government*. You can't just decide to disobey your orders. It simply isn't done!'

Lil lifted her chin stubbornly. 'Just because I work for the government doesn't mean I'll blindly follow orders. Sophie and I, we make up our *own* mind about things and –'

She could have said a great deal more, but just then she broke off abruptly. From outside came the shrill of a whistle, followed by the unmistakable sensation of the train beginning to move forward, picking up speed. Carruthers darted at once to the door – but when he flung it open, it was clear that the train was already moving too rapidly for him to think of jumping back down on to the tracks.

'Oh, this is just absolutely *marvellous*,' he muttered bitterly.

Lil ran over to the window and peered out. Even in the dark, she could see that the train was going faster and faster, carrying her towards St Petersburg and Sophie. She felt a sudden fizz of excitement.

Carruthers, on the other hand, looked utterly dejected. He flopped down, holding his head in his hands. Lil could hear him muttering to himself: this was a nightmare; they were certain to be discovered; he was hungry and thirsty; this wretched luggage car was freezing cold; he'd left his bag behind on the Hamburg train; and thanks to her, his first assignment was completely ruined.

'You aren't behaving much like a secret agent on a government mission, you know,' Lil told him eventually, losing patience.

'I'm not *on* a government mission,' Carruthers snapped back. 'I'm on a *circus train*.' He screwed up his face. 'No doubt full of drunken and dissolute ruffians! I'd go straight to whoever is in charge here and demand they let us off at once but who knows how they might react? You can't trust these kinds of people to behave properly.' He shuddered, as if imagining the very worst criminal behaviour.

'You really are a dreadful snob,' said Lil. 'That's a lot of rot. And there's no need to be so dramatic. It's your own fault you're here, you know: I didn't tell you to follow me. If you'd stayed where you were, you'd be on the way to Hamburg by now to complete the assignment. Anyway, as soon as the train stops at a station, you can simply get out there and catch the next train back to Cologne. It's really quite easy.'

But as it turned out, it wasn't easy at all. Through the small hours of the morning, the train bumped and rattled onwards, without any sign of stopping. They steamed straight through the station at Hanover, and then at Berlin, without even slowing down. As the night drew on, Carruthers grew crosser and crosser, and by the time dawn had broken and a watery sunlight was beginning to filter through the window, he was positively fuming.

Lil was beginning to feel bad-tempered herself. She'd hoped to leave Carruthers behind at Cologne: now it seemed she would be saddled with him all the way to St Petersburg. Last time she'd travelled in Europe, it had been with Captain Forsyth, and now she reflected that she'd quite happily swap him for the grousing, grumbling Carruthers – even if Forsyth would no doubt have spent the entire journey showing off about his important role at the Bureau, and telling long, boring stories about all his derring-do.

For a moment, she allowed herself to think of how much better this journey would be if Joe had come with her, as he'd suggested at the station. Joe was the least complaining person she'd ever met: and besides, she knew he would be focused on supporting her, helping her plan what they'd do when they arrived in St Petersburg, and how they'd find Sophie – not fretting and fussing. He was someone who could be absolutely relied on, she thought, smiling in spite of it all.

She was beginning to feel hungry, so she took out the package of sandwiches she'd bought at Ostend and opened it. They were filled with some kind of sausage, strongly flavoured with garlic – unfamiliar, but rather tasty. She offered Carruthers one but he just stared at her as though she'd insulted him.

'You don't even care, do you? You're absolutely brazen. You're not even *considering* the fact that you've wrecked my entire career. Do you know how long I've waited to do something that isn't *filing*? Now it's all ruined and I'll probably never be trusted to go out into the field again – and it's all your fault!'

But Lil didn't reply. Instead, she put down her half-eaten sandwich. 'Shhh!' she hissed suddenly. She'd heard something over the rattling of the train – a sound which seemed very much like footsteps, coming closer towards them. 'I think someone's coming!'

There was no time to find a better hiding place. They crouched down where they were, behind an enormous wooden crate. Lil listened intently, her ears straining, as an interconnecting door that led into the luggage car squealed open. A single set of footsteps entered and crossed the carriage, making straight for the corner where they were hiding.

Lil stiffened, and Carruthers shot her a quick, horrified glance. But before the footsteps could reach them, they came to a sudden halt. Whoever had come in was standing very close to them – so close that Lil could hear the sound of heavy breathing. There was silence, and then the creak of a wooden lid being lifted – and she realised that the crate they were hiding behind was being opened.

'Rogers!' came a crisp, curt, English voice from across the room. 'What are you doing in here?'

The lid dropped suddenly shut. 'Er . . . just checking everything's all right, sir,' said a man gruffly. 'Making sure nothing's been damaged in transit.'

'Well, I must say, it's good to hear that one of you fellows has some initiative,' said the first voice, sounding rather surprised. 'The rest of your colleagues are still fast asleep after last night's revelries. You'll have to wake them up, sharpish. We're almost at Virballen, and the guards will need to check everyone's papers at the border crossing.'

At her side, Carruthers let out a little groan. Lil elbowed him as sharply as she dared. They must certainly not be caught now: the last thing she wanted was to be handed over to the border officials, who she was certain would not be friendly towards stowaways trying to cross the border illegally.

'Well, hurry along then,' said the first voice impatiently.

'In a moment, sir.'

'Not in *a moment*, Rogers. *Now*,' insisted the first voice, muttering: 'Goodness me, these fellows!'

To her relief, Lil heard Rogers' footsteps padding reluctantly away from them. A moment later the two men were gone, and the closing door had been slammed shut behind them.

'I can't go into Russia!' Carruthers wailed. 'I haven't got a visa!'

But Lil could already feel the train was slowing. Sure enough, when she went over to the window, she saw that they were chugging into Virballen station, at the very edge of Prussia, the easternmost province of the German Empire. She knew that this was the border of the vast Russian Empire, a place where all trains must stop; passports must be shown; trunks must be opened and inspected. As they came to a shuddering halt on the platform she ducked out of sight – but not before she'd had the chance to take in the uniformed policemen with rifles, the customs men and border officials, and an immense flag bearing the sign of the Imperial Eagle, fluttering against a chilly blue sky.

'Perhaps I can get out and explain this is all a dreadful mistake,' said Carruthers desperately. 'I'm an Englishman, after all – surely they'll believe me? Or perhaps I can just slip off somehow, before they catch sight of me . . . ?'

'Don't be an idiot! Have you seen how many armed men are out there? You don't want to mess about – they might arrest you. What we need is a really good hiding place. Look – what about this crate? It's easily big enough to hide a person.'

She pointed to the large wooden crate that Rogers had opened and flung back the lid. The top part of the box was packed with straw, but as she felt about beneath it to see what was inside, her fingers closed unexpectedly on something that felt cold and metallic. Grasping hold of the strange object, she drew it out from beneath the straw – and at once, almost dropped it in surprise.

It was a gun! A long black gun! The big crate was full of them – pistols, revolvers, rifles and ammunition, all carefully packed amongst straw. 'I say, look at this!' she exclaimed aloud. 'Dozens and dozens of guns!' She turned over the luggage label attached to the crate: sure enough it was clearly marked for the Circus of Marvels. 'Whatever could the circus need those for?'

'Goodness knows,' retorted Carruthers. 'Maybe for some kind of Wild West cowboy number – one of those idiotic things where they shoot apples off the top of some poor fool's head? Or perhaps they have a delightful little sideline in illegal gun-running? I honestly don't know – and just now, I don't much care.'

Much as she hated to admit it, he had a point. Lil was not about to hide in a box full of guns, so she let the lid fall closed, and then looked around to where Carruthers was opening what looked like an enormous dress basket. Inside, she saw a heap of shimmering costumes – spangled ballet dresses, frilly petticoats, a feather boa. There would be plenty of room for someone to squeeze in amongst them. 'That's perfect – get in, quickly!'

Carruthers clambered inside, and Lil hastily covered his

head with two or three of the frilly petticoats. If anyone opened the lid, they would have no idea there was someone hiding underneath.

'Ugh! You're smothering me!' came a bad-tempered voice from somewhere beneath the petticoats. 'And by the way, can I just make it clear that I still think this is the most *terrible* plan in existence.'

'Oh shush!' said Lil, closing the lid of the basket over his head.

She looked swiftly around for a hiding place of her own, but before she had the chance to find one, she heard voices and footsteps approaching along the train once more. There was no time left. 'Move over – I'm getting in too!' she whispered to the dress basket urgently – and before Carruthers could argue, she hurriedly squeezed herself in beside him, pulling the lid closed over both their heads.

Inside it was hot, dark and very uncomfortable. 'What d'you think you're doing? This is *my* hiding place,' Carruthers hissed in her ear. 'You *reek* of garlic sausage, do you know that? It's positively revolting.'

'Shut up and stay still – they're coming in!'

But staying still when you were squeezed tightly into a dress basket was not easy. It might be an unusually large dress basket, but it was still not nearly large enough for two tall people. Carruthers' bony knee jabbed painfully into Lil's side, and she had to bend her neck at an unpleasant angle in order to keep her head covered with the petticoats she'd hastily pulled over it. She could feel one of her legs cramping, but there was nothing she could do. The connecting door had opened, and what sounded like a whole crowd of people were coming in.

'And this is another of the luggage vans . . .' came the same crisp English voice they'd heard before.

Someone said something short and forceful, in what Lil assumed was Russian.

'Sasha – what's he saying?' asked the English voice.

'He wishes to know what is inside the boxes,' came another voice, softer and speaking with an accent.

'Well, tell him they are circus costumes and properties.'

'He says he must open them all. To survey them.'

'Oh, heavens above – really? We'll be here all day! Fanshawe is going to be hopping mad if we don't make it to St Petersburg on time.'

'I am very sorry, Max, but it is what he says he must do.'

'Well, look here, does he really need to check every single one? Couldn't he just inspect a few at random? We've got all the documentation – Imperial seals, declaration that the circus is to perform for the Tsar, and all that – great reams of the stuff!'

There was the rustling of paper as documents were passed around, then Sasha said something again in Russian. Lil tried to keep quiet and still as a mouse, all the time very conscious of how loud Carruthers' breathing sounded, and the way the wicker basket creaked and rustled with even the tiniest movement.

The connecting door opened again, and a girl's voice said: 'Here's the refreshments you wanted, Max.'

'Thanks, Hanna. Here, Sasha – ask the fellow if he'll have a drink with us.'

The soft-voiced Sasha said something else in Russian, and there was an appreciative grunt from the official, followed by the *glug-glug-glug* of liquid being poured, and glasses clinking.

'There,' said Max. 'Cheers! I say, what do they say in Russia for "cheers", Sasha?'

'*Za Zdarovje.*'

Max repeated the words clumsily, and then there was silence for a few moments, but for lip-smacking and the sound of glasses being refilled.

'Well, I can't say I care much for vodka – especially at this time in the morning. But *he* seems to be enjoying it, and I suppose that's what matters. Now then, Sasha – all well?'

Sasha spoke again, and this time the official made some approving noises, and then said a few words in a more cheerful voice.

'Yes, all is well,' Sasha explained. 'He says your paperwork is in order. No need to inspect the boxes since you are travelling under the protection of His Imperial Majesty the Tsar. He thanks you for your hospitality. Now, the other men must finish the checking of the passports, and then we may go.'

'All right – very good – let's get that over with,' said Max. There was the sound of feet shuffling out again. The door slammed shut, and Lil realised that she and Carruthers were alone in the luggage car once more.

'Thank goodness!' she exclaimed with feeling, pushing herself upwards out of the box, shaking out her cramped limbs. 'That was a narrow escape – but I believe everything's going to be all right now.'

'*All right?*' repeated Carruthers, as he burst to the surface from beneath a foamy sea of petticoats. 'How can you possibly think this is going to be all right?'

'The train will soon be on the move again, and we'll go on to St Petersburg. From there, you'll be able to get a train to Hamburg.'

'No I won't! I'll be in Russia illegally – without a visa, remember? They'll probably clap me straight in handcuffs and have me shipped off to prison in Siberia!'

'Don't be so silly,' Lil scoffed. 'They won't do that. Anyway, all you have to do is let the Chief know where you are and what's happened, and I'm sure he'll arrange for the papers you need.'

Carruthers looked more furious than ever. '*The Chief?* Oh yes, I have no doubt he'll be absolutely thrilled when I tell him we're in St Petersburg, having completely disobeyed his orders and gone to the other side of Europe on a *whim*. This was my chance to show him what I'm made of, and now I'll have to go to him cap in hand, to beg for his help like some naughty schoolboy. He's going to be so disappointed.'

'It *isn't* a whim,' said Lil crossly. Just then, she heard a whistle on the platform, and the slamming of doors. 'I say – here we go! I think we're moving off again. We've done it! We're going over the border!'

'Oh, we've *done it*, all right,' muttered Carruthers sarcastically.

Before he could say another word, Lil lunged forward, clapping a hand over his mouth and dragging him down into the dress basket once more, then pulling the lid closed over their heads. Carruthers gave an indignant squeak of protest, but the connecting door opened yet again.

This time, the voices were different. 'I gotta make sure everything's all right,' an American voice was saying fussily. 'Who knows what kind of a mess those guards might've left behind 'em, if they've been rummaging through my baskets?'

Lil was still hanging on to Carruthers. She could feel him twisting away, trying to wriggle out of her grip. The basket rocked from side to side.

'Stop it!' she hissed.

'Well, let go of me then!' He shook her away, but in the cramped dark, there was nowhere for her to go. The basket rocked a little more.

'Hey! What was that?' said the American voice.

'I think I heard something.'

'Oh goodness – you don't suppose one of the animals could have got loose somehow, and got in here, do you?' said another voice – a girl's voice this time.

'Maybe one of the guards opened a cage,' said the first voice. 'Hey, Ravi, you take a look. This is your department. Maybe it's one of your snakes.'

Lil gripped Carruthers' shoulder harder. Light footsteps were crossing the floor towards them – and then suddenly, the lid of the basket was lifted up, and light flooded in.

The Circus of Marvels

Someone was staring down at them – startled, but not really half as shocked as you might expect, given that he'd just found two stowaways in a dress basket.

'Hello,' said an amused voice. '*You* are certainly not my snakes.'

A boy was grinning at them. He was small, brown-skinned and black-haired, and his dark eyes were gleaming with high spirits. 'And I think you are rather too old to be running away to join the circus,' he observed.

'What is it?' said the girl's voice, and then two more faces appeared above them. Not one of them looked in the least like Carruthers' description of 'drunken and dissolute ruffians' but then again, nor did they look much like the circus folk of Lil's imagination, who were dressed in sparkling sequins and feathered plumes.

One of them was a tall girl of about Lil's own age – though *tall* scarcely covered it. Lil knew that she herself was tall, but this young woman would make her look positively tiny. She must have been at least six foot, with strong rounded arms, and a figure which looked as though it had been carved out of marble. A thick plait of corn-coloured hair fell over one shoulder as she peered down at them, intrigued.

'That's a clever hiding place,' she observed.

'*Clever?* They're crushing my costumes!' protested the young man at her side. He was the American they'd heard before: short, plump, and rather well dressed, in a crisp white shirt with a silk cravat at the neck. 'Have you any idea how long it takes to iron the frills in those skirts?' he exclaimed angrily.

There was nothing else for it: Lil climbed out of the basket, shaking off petticoats, which the young man began to gather up protectively. 'I'm awfully sorry. We didn't mean to do any damage.'

Carruthers was scrambling out of the basket too, almost tripping himself up with a long feather boa that had become tangled around him as he did so. 'Utterly mortifying!' Lil heard him mutter, as the young American began untangling him, clucking like an irritable hen. Beside them, the boy stifled a giggle.

'We can explain,' she began, thinking quickly. She knew that if these three were to report them to whoever was in charge, her plan would be ruined – and she and Carruthers might find themselves handed over to the Russian police.

But the girl held up a hand. 'No need,' she said, with a beaming smile. 'We understand.'

'You do?' Lil asked in surprise.

'Of course. You're eloping.'

'*Eloping?*' choked Carruthers.

'Yes – I think it's awfully romantic to run off to get married in secret. It's lucky for you that Fanshawe is secretly a soft touch. You'd never know it, of course – but I'm sure you'll be allowed to stay until St Petersburg. I suppose that's where you're headed?'

'Yes it is. Do you mean it – will we really be allowed to stay?' Lil hadn't the least idea who 'Fanshawe' was, but this sounded unexpectedly promising.

'Well, you'll have to muck in and help, of course,' the girl added.

'And you can start by helping me sort out these petticoats,' interjected the American, who was shaking them out fussily. 'It's really the least you can do.'

'But even if you do have to become Cecil's wardrobe assistant, at least you won't have to spend the rest of the journey in a dress basket,' put in the boy, with another wide grin.

'No need to look so surprised,' the girl went on. 'You're not the first eloping couple we've found hiding on one of our trains, you know. Far from it! We're used to it. It's usually either that or kids with dreams of running away with the circus, to become a bareback rider or a clown.

Come on – I'll take you to Fanshawe, and you can say your piece.'

Lil shot Carruthers a desperate glance. His face seemed to have turned an unusual shade of purple. 'Yes, come on, *darling*,' she improvised, grabbing him purposefully by the arm. 'Let's go and get this sorted out.'

She didn't dare look at him as the girl led the way out of the luggage car, and along the passage through the swaying, rattling train. She knew he would loathe and despise the idea of pretending to be sweethearts – no doubt he'd think it even worse than masquerading as brother and sister. But they had no choice now.

She glanced around as they went along the train, catching glimpses of more luggage cars loaded with boxes and trunks; and then a series of living compartments. Inside each, a group of people was sitting – playing cards, or eating breakfast, or in one compartment, snoozing on bunk beds. In spite of all that was happening, Lil found herself peeping in, fascinated by these snatches of life with the circus – although their companion was not giving them much chance to stop and look.

'What are your names?' she asked, as she led them briskly onwards.

'I'm Lil. And this is er . . .' It struck Lil suddenly that she had no idea what Carruthers' first name was. But surely she couldn't introduce a man who was supposed to be her *fiancé* as 'Carruthers'?

'Samuel,' interjected Carruthers, giving their new friend what Lil was surprised to see was rather a pleasant smile. 'Samuel Carruthers. But you can call me Sam.'

'Sam – that's a nice name,' said the girl, smiling back.

'I'm named after my grandfather,' said Carruthers cheerfully. Lil felt rather astonished. Was it her imagination, or was Carruthers actually being friendly and decent, for once?

'You've changed your tune about people from the circus,' she muttered – so low that only Carruthers could hear her.

'Right now, that girl is all that's standing between me and a Siberian prison,' Carruthers muttered back, sounding far more like his usual self. 'Thanks to you and your *plan*.'

'I'm Hanna,' the girl was saying, as she strode ahead of them along the passage. The other two, she explained, were Cecil – 'who looks after all our costumes' and Ravi – 'who's awfully good with snakes'.

'I beg your pardon – did you say *snakes?*' repeated Carruthers, looking all around him as though he expected a boa constrictor to drop from the ceiling at any moment.

Hanna laughed. 'That's right! You must see his snakes – they're beautiful. He has a wonderful snake-charming act. It's terribly popular.'

'And what do you do?' asked Lil curiously.

Hanna grinned over her shoulder. 'I'm a strongwoman. They call me "Miss Hercules"!'

Lil stared in surprise. She knew that circuses often had strongmen: she'd seen pictures of them plenty of times, usually posing in a skimpy outfit, flexing their enormous muscles or lifting an immense weight over their heads. But she'd never heard of a strong*woman* before. 'I perform feats of strength,' Hanna was explaining. 'I lift weights – or sometimes I'll get men from the audience to volunteer, and I'll hold them above my head.'

'How marvellous!' said Lil, thinking of how all her suffragette friends in London would adore the idea of a circus strongwoman.

'Oh, it is! I couldn't imagine doing anything else,' said Hanna proudly. She told them she was part German, part Swedish and part English: she'd been born in a circus wagon in Bavaria and had been performing since she was two years old. 'My father was a strongman. He taught me gymnastics and wrestling, and then weightlifting. Two years ago, when I turned sixteen, he offered a prize of one hundred gold marks to any man who could defeat me in a wrestling match. Plenty of them tried, but none of them could,' she said with a giggle, pushing back the sleeve of her blouse to show Lil her powerful arm muscles. 'That's when Fanshawe heard about me, and invited me to join the Circus of Marvels. Of course, I couldn't resist the chance. It's one of the best circuses there is.'

'They call it "the Greatest Show on Earth", don't they?' said Lil, thinking of what she had read in the newspapers.

'That's right,' said Hanna proudly. 'And you'll have heard of Fanshawe, of course. It was actually Felix Fanshawe who started the circus, oh, twenty years ago or more. When he died, Freddie Fanshawe took over.'

As she spoke, she tapped on a door – and a moment later, Lil and Carruthers found themselves standing in front of a large desk, in a private train compartment fitted out like an office. Behind the desk sat a woman, so absorbed in a stack of paperwork that she scarcely took the trouble to look up at them. Whilst everyone else on the train was dressed in quite ordinary clothes, Lil saw that the woman was very smart. She wore what looked like a man's black suit, with a snow-white shirt, her dark hair pulled back into a glossy bun.

Carruthers glanced around, obviously looking for the 'Freddie Fanshawe' Hanna had described. But when the woman behind the desk looked up, giving them a fierce, imperious glance, Lil felt quite certain that *this* was Fanshawe. She found herself beginning to smile. Suddenly it did not seem so very surprising that the Circus of Marvels played host to a young strongwoman like Hanna, when the owner of the circus was a woman herself.

'What's all this then, Hanna?' Fanshawe demanded – then sat frowning while Hanna quickly related their story.

'Lil and Sam need to get to St Petersburg. Couldn't they stay with us until then?' she finished, in a pleading voice.

'I'm not providing a transportation service for waifs and

strays here, you know. I have a business to run,' said the mistress of the circus, in a brusque voice. 'But . . . since we're behind schedule already, I have no plans to stop until we arrive in St Petersburg. With that in mind, I suppose they will have to stay.' She fixed them with a steely expression. 'Count yourselves lucky I'm not dropping you off in the wilds of the Russian countryside. Hanna will look after you and see you make yourselves useful. But after we get to St Petersburg I don't want to see you on this train ever again – do I make myself clear?'

She looked at them grimly, but it was all Lil could do to conceal her delight. This was far better than anything she could have imagined. Now, there would be no need to hide in the luggage van and sneak off the train in the station at St Petersburg. Now, they would arrive in the city amongst the crowd of circus folk – it was absolutely the perfect cover. And while she knew that Carruthers hated the idea of pretending to be her fiancé, even he looked suddenly cheerful as Hanna led them away to one of the living compartments – a comfortable little place with cushioned seats, which smelled wonderfully of coffee and warm bread.

'I brought you breakfast,' announced Ravi, who was lounging in a corner. 'I thought you would be hungry.'

The sandwich she'd only half eaten seemed like years ago: Lil fell hungrily upon rolls, butter and honey, and Ravi looked pleased.

'I told you Fanshawe would be all right,' said Hanna. 'Now, tell us all about yourselves. We want to hear *everything*. How did the two of you meet?'

Carruthers and Lil exchanged a quick, awkward glance. 'I suppose . . . through work,' said Lil at last.

'What is your work?' asked Ravi curiously, munching on a roll.

Of course, they couldn't mention the Secret Service Bureau – and announcing that she was a private detective didn't seem quite the thing to do either – so Lil fell back on her old career. 'I'm an actress, and a dancer,' she explained. 'On the London stage.'

In other company, people might have responded to this with surprise, or excitement – or perhaps even disapproval. But Hanna and Ravi accepted it without even as much as a raised eyebrow. 'And are you on the stage too?' Hanna asked Carruthers.

Carruthers looked appalled by the very idea. 'Me? Oh no!' he replied at once.

'He was one of those fellows waiting by the stage door, for an autograph,' Lil invented hurriedly. 'That's where we first met – and then we fell in love!' She grabbed Carruthers' hand, and fixed him with a suitably adoring look.

'How romantic! I suppose that's why you had to elope?' Hanna exclaimed, nodding sympathetically to Carruthers. 'Your family didn't approve of you marrying an actress? Are they awfully traditional?'

161

'Something like that,' said Carruthers uncomfortably, pulling his hand away from Lil's.

'So why do you wish to go to Russia?' asked Ravi, beginning on his second roll.

To Lil's relief, the door of their compartment banged open, and a man burst in. 'Does anyone here read Russian?' he demanded. 'I've got a dozen of these dashed official documents to get through before we arrive in St Petersburg, and I can't make head nor tail of the beastly things. I've never known a country for so much paperwork!' Lil knew the voice at once: it was Max, the man with the crisp English accent who she'd heard earlier in the luggage compartment.

'I thought Sasha was helping you,' said Hanna in surprise.

'Yes, he *was* helping me,' said Max impatiently. 'And I must say, he didn't do a bad job when it came to dealing with those customs fellows. But he's no help at all with these documents!'

'Why not?' asked Ravi, his mouth full of bread.

'He can't read or write! He speaks Russian like a native – well of course he does, he *is* Russian. But he can't *read* a word – and if I don't get these sorted out we won't be able to go ahead with the show, and Fanshawe will be furious.'

'Er . . . I can read Russian,' spoke up Carruthers tentatively.

Max looked him up and down. 'And who the devil are

162

you? No – on second thoughts, I don't want to know. If you can read Russian and you've got half a brain, you might be the answer to my prayers. Well – come on then!' Carruthers hurriedly put down his coffee, and followed Max out of the room.

'Sam can read Russian? He must be *awfully* clever. He definitely looks clever. You are lucky – I wish a clever, handsome man would fall in love with *me* at one of our shows.' Hanna stared dreamily after Carruthers, and Lil felt rather startled at the idea of anyone finding the scowling Carruthers handsome.

She was kept very busy for the rest of the day by Cecil, who reappeared to demand that she help refold and repack the costumes in the dress basket, and then assist him by sewing hundreds of red and gold sequins on to some ballet dresses. He was extremely particular about how this must be done, and Lil, who loathed sewing, would have found it terribly dull – but luckily, Hanna and Ravi kept them company, chatting about the circus, and only occasionally asking an awkward question that Lil found difficult to answer.

Now and then, she found an opportunity to squeeze in a question of her own. 'What about that journalist who's writing about the circus – Miss Russell? I read her pieces in *The Daily Picture*. Is she travelling on the train too?'

Ravi snorted. 'Of course she isn't!'

'The newspaper people don't bother hanging about

with us to pack up the show,' explained Hanna. 'They travel separately.'

'First class all the way. Then she and her photographer will no doubt be staying in some fancy hotel suite while we slum it in whatever awful digs Max has found for us,' said Cecil, with a plaintive sigh that suggested he would very much rather have enjoyed a fancy hotel suite himself.

Lil bent her head over her sewing to hide her relieved expression. She felt very glad indeed that she wouldn't have to worry about dodging Miss Russell and Charlie Walters for the rest of the journey to St Petersburg.

It was teatime before Carruthers and Max reappeared: Lil noticed at once that Carruthers was looking extremely pleased with himself.

'I must say, old fellow, you really have been a tremendous help,' said Max, shaking his hand vigorously.

'Did you get all your paperwork done?' asked Hanna.

'Get it done? This fellow absolutely *breezed* through the lot of it – I've never seen anything like it! My paperwork has never been in such marvellous order. And it turns out he doesn't just know Russian – but French, German and Italian too!'

'Well, that and a bit of Hindustani,' said Carruthers modestly.

Max guffawed and slapped him on the back, as though he'd made a most amusing joke.

'You'll be sorry to say goodbye to Sam when we get to

St Petersburg tomorrow,' observed Ravi.

'Say *goodbye* to him?' Max demanded. 'Oh no. I'm not saying goodbye to this chap now. I *need* him. I'll do whatever it takes to keep you, old fellow. I'll pay you – put you up in lodgings, whatever you like. But you simply mustn't *go* anywhere. I can't have that.'

'Yes, do stay!' burst out Hanna excitedly. 'And Lil can stay too, of course.'

'Lil? Who's Lil?' demanded Max.

'She is,' said Carruthers, pointing at the corner where Lil was sitting. 'She's my . . . er . . . fiancée.'

Max shrugged. 'Bring her. Bring whoever you like – bring your grandmother, if you want! Just as long as I get to keep you as my right-hand man.' He clapped Carruthers on the shoulder again, and Carruthers looked smug.

Well, Lil thought. Of all the things she'd expected might happen on this journey, Carruthers joining the circus had certainly not been one of them. But perhaps this would work out rather well, she mused. Being part of the circus would certainly offer an excellent cover while they were in St Petersburg – and what's more, she speculated, if Carruthers was being kept busy by Max, he'd be out of her hair while she went in search of Sophie.

Hanna and the others were even merrier now that they were officially part of the circus. They ate supper together, and when night fell, Ravi showed them how to fold down bunk beds from the walls of the compartment, while Hanna got out blankets and pillows. Soon, they were all tucked cosily in their bunks, and Lil could hear the now-familiar sound of Carruthers' snores.

But Lil herself couldn't sleep. She was too excited, tossing and turning restlessly in her bunk, listening to the train steaming onwards through the night. The early hours of the morning found her standing alone in the passageway, gazing out of the open window, watching the starry lights of St Petersburg draw closer.

As the rose-gold dawn began to seep across the sky, she felt a thrill, watching it light up the shapes of domes and spires. The city rose up before her, wreathed in mist, growing larger and more real, as the train chugged towards it.

At eight o'clock they came at last into the station. Lil was one of the first to disembark, her suitcase tucked under her arm. In the smart, modern surroundings of the Vitebsky station she gazed around her – taking in the high, arched ceilings, the grand staircases, the gleam of gilt. Stern, uniformed guards marshalled the crowds of people hustling through the station – many of them pausing to point and exclaim over the scarlet and gold circus train, their voices a buzz of unknown languages. The light gleamed pale gold; the air was cold and smelled of smoke; and pigeons flapped above her head. All around her, the circus folk were descending from the train too – stretching, yawning, calling out to each other.

Excitement stirred in the pit of her stomach. She had made it. She had arrived in St Petersburg – and now she could set out to find Sophie at last.

CHAPTER FOURTEEN

Taylor & Rose Detective Agency
Sinclair's Department Store, London

'Telegram for Taylor & Rose!' Mei accepted the envelope from the uniformed Sinclair's porter as he hurried into the Taylor & Rose office, before rushing off to deliver his next message. It was another busy day at Sinclair's and, as always, London's most famous store was full of eager shoppers and admiring tourists. As the door swung shut behind the porter, Mei caught a glimpse of visitors outside the office door, keen to peep in and see what might be happening inside. There were rumours that the young lady detectives of Taylor & Rose had many important clients – from aristocrats to West End stars like Mrs Kitty Whitman, who had recently been spotted paying them a visit, to the delight of London's gossip columnists. Now, they lingered hopefully on the threshold, hoping to catch a glimpse of some illustrious personage going in or coming out.

Of course, to these excited visitors Taylor & Rose

was just one of the unusual attractions they could see at Sinclair's. A detective agency run by young ladies was simply another intriguing feature of the store, to go alongside its glamorous Beauty Salon, its exotic Pet Department where you could purchase anything from a poodle to a python, and its famous Marble Court Restaurant, where the crème-de la crème of London society could be seen enjoying one of the chef's famous ice puddings.

Most of the time, Mei was far too busy to pay any attention to the watchers outside the office and today was no exception. The telephone bell had been ringing all morning, and she had a stack of reports and letters to type. But she forgot all about the work she had to do when she saw the telegram, and quickly ripped open the envelope.

Inside was exactly what she had hoped for. The message might look like no more than a string of incomprehensible numbers, but Mei knew what it was at once. They'd planned that Lil would send a coded telegram as soon as she arrived in St Petersburg. They'd agreed a secret code in advance, which would make it impossible for anyone to decipher her message, unless they had the pre-arranged key word.

Now, Mei quickly took out a pencil, and began working out the solution, starting with writing out the alphabet in full. The key word they had agreed was MONTGOMERY after Billy's favourite fictional detective, Montgomery Baxter. She wrote it down carefully in capital letters, removing any repeated letters: MONTGERY. Then after it she wrote the rest of the alphabet, leaving out the letters she'd already used. Underneath she wrote the numbers 1 to 26 in order, so that the number '1' was positioned directly beneath the letter 'A'.

TAYLOR & ROSE
PRIVATE DETECTIVE AGENCY
4TH FLOOR, SINCLAIR'S DEPARTMENT STORE, PICCADILLY W1

A	B	C	D	E	F	G	H	I	J	K	L	M	N	O	P	Q	R	S	T	U	V	W	X	Y	Z
M	O	N	T	G	E	R	Y	A	B	C	D	F	H	I	J	K	L	P	Q	S	U	V	W	X	Z
19	20	21	22	23	24	25	26	1	2	3	4	5	6	7	8	9	10	11	12	13	14	15	16	17	18

CHARGES TO PAY

RECEIVED

POST OFFICE TELEGRAM

No. 1704

OFFICE STAMP

01.10.1911   Prefix. Time handed in. Office of Origin and Service Instructions. words.

BAXTER, ST PETERSBURG, RUSSIA   87

TAYLOR & ROSE DETECTIVE AGENCY, SINCLAIR'S, LONDON, ENGLAND   To

From

19-10-10-1 14-23-22-11 19-24-23-4 17-1-6-11 12-8-16-21 19-10-10-14
ARRI VEDS AFEL YINS TPXC ARRU

12-26-24-10 13-26-23-10 23-12-7-7 15-7-10-11 23-4-13-21
THER SHER ETOO WORS ELUC

9-17-16-7 4-4-15-10 1-12-23-15 1-12-26-6 23-15-11-15
KXWI LLWR ITEW ITHN EWSW

26-23-6-1 21-19-6-16 4-16-16
HENI CAN X L XX

ARRIVED SAFELY IN ST P X CARRUTHERS HERE TOO WORSE LUCK X WILL WRITE WITH NEWS WHEN I CAN X L XX

Mei was so absorbed in solving the cipher, that for a moment she didn't notice that the office door had opened again. She looked up to see that two men she'd never seen before had strolled into the office.

'Hello there,' said one of them – a tall, fair, suntanned fellow, who swaggered over to her desk and swept off his hat with a flourish. 'Captain Forsyth, at your service.'

'Philip Brooks,' said the other, who wore a black raincoat and carried an umbrella.

'We're here on behalf of Mr Clarke, of Clarke's Shipping Agents,' said the first man, Forsyth. 'You know what that means, I'm sure.' He gave her a quick wink.

Of course, Mei knew exactly what it meant. *Clarke's Shipping Agents* was the code name for the Secret Service Bureau, and *Mr Clarke* meant the Chief himself. Forsyth took a wallet from his pocket and flipped it open – quickly flashing her an identity card indicating that he was indeed Captain Harry Forsyth, of His Majesty's Army.

Brooks looked sharply around at the reception area, taking in its comfortable chairs and elegant flower arrangements, before coming forward to lean over her desk. The telltale telegram from Lil was still lying there, but Mei quickly opened her big leatherbound appointment book, covering it up.

'Do you have an appointment?' she asked, studying the pages as though she were looking for their names – though she knew quite well they were not there.

'Look here, *miss*,' said Brooks in an insolent tone, which seemed to imply the polite address could not possibly fit someone like her – a young, half Chinese girl with an East End accent. 'We're not messing about with appointments. We need to speak to whoever is in charge here, urgently. Understand?'

Mei felt her cheeks turn pink, but she was determined not to let this man see he had rattled her. 'And what will that be in reference to?' she demanded, in her haughtiest voice.

'Don't mind my colleague,' said Forsyth, with another warm grin. 'His bark is worse than his bite. It's just this is rather important, you see. It's about Miss Rose and her current assignment.'

It took all of Mei's nerve not to let her eyes slide back to the telegram – a corner of which she saw was still visible from under the appointment book. 'Very well,' she said, getting to her feet. 'Please follow me.'

She led the two men out of the reception, and through to Sophie and Lil's empty office. 'Take a seat, if you please,' she said, prim and polite.

But the moment she had closed the door behind them, her formal manner vanished and she ran helter-skelter in search of Billy and Joe. To her relief, she found them both sitting at Billy's desk, drinking tea and eating jam tarts: Billy was reading bits of a case-file out loud, whilst Joe stretched out in a chair with Daisy the guard dog curled contentedly at his feet.

'Oh, hello,' said Billy, looking up and holding out the plate of tarts. 'Want one? They're jolly good.'

But Joe could see from Mei's flushed face that something was wrong. 'What is it?' he asked.

'Two men have turned up from the Bureau. Captain Forsyth and another man called Brooks!' she burst out. 'They said they're here to talk about Lil.'

Billy choked on his jam tart and had to be thumped on the back. 'That doesn't sound good,' he said, coughing and swallowing. 'You don't suppose something could have gone wrong on the journey, do you?'

Mei shook her head vigorously. 'A telegram came just a moment ago. I was working it out when they came in. Lil's made it safely to St Petersburg – though she did say that Carruthers is there too, which is strange. That wasn't part of the plan.'

Joe and Billy exchanged troubled glances. 'So do these fellows know she hasn't gone to Hamburg then?' asked Joe.

'Surely they couldn't possibly – not so quickly,' said Billy, puzzled. 'She's not due back in London for days yet.'

'They said they had to speak to whoever was in charge. They said it was *urgent*,' Mei went on. 'I've put them into Sophie and Lil's office.'

'Well, I s'pose we'd better go and talk to them then,' said Joe, getting to his feet. 'We need to find out what this is all about.'

In Sophie and Lil's office, they found that Captain Forsyth was perched on the edge of Sophie's desk, whilst Brooks was sitting in her chair, flicking through one of their case files. Billy turned scarlet at the cheek of it – but Joe knew at once that getting angry would do them no good. His instincts were telling him to go very carefully. Before either of them could say anything, Forsyth spoke up.

'Oh – here to fetch the tea are you? Mine's with milk and sugar. Brooks, what about you, old fellow?'

'No tea for me,' said Brooks, without looking up from Lil's papers.

Billy's cheeks burned redder than ever. He took a step forward. 'I understand you want to speak to whoever is in charge. Well – that would be us,' he declared, gesturing to himself and Joe.

The two men looked back at him – Forsyth amused, Brooks frankly disbelieving. For a moment, Joe saw themselves quite clearly through their eyes. Billy might be neatly dressed in a suit and tie, but it was plain to see he was not yet seventeen – a more usual age for a junior clerk than an office manager. What was more, his fair hair was sticking up at the front, and there was a small blob of strawberry jam visible on the front of his white shirt. As for Joe himself, he'd come straight from the stables, and was wearing an old pair of corduroy trousers with boots and an open-necked shirt. Daisy had followed him, as she did everywhere he went, and was now nosing at his hand, obviously hoping that he might have some jam-tart crumbs for her.

Forsyth gave a jolly laugh. 'Nice try, boys!' he said. 'Now, can you send in whoever is *really* in charge?'

'We're rather busy, you know,' said Brooks shortly. 'We haven't time to waste.'

'We aren't wasting your time,' replied Billy indignantly. 'I'm William Parker, and I'm the office manager here,' he announced, stepping forward and offering them his hand.

'Stop messing around,' said Brooks, ignoring the hand altogether. 'You can't be serious – you're just a kid.'

'Kid or not, it's the truth,' said Joe. 'We're in charge here while L . . . er . . . Miss Rose and Miss Taylor are away.'

'Look, that's enough,' said Brooks, getting up and moving towards him aggressively. 'Fetch your boss – go on, get on with it. This is serious.'

'We're quite serious,' said Joe, taking a step towards him in response. 'Look – why don't you just tell us what this is about?'

Forsyth intervened. 'I say – do you really mean there isn't anyone more senior we can talk to?' He chuckled to himself. 'I knew that this place would be a little unusual, but I must say, I didn't expect that! Oh, I know – what about McDermott? He's got an interest in this place, hasn't he? He'd be the fellow for us to speak to.'

'It is true that Mr McDermott is an associate of Taylor & Rose,' Billy replied, in his grandest office-manager voice. 'But he's away in America at present.'

'Sorry, gents, but it's us or nothing,' said Joe, settling himself down in Lil's chair, where Daisy laid her head on his knee at once. 'What can we do for you?'

Brooks frowned and crossed his arms, but Forsyth nodded. 'All right. We need to talk to you about Miss Rose.'

'What we need to know is *where she is*,' interrupted Brooks curtly. 'And what the devil she's playing at. We know she isn't in Hamburg.'

'She isn't?' said Joe, feigning surprise. 'Perhaps they were delayed on the journey. Train problems. Or some issue with their papers.'

'There couldn't possibly be any issue with their papers,' scoffed Brooks at once.

'But any number of things could have delayed them. I'm sure they'll get there as soon as they possibly can.'

Forsyth and Brooks exchanged a quick glance, and then Forsyth asked: 'So you haven't heard anything from her, then? No letters – no telephone calls – nothing to say she's had a change of plan, or to explain the delay?'

'Nothing,' said Joe coolly.

'No telegrams?' added Brooks sharply.

'Not a peep.'

'Which of course is perfectly normal. We don't expect to hear much from her when she's away on an undercover mission like this,' added Billy. 'After all, she wouldn't want to compromise her cover, would she?'

Forsyth looked thoughtful for a moment, then handed

Joe a small white card, printed with a telephone number. 'If you hear anything from her, then call this number at once and notify us,' he said.

The two men got up to go. But by the door, Brooks paused. 'What about St Petersburg?' he rapped out suddenly.

'St Petersburg?' Billy squeaked. Joe gave him a warning look.

'What's St Petersburg got to do with anything?' he replied casually.

Forsyth and Brooks exchanged glances again. 'St Petersburg is where Miss Taylor is,' said Forsyth after a moment. 'Or was.'

'Oh, is that right? We don't know anything about that – do we, Bill?'

'Nothing at all,' said Billy, picking up the cue. 'Last time we heard from her, she was in Zurich.'

'All we know is that she's on an important assignment for Mr Clarke,' Joe added. 'And that she may not be back for a while. Miss Taylor and Miss Rose – well, they tend to keep the details of those assignments to themselves. After all, they are top secret.'

Brooks sniffed. 'Seems to me that you fellows don't know an awful lot. So much for being *in charge*. But then I suppose that's how it goes in a place like this – a detective agency run by *young ladies*, if that's what you call them.' He snorted as he went out of the door. 'If you ask me, this operation isn't much more than a joke – a publicity stunt for Mr Sinclair. I really don't know why the Chief bothers with it.'

Forsyth followed in his wake, looking a little awkward. 'We'll see you again soon, I'm sure,' he murmured, and then he was gone.

'Phew!' Billy exclaimed. 'What d'you suppose all that was about? How on earth did they know so soon about Lil not being in Hamburg?'

Joe was still sitting in Lil's chair, stroking Daisy, and thinking hard. Normally friendly with everyone, he'd noticed the dog had been unusually wary while the two men had been in the room and he understood just how she felt. There was something about the whole encounter that made him twitchy, as though he himself was a dog whose hackles had gone up.

'I'll tell you what, I didn't like that Brooks fellow one bit. I know Lil has worked with Captain Forsyth before, but she's never said a word about *him*. Why d'you think he brought up St Petersburg like that?' Billy was saying. 'D'you think he knows that Lil's gone there? Perhaps he was trying to take us by surprise – and trick us into giving her away.'

'If Carruthers really is with Lil, perhaps he blew the whistle to the Bureau?' suggested Joe, trying to think it out. He hadn't taken much of a shine to Carruthers on their brief meeting at the railway station: he'd seemed exactly the kind of fellow who'd drop you in it, if you gave him half a chance.

'And why did they bring up Sophie?' Billy went on anxiously. 'The Chief didn't tell Lil where Sophie was, or anything about her being missing. So why did Brooks start talking about her being in St Petersburg, if we aren't supposed to know anything about it?'

'I don't know,' said Joe slowly. 'But I think you're right. I think they were trying to trip us up.'

He looked down at the card in his hand – a simple white card, with nothing on it but a number, not even the name *CLARKE* to identify it. He knew he wouldn't be calling it anytime soon. And yet, he felt a sudden, powerful urge to take action – to do *something*. He was certain that there had been something peculiar about their visit and his instincts were shouting to him that even if Lil had arrived safely in St Petersburg, her mission to find Sophie could well be far more complicated and precarious than they had anticipated. He wished more than ever that he had climbed aboard that train with her. For now she was a thousand miles away in St Petersburg, knowing no one she could trust. As he sat in Lil's chair, smoothing Daisy's fur, he felt a growing sense that *something wasn't right* – the problem was, he didn't have the slightest idea what it was.

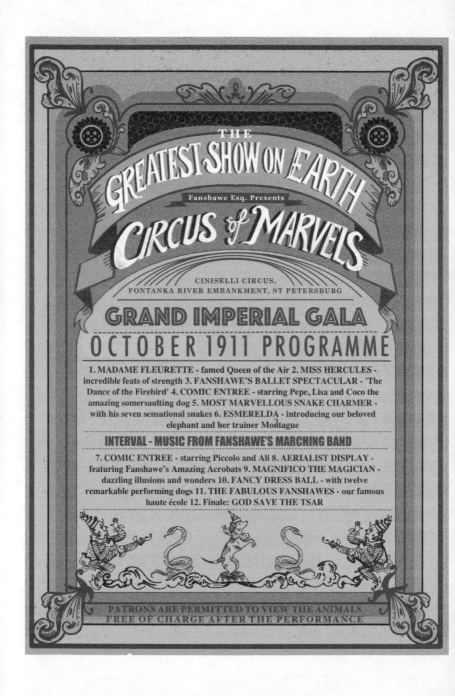

PART IV

'St Petersburg is full of the most marvellous entertainments! Already, Papa has taken me to the opera at the Mariinsky Theatre, to the wonderful Imperial Ballet, and to see a magnificent exhibition of Russian art. Tomorrow we are to go to the famous Ciniselli Circus, of which I have heard so much – and I am so excited I don't believe I shall sleep a wink tonight!'

– From the diary of Alice Grayson

CHAPTER FIFTEEN

The House on the Ulitsa Zelenaya, St Petersburg

Sophie woke suddenly to the sound of the book in her hands slipping from between her fingers and falling to the floor.

She'd been dreaming she was back in the Taylor & Rose office. She'd seen the light slanting through the tall windows, heard the hum of traffic from Piccadilly Circus below, felt the smooth texture of Daisy's fur beneath her hand . . . But gradually she became aware that she was instead curled up in the armchair in the empty, darkened cellar room. Earlier that evening she'd been sitting reading while Nakamura worked on his aeroplane designs: now, his work table was empty.

She sat up and rubbed her eyes: she must have fallen fast asleep. And really, that wasn't so surprising. After all, the last few months of travelling across Europe, and her undercover existence in St Petersburg, had been exhausting. But now, at last, the end was in sight. The precious notebook was locked away in the safe at Rivière's. The spyglass was almost ready: Boris had told her only that morning that he was putting the finishing touches to it, he'd managed to make it in a matter of days, ready to deliver to her mysterious 'customer'. Very soon, it would be time for her to go home.

The night-time house was still. She could hear the faint plashing of the canal outside, and from the next room, the low hum of voices. It must be Mitya and his friends having one of their late-night meetings. He was talking now, his voice raised, as though he was arguing with someone:

'Surely this is a step too far! There are plenty of other ways we can take action,' she heard him say.

'What – printing more leaflets, you mean? Painting slogans on walls? We've done all that a hundred times. You know it won't get us anywhere!' she heard Viktor's familiar, more forceful voice reply. 'We ought to be honoured that *our* group has been chosen for a task of such importance. These orders come from a very important man – someone at the highest levels of the revolutionary movement.'

'Who is he, Viktor?' interrupted Nikolai eagerly.

'You know I can't tell you that. But he's at the centre of everything – and now he wants *us* to help him. He's noticed us and this is our chance to prove ourselves. We must show him that we'll do whatever it takes to make *real* change – more than just posturing and empty words.'

'*Whatever it takes?*' Mitya repeated, his voice troubled. 'Even if that means danger and violence?'

'And what about the risk . . . if something went wrong . . .' piped up another voice, one that Sophie didn't recognise.

'But that's what working for the cause *means*,' argued Viktor. 'It means action. It means danger – and yes, it means risk. But it's our duty to take risks, isn't it? Revolution will not happen without them! We can't afford to be weak any longer; we must make a show of strength. A grand gesture. Something that will make everyone see that change is coming.'

There were murmurs of assent, as though the others in the room liked the sound of this very much indeed. But then Mitya cut in again. 'A show of strength is all very well – but we can't put innocent people in danger.'

'Aristocrats and rich factory owners? They're not so very innocent, if you ask me,' snorted someone else. 'They're the ones living in luxury, while the workers toil all day for only a few coins – not even enough to feed their families.'

'But there will be children there!' Mitya protested. 'That cannot be right!'

There was another murmur, but this time the voices sounded more doubtful. Much as they liked Viktor's stirring words, it seemed that some of the students also saw sense in what Mitya had said. But Viktor calmed them down at once. 'You're making too much of this, Mitya, old friend. You're being too dramatic. There's no intention for anyone to come to harm. This operation is simply about *frightening* our target – showing that we mean business, you see? He must understand he cannot continue to simply do just as he likes, without thought for the people, without consequence. He must understand that he is not *safe*.'

'He's right,' said Nikolai excitedly. 'We won't hurt anyone. But we *will* make them sit up and take notice of us. Come on, Mitya. You must see we have to take action.'

'I have no objection to taking action,' said Mitya gravely. 'As long as you are certain that no one will get hurt.'

'We'll make sure of that,' said Viktor. 'Don't worry. Now let's put it to the vote.'

There was silence for a moment, and then she heard him say in a pleased voice: 'That's settled then. We'll follow our orders.'

There was a buzz of excited discussion, and Sophie took advantage of the sudden burst of noise to get up from her chair, and creep out of the room and up the stairs. She had a feeling that Mitya and the others did not want to be overheard, not by her and certainly not by Vera and Boris – who after the run-in with the police would no doubt disapprove of this latest scheme, whatever it might be. For a moment, she wondered if she ought to say something to them – or perhaps she should talk to Mitya about it? But then she reminded herself that she was a stranger in this house, and in St Petersburg. What did she know of Russian politics? Besides, she knew Mitya was an intelligent, good-hearted fellow: she could trust him to do the right thing.

But back in her bedroom, she found herself suddenly wakeful. Even once she'd undressed and clambered into bed she was unable to fall back to sleep. She felt suddenly wary, though she didn't quite understand why. She was *so close* to doing what she'd intended all this time – taking the notebook and spyglass safely back to the Bureau. And yet lying awake in her bedroom, she felt plagued with superstitious anxiety – as though something was about to go terribly wrong.

She found herself staring up into the darkness, thinking about the *Fraternitas*. Why hadn't they come after the Count? Was it simply because they knew there was no chance of getting the notebook while it was locked away? Or could it be possible that they had already got the information it contained in some other way and that they were even now on the trail of the paintings, with a spyglass of their own? Or then again, might they be waiting for her to return home, and be poised to intercept her on the journey back across Europe – lying in wait to seize the notebook and spyglass from her, in some train carriage or hotel room?

She rolled over and buried her head in the pillow. She was overthinking things and being silly. She'd been lucky, that was all – and now she must take advantage of it.

She tried to lie still and listen to the sounds of the canal outside, a bird hooting in the night. She made herself think of Taylor & Rose, imagining that she was back in the office, pacing up and down, talking everything over with Lil as she always used to do. As she did so, her anxiety began to drift away, but it was very late before she at last fell into a troubled sleep.

CHAPTER SIXTEEN

The Ciniselli Circus, St Petersburg

Lil stared around her, dazzled by bright lights and the sweeping richness of velvet, giddy with the magnificent gleaming of gilt.

'Isn't it wonderful?' said Hanna, stretching out her arms with as much pride as if she'd built the place herself.

St Petersburg's Ciniselli Circus was full of splendour. Immense crystal chandeliers hung from a high-domed ceiling and rings of comfortable seats, upholstered in rich crimson plush, sloped steeply upwards. At one end, high above everything else, was the Imperial box, draped extravagantly with deep-red curtains, the Imperial Eagle watching over it from above. Hanna had already pointed this out as the place the Tsar and his family would sit, when they attended the grand gala performance.

For now though the circus was empty of spectators. There was no one here but the team of men hard at work covering the central ring with a thick layer of sawdust, raking it smooth and even. From above, they could hear the sound of hammering, and an occasional yell of 'Up to your right!' or 'Try it now, Tommy!' Lil caught glimpses of silhouetted figures high up in the rafters like shadow puppets, busily setting up ropes and pulleys, whilst a woman watched them critically from the top row of seats, her arms folded, occasionally shouting out a curt instruction in French.

'That's Madame Fleurette. The Queen of the Air herself. She always supervises the men when they're putting up the rigging.'

'I would have thought she'd leave all that to the circus hands,' Carruthers observed.

'Oh no, she must see to it herself,' said Ravi seriously. 'If one of those ropes was to snap – poof! She would fall and break her neck.'

'But surely she isn't going to be on the flying trapeze all the way up *there* – not without a safety net?'

Ravi laughed at his astonished face. 'A safety net? This is the Circus of Marvels! We do not have *safety nets* here.'

Outside, they saw that the exterior of the circus building was quite as grand as the interior, with its statues and balustrades, its arched windows and lamps. At night, Hanna said it would look even grander, all lit up with electric lights. To one side lay the sweeping blue-grey water of the Fontanka River, and here they stood for a moment, looking out at the bridges and the elegant butter-yellow mansions on the opposite bank.

'St Petersburg looks almost like Paris,' said Lil in surprise, looking at the graceful buildings with their tall, narrow windows and slate-grey roofs.

'It does,' said Carruthers, leaning on the railing. 'But then, it's meant to. Peter the Great designed St Petersburg to look like a European city, you know. He wanted it to be just like Paris – or Venice, or London, or Rome. People called St Petersburg his "window on Europe".'

Hanna was listening intently. 'How do you *know* all that?' she asked.

Carruthers shrugged casually. 'I'm interested in that sort of thing. History, architecture.'

'You are *clever*,' said Hanna. 'I wish I knew about history.' She pulled her coat more closely around her, her cheeks very pink in the brisk air. 'Brr! It's cold, isn't it?'

'That's not so surprising either,' Carruthers informed her, with the manner of a learned professor. 'We're on about the same latitude as Greenland here, after all. A mere five hundred miles from the Arctic Circle.'

Lil rolled her eyes, but Hanna only looked even more admiring. Behind Carruthers, Ravi snorted. 'It's too cold to stand about here talking of *miles* and *latitudes*,' he interrupted, before Carruthers could recite any more facts. 'Come on. I must make sure my snakes have arrived safely.'

The others followed Ravi around to the big yard at the back of the circus building. The tall gates stood open, and a whole parade of carts and motor-lorries were crowding in, laden with the boxes and crates that had come from the train. Lil had never considered how many people would be needed to set up a travelling circus, but now she found herself watching, fascinated, as gangs of people worked busily, unloading the boxes on to trolleys and shifting them rapidly inside, like the cogs of some enormous machine.

Across the yard, Cecil was bossily directing several circus hands carrying dress baskets, whilst a string of beautiful horses were being led carefully out of a horsebox by a team of grooms. From the largest van of all, Lil could see the elephant slowly emerging, swinging its great trunk to and fro, as it lumbered towards the large bun that its trainer was holding out to it. Max hurried past with a stack of papers, looking harried and important. Close to him, Lil caught a quick glimpse of Charlie Walters the photographer, busy setting up a big camera. At his side was a young woman who was pointing over at the horses and then to the elephant, obviously giving him directions on the pictures she wanted. It was Miss Russell: Lil ducked quickly behind Carruthers as they crossed the yard, keen to stay out of sight.

Just ahead of them, one of the circus hands was pushing a trolley loaded with a large wooden crate. He was a broad-shouldered, hard-faced fellow, red and puffing with the effort. As he passed them, he stumbled a little, and the big crate slid forward as though it was about to slip off the trolley. But Hanna was there in an instant – catching the crate before it fell and pushing it back into position as though it contained nothing more than feathers. Lil marvelled at her strength, but the circus hand didn't look so impressed. 'Leave that!' he demanded roughly.

'Well, *what* a charming fellow,' said Carruthers sarcastically.

Hanna brushed off her hands on her skirt, as if she was brushing off his rudeness, as he went away with his crate, without looking at any of them. 'Rogers, I think his name is. One of the new circus hands – *not* very friendly.'

'Some of these men don't like the idea that a girl could be stronger than they are,' observed Ravi. 'But they are *nincompoops*.' Seeing the surprise on Lil's face, he added: 'That is the right word, isn't it? *Nincompoop?* It is a very good word to say.'

'Well, it's one word for them,' said Lil, chuckling to herself. 'But there are lots of others I can think of.'

'You'll have to teach me some more then,' said Ravi decidedly. 'But now hurry up, please! I need to see my snakes. I will introduce them to you.'

Carruthers turned a little pale at this idea, and Ravi flashed Lil another mischievous grin. She grinned back at once, although her thoughts were elsewhere. *Rogers* – wasn't that the name of the man who had come into the luggage car, when she and Carruthers had been hiding in the train? She thought that crate he'd been pushing had been the one they'd hidden behind – the crate he'd opened, and that she knew was full of guns . . .

'Lil! Hurry – you do not wish to miss Sam making the acquaintance of my snakes!' Ravi called out.

Lil hastened to catch up with the others. Ravi had led the way into one of a number of outbuildings adjoining the stables: here were an assortment of large baskets and cages, some of which were emitting a distinct hissing sound.

'So . . . Lil and Sam, *this* is Shesha, my python,' Ravi announced proudly, unbuckling a large basket and lifting out a simply huge snake, beautifully patterned in rich brown and black. He draped the enormous creature around his narrow shoulders as though it was one of Cecil's feather boas. 'He's very clever, and he loves to perform.'

Carruthers stared at the snake, curling itself lovingly around Ravi's shoulders, with an expression of horrified fascination. 'Surely a creature like that can't possibly enjoy performing,' he said, with a shudder. 'Isn't it cruel to take it into the circus ring? Shouldn't it be free to – you know – slither off?'

Ravi looked highly insulted. 'My snakes are treated very well! I would never be cruel to them. They are my friends and they would choose to stay with me even if I set them free.'

Lil thought this sounded rather unlikely, but Hanna nodded at once. 'It's true. The snakes do love Ravi. They do whatever he asks them.' She stroked a hand gently over the snake's scaly skin. 'Besides, Fanshawe is awfully particular about how the animals are looked after. The Circus of

Marvels isn't a bit like some circuses, where they have awful things like bear fights, or tigers jumping through flaming hoops – poor things.'

Ravi beckoned them forward and pointed to another cage, where Lil could see a dark-coloured snake, striped vivid yellow. 'This is one of my king cobras, Vasuki. And beside him is Manasa. The king cobra is the world's longest poisonous snake. Each can grow to as long as nineteen feet.'

Carruthers shuddered again, and Ravi shook his head. 'You shouldn't make this face,' he said, imitating Carruthers' disgusted expression. 'Snakes are to be admired and respected. If you don't see that then I think you too are a *nincompoop*. The snake is a sacred creature: these two cobras are named for the king and queen of the snakes themselves.'

He whispered something through the cage bars to the cobras and they hissed back, just as though they were answering him.

Lil took advantage of Carruthers backing away from the cobras' cage to whisper in his ear. 'Look, I'm going to slip off and do some investigating.'

'Well, make sure you're back here in time to meet Cecil, like we agreed,' Carruthers instructed her.

Lil rolled her eyes. 'That's not important. Have you forgotten why I'm here? I'm *looking for Sophie*, remember.'

'That may be so, but you can't just abandon your commitments,' said Carruthers primly. 'Anyway, I don't know how you think you're going to find Miss Taylor. We don't have the first idea where she is – if she's still here at all. It will be like looking for a needle in a haystack.' Before Lil could argue, he went on: 'I'm going to find a post office and send the Chief a telegram to let him know where we are, and ask for his orders. He *may* authorise us to search for Miss Taylor since we are here, but I'm not going to do anything without his say-so.'

Lil glared at him. She knew quite well that there was a post office only a minute or two away from the circus: she'd been there herself already, to send a telegram back to Taylor & Rose. She knew that if Carruthers sent a telegram to the Chief then they would probably be ordered straight back to Hamburg – or even London. 'Can't you at least give me some time to start looking for Sophie first? The Chief won't even have missed us yet,' she asked him. 'Give me another day – or two days – and then send your telegram and tell the Chief whatever you like. But you might at least give me a chance to find her!'

Carruthers hesitated, but just then Sasha came running up – rather pink and out of breath. 'Sam, will you come quickly, please? Max has need of you.'

Carruthers nodded. But as he turned to follow Sasha, he glanced back at Lil. 'You must see I can't possibly wait,' he said in a low voice. 'It's not just about what *you* want. Any more delay could compromise our assignment – it might even put our man in Hamburg at risk. I'm sorry, but

I have no choice. I have to send the telegram, whether you like it or not.'

Lil stared angrily after him. If the Chief sent word that they must leave at once, would she be able to disobey his direct order again? Would Carruthers let her? But there was no sense worrying about it now. There was one thing and one thing only for her to do – and that was to find Sophie.

CHAPTER SEVENTEEN

The House on the Ulitsa Zelenaya, St Petersburg

At that precise moment, not far from the Ciniselli Circus, on the busy Nevksy Prospekt, Sophie was in the workshop at Rivière's, where Boris had presented her with a small blue velvet box.

'Go on – look,' he said, his voice rumbling with pride. 'I must admit, it wasn't easy, especially at short notice. Those designs you gave me – most unusual! But I believe your mysterious customer will be well satisfied with this.'

Sophie opened the box with careful fingers. Inside, lying on the softest cushion of snow-white satin, lay a perfect golden spyglass. It was decorated with narrow bands of mother-of-pearl and sparkled all over with precious stones.

'Boris – it's exquisite!' she exclaimed in delight.

Boris gave a booming laugh, obviously well pleased. 'But of course it is. This is Rivière's, you know, Alice. Everything we make here must always be beautiful.'

Lifting it gently out of its box, Boris showed her the delicate mechanism. Sophie marvelled at the series of tiny golden levers, which allowed each of the coloured glass lenses to be raised and lowered in turn. She put the spyglass to her eye, and watched in astonishment as the world turned first red, then blue, then purple.

'It's a fascinating device. What did you say your customer wanted to use it for?' he asked, with interest.

But Sophie only shrugged. Even to kindly Boris, she dared not give even the smallest hint about the purpose of the spyglass. 'I don't know. He didn't say much.' She'd described the customer as an eccentric, aristocratic gentleman, who refused to give a name, and only paid in cash.

'Well, he has certainly paid well,' said Boris approvingly. 'Now, you will take this to him, and tell me what he thinks of it, won't you?'

Sophie smiled and said that of course she would, although it gave her a brief pang of conscience. For of course, Boris would never know what her imaginary 'customer' thought. This was it: her work at Rivière's was done. As she prepared to leave the shop that afternoon, she knew that her mission in St Petersburg was almost at an end. All that was left was to take the spyglass and the notebook safely back to London. She would go the next morning, she decided, if she could get a ticket. *Mademoiselle Alice Grayson* was about to disappear from

St Petersburg, for good.

Before she left, she went to the safe and retrieved the small parcel wrapped in brown paper, placing it carefully into her pocket beside the spyglass. She took one last glance around before she left. The shop had been even busier than usual that day, crowded with wealthy customers who had travelled in from Moscow and Riga and Ekaterinburg for the Imperial Gala of the Circus of Marvels, which would be taking place at the Ciniselli Circus that evening. Of course, all the visiting aristocrats wanted to come to Rivière's, and as she left she could see Irina showing an expensively dressed couple some of the splendid music boxes – the peacock, the parrot, and of course, the wonderful firebird. Sophie smiled and then turned away, stepping out into the chilly street. Her time of Russian firebirds was over now: it was time to think of home, and London sparrows.

Although she had paid for the spyglass with her money from the Bureau, she felt rather like a thief as she went down the Nevsky, very aware of the weight of the velvet box in her pocket next to the notebook. She wrapped her gloved hand securely around them both as she walked, thinking as she did so that she might not walk this way again, and looking all around her, as though she was seeing it for the last time.

As she turned away from the bright shop windows and the glitter of the palaces towards Vera's, she felt a wind of change blowing – a bitter winter wind, bringing with it a new sharpness, something fierce. The canals were clouded with mist, and the skies were growing dark already. Perhaps it would be cold enough to freeze tonight? She found herself walking a little faster than usual, glancing back over her shoulder, alert to anyone lurking behind her in the gloom. But there was nothing to be seen but the mist, and she put her head down and walked onwards, suddenly eager to get inside and close the door on the murky St Petersburg night.

At Vera's, all was snug and warm and familiar. She could hear the pleasant sounds of the house: Vera humming to herself in the kitchen, the children's footsteps above as they played. In the parlour she found that the Count was ensconced in an armchair, sipping tea and chatting to Nakamura. She felt glad that Vera had found a room for the Count – or 'Herr Schmidt', as she was careful to call him. In spite of everything he had done she didn't like the idea of leaving him alone and frightened, in that dingy, depressing hotel, looking over his shoulder for the *Fraternitas* at every turn.

For now though, she didn't go and join them. Instead, she went straight up the dark stairs to her room. She wanted to examine the spyglass again before supper, and what was more, she needed to start making her plans for the journey back to London. How peculiar it would be to leave this house, which had been her home for the past few weeks – and to say farewell to Boris, and Vera and Mitya.

She would have to say goodbye to Nakamura too,

she realised, with a sudden stab of regret. He might have come with her to St Petersburg, but she knew he would have no reason at all to accompany her all the way back to London. When he'd finished his work at the Aero Club, she knew he was planning to travel east, across Russia and then home to Japan. The thought of saying goodbye to him after so many months seemed very strange indeed.

But as she came to the top of the stairs, Sophie stopped abruptly, forgetting all about her farewells. She could hear a noise ahead of her: an odd, furtive, rustling sound. All at once, her skin prickled. Acting on instinct, she slid into the shadows. At the top of the stairs, the door to her room stood ajar – although she was quite certain she had left it closed that morning. Inside, she could see a small light flickering, like a candle flame, moving about in the dark.

Sophie crept silently towards the door, until she was close enough to peep inside. She saw a dark figure moving around her room – opening drawers, rummaging through her clothes, rifling quickly through the things she'd left on the table by the bed – a London newspaper, the Russian-English dictionary Mitya had loaned her, a brooch, a few hair-pins. The candle flame illuminated a sharp nose, a pointed face and close-cropped hair – and at once, Sophie recognised Mitya's friend Viktor.

What was he doing, poking about her room? Was he looking for money, or jewellery, she wondered? She watched in growing alarm as he lifted her pillows, as though searching for anything that might be hidden under them, and then began feeling about under her bed. To her horror, she saw him reach forward and pull out her attaché case, containing all her remaining money from the Bureau – not to mention her papers and her mother's diary. It was locked, but Viktor gave it a shake, listening intently to hear the contents rattle. He smiled and the candle lit his face from beneath, making his eyes hollow and black.

Sophie hesitated. She couldn't possibly let Viktor take her attaché case – apart from the money, it was full of confidential papers from the Bureau. And yet somehow she didn't want him to know she had seen him. As she stood, wondering what to do, a voice called out from the stairway below her.

'Alice! Are you there?'

It was Nakamura – and then came the sound of his feet on the stairs. At once, Viktor dropped the attaché case, cursing under his breath. He pushed it back under the bed, blowing out his candle and dashing for the door. Sophie pressed herself back into the deep shadows behind it, but she didn't need to worry about being seen. Viktor didn't pause even for a moment but darted quickly down the stairs.

Sophie crept after him. She was in time to see Viktor pass Nakamura on the stairs, pushing by him and hurrying downwards. Nakamura came to the top of the stairs to see Sophie standing watching him.

'Are you all right?' he asked in surprise.

Sophie nodded. 'But I just saw Viktor sneaking about my room. It looked like he was trying to steal something.'

Nakamura frowned. 'He's been hanging about here all day. Asking odd questions about all sorts of things, including you – and Herr Schmidt. I think he might have been poking about in Herr Schmidt's room too.'

What was Viktor up to, creeping about the house, poking around in the lodgers' bedrooms and asking questions? Was he a thief? Or, Sophie suddenly wondered, could there be any connection with the mysterious scheme she'd heard him discussing with the other students in the cellar? Whatever the reason, she most certainly did not want Viktor going through her things. She would have to keep the spyglass safely with her until she left for London.

She knew she should go and check her room and make sure that nothing had been taken, but she couldn't resist showing the spyglass to Nakamura first. 'I've got it,' she whispered. 'The spyglass – it's here in my pocket. Boris finished making it today. Come and see!'

Down in the cellar room, Sophie made sure the door was tightly shut before taking out the blue velvet box and opening it.

'What an instrument!' Nakamura exclaimed in admiration, sinking down into a chair to admire it more closely.

'I'm going to take it back to London straight away,' said

Sophie. 'Together with the notebook, it will allow us to examine the paintings, track down the secret weapon – and destroy it, for good!'

Nakamura looked up at her quizzically. For a moment he paused as though uncertain, and then he spoke: 'You told Herr Schmidt – the Count – that you would see this weapon destroyed. But Sophie, let me ask you this. How can you possibly be so sure that your government will not want to claim it for themselves, and use it for their own ends?'

Sophie frowned. She felt sure that the Bureau would destroy the weapon. It was clearly the right thing to do. But it occurred to her now that the Chief had never actually said so. All he'd ordered her to do was to have the spyglass made, and to bring it back to London as soon as possible.

'An unknown, deadly secret weapon – lost for centuries? It's like something from a strange old legend. I know my government would certainly want it for themselves,' Nakamura went on. He saw her stricken face and then laughed. 'Don't look so worried. I haven't said a word to them. If I did, they might try to claim it and use it against their enemies. At one time, I might have wished to help them do that – but now . . . well . . . I'm no longer so sure that would be a good thing.'

Nakamura was right, Sophie realised. She'd spent so much time thinking about the *Fraternitas*, when of course they would not be the only ones who would want a weapon like this one. There were many people – powerful people all over the world – who would want it, if they knew it existed.

'Can you really be certain your government will be any different from mine?' asked Nakamura gently.

Coldness began to wash over her, like icy water. *Could* she be absolutely certain? The Chief had never said anything to her about his plans. Was it possible that he was going to hand the information about the weapon over to the Generals in the War Office? She knew how closely the Bureau worked with the Army and Navy; after all, everything she'd done for them so far had been to help give them a military advantage. What if they planned to take the weapon for themselves, and to use it against Germany, or another of their enemies? The thought gave her a sudden, sharp chill.

But before she could say anything in reply, Vera's voice came suddenly from above them. 'Supper is ready!'

It felt strange to put talk of secret weapons and governments aside to join the others for supper. She tried to keep her mind on the conversation, but her thoughts kept drifting back again and again to the weight of the spyglass in her pocket – and especially to what Nakamura had said. It didn't help much that the supper table was quieter than usual – Boris had not yet returned from the Rivière's workshop where he often worked long, unpredictable hours, and Mitya and Viktor had left to attend a lecture.

Nakamura and the Count discussed new innovations in aeroplane engines, whilst Vera scolded Luka and Elena on their table manners, and at the same time tried to get the shy Ukrainian girl, Alina, to talk – but Sophie found herself saying very little at all.

'Are you all right, *lapochka*?' Vera asked her, after a little while.

'Oh yes, of course – I'm just rather tired,' she explained.

Vera nodded understandingly. 'You must have worked hard at the shop today! The city is so full of people for the Imperial Gala at the circus tonight.'

'I wish *we* could go to the circus,' said Elena wistfully.

But Vera shook her head. 'The Imperial Gala is not for the likes of us. It's a special performance for the Tsar and his family – and all the most important members of the Court! No doubt they all wished to visit Rivière's while they are in town,' she added to Sophie. 'I expect that's why Boris is so late tonight, no doubt there are many new commissions –'

But almost as the words came out of her mouth, the door opened and Boris himself came striding in, still wearing his outdoor coat and muffler.

'Everyone – we are going to the Imperial Gala!' he announced in delight, beaming around at them, flourishing a handful of paper. 'I have tickets for all of us – we're going to the Circus of Marvels, tonight!'

CHAPTER EIGHTEEN

A Night at the Circus, St Petersburg

'The circus? We're really going to the circus?' gasped Elena, her eyes as wide as the dinner plates. 'But *how?*'

'One of our clients is the owner of the Ciniselli Circus building,' Boris exclaimed, tremendously pleased with himself. 'I did a special favour for him – a present for his wife's birthday. As a thank-you, he has given me these – complimentary tickets to the Imperial Gala. So, we shall be going to the circus in the company of His Imperial Majesty himself! How about that, Vera my dear?' He set the stack of tickets down on the table amongst the dishes, with a dramatic flourish.

'The circus?' tutted Vera at once. 'Do you really think that I have time to go gadding about to the circus of an evening? I have work to do – a house to run. You should go, and take the children.' But in spite of her protests, Sophie could already see that her eyes were sparking with excitement.

'*Babushka*, you cannot miss seeing the Tsar!' insisted Luka.

'Pah! Do you think I care anything for *him*?' said Vera. 'I would not wish to see all those people, bowing and scraping and making fools of themselves.'

But it didn't take very much persuading from Luka, Elena and their grandfather before Vera had agreed that for once the dishes could wait – and had begun scolding them all to hurry up and finish their supper, so that they wouldn't miss the beginning.

'And the rest of you?' said Boris, looking around the table. 'I have plenty of tickets – you will all come, won't you?'

Alina looked terrified at the thought; and the Count only smiled and shook his head. But although Sophie's mind was still whirling with thoughts about the Bureau, she could see no reason to refuse a ticket. Boris was so eager to share his good fortune, and after all, she remembered, this would likely be her last night in St Petersburg. It would be pleasant to spend it enjoying an exciting circus performance with Boris and Vera, and the children. She was pleased when Nakamura accepted a ticket too: they could go along and enjoy the circus together, and then finish their talk when they got back.

'But Mitya isn't here!' said Luka suddenly. 'He's going to miss it.'

'Well, he is spending his evening at a lecture,' said Vera

proudly. 'That's more useful to him than a circus. It's good that he's paying attention to his studies.' Anyway, Sophie thought, Mitya wasn't likely to enjoy a grand Imperial celebration very much, given his views on the Tsar's extravagance, and the pomp of the Imperial Court.

Vera hurried them up to their rooms, to dress for the evening. 'You must wear your very best clothes,' she explained. 'This is an Imperial Gala, after all.'

Sophie didn't have many grand outfits to choose from, but she was glad of the chance to go back to her room and check everything after Viktor's snooping. Feeling that she couldn't risk leaving either the notebook or the spyglass behind at home, she decided to bring them with her. As an extra precaution she opened her attaché case and took out one or two of the most important papers from the Bureau – papers that would certainly give away her true purpose here in St Petersburg – and slipped them safely inside the notebook, before putting the attaché case carefully away in a new hiding place, under a loose floorboard.

Just as she'd replaced the floorboard and pushed the braided rug back over it, there came a tap at the door. She thought it would be Nakamura, telling her it was time to go, but instead she saw Vera was standing on the threshold.

'I thought you might like to borrow something special to wear tonight,' she said, holding out a pretty blue embroidered scarf. 'This will suit you perfectly, I think.'

Sophie took it. 'Thank you – that's very kind.

What a beautiful scarf!'

Vera arranged it gently around her shoulders. 'It belonged to my daughter, Natasha,' she said, in a low voice. 'Luka and Elena's mother. She had hair just like yours – such a pretty golden colour!' She touched Sophie's hair with a gentle finger. Sophie knew that Vera's daughter Natasha had died a few years ago and that, although she rarely mentioned it, Vera missed her very much.

'Here, let me plait it for you,' said Vera now, reaching for Sophie's brush and comb. It was a very long time since anyone else had combed Sophie's hair, but she found herself sitting down and allowing Vera to carefully brush it out in long, gentle strokes. It was like being a child again. Her own mother must have done this for her once, Sophie realised – though she had been far too young to remember it. As Vera's fingers carefully wove her hair into two long braids, she felt tears coming suddenly into her eyes and she had to blink them away.

Vera carefully pinned the long braids around her head, into a crown. 'There! Now you look like a good Russian girl,' she said. 'We'll show the Tsar that his daughters aren't the only ones who can look splendid at the Imperial Gala, hmm?' She gave Sophie's shoulder a little squeeze, and then hurried out of the room.

The ground was already glittering with frost when they set out, well wrapped up in coats and hoods. The canal was still and dark as they hurried over the little bridge, but as they came towards the Nevsky, they saw that they were not the only ones headed to the circus. Grand carriages rattled past, carrying elegantly dressed people; several expensive motor cars sped by them. There was a sparkle of excitement and merriment in the air: Elena skipped ahead, holding Boris's hand, pointing eagerly to the brightly coloured posters advertising the circus, whilst Luka strolled just behind them, his hands in his pocket, sniffing the scent of caramel apples and candied nuts that hung in the air, and pretending he wasn't just as thrilled as his smaller sister.

'Do you know, I haven't been to the circus since I was a girl!' exclaimed Vera, who had her arm tucked into Sophie's. 'What a place it is – just as splendid as I remember.'

The circus building was a dazzle of golden light in the dark evening. Stylishly dressed ladies in glittering diamond necklaces, and gentlemen in rich furs, could be seen clambering out of their carriages, whilst ordinary folk had gathered close by to stare in at the immense building, hung with great red and gold banners reading *The Circus of Marvels*. At the entrance, Boris presented their tickets with a flourish to an usher in a frock coat; guards were checking people's bags and pockets as they entered. 'That's because of the Tsar, of course,' Vera observed with a sniff. At last they were allowed inside the grand foyer, where they were each presented with a large programme in a silk cover and directed towards their seats.

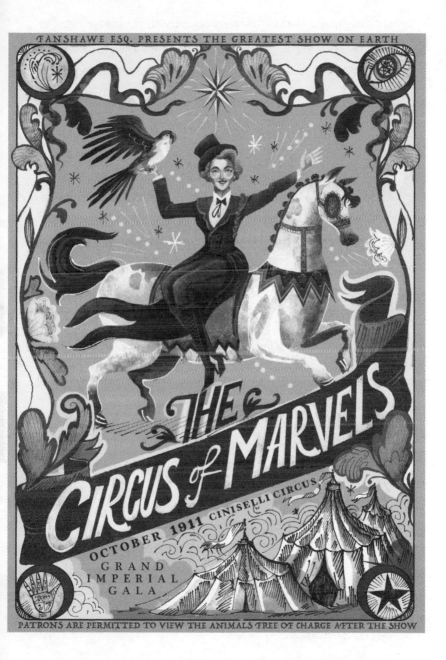

The magnificent auditorium thronged with people – elegant ladies in evening frocks, gentlemen with roses in their buttonholes, children in frilly frocks or sailor suits – although the Imperial box, draped in its grand red velvet curtains, was still empty. Sophie and Nakamura found themselves sitting side by side at the end of the row, with a fine view of the circus ring below them, as well as all the people in their finery. As they took their seats, Sophie gave Nakamura a quick nudge. 'Look!' she whispered.

Sitting across the auditorium from them, on the other side of the ring, she had spotted someone familiar. It was Viktor, sitting by himself. What was *he* doing here, Sophie wondered? Wasn't he supposed to be at the lecture with Mitya? A grand gala performance for the Tsar was the last place she would have expected to see him. She saw that he hadn't noticed them, but instead kept glancing over his shoulder, as though waiting for someone to arrive. In his green cap, he looked rather out of place in an auditorium filled with silk top hats and satin gowns.

'And there's someone else we know,' said Nakamura in a low voice, gesturing to one of the seats just beneath the Imperial box, where a young woman was sitting with a notebook and pencil in her lap. At once, Sophie opened her programme and whisked it up to hide her face. It was Miss Roberta Russell! She'd forgotten that Miss Russell was following the circus on their grand tour. Even though Sophie had managed to dodge her for most of the air race, she knew that Miss Russell would not have forgotten her.

To her relief, at that moment a trumpet fanfare sounded and the audience stood up, all of them looking up at the Imperial box, where the upright figure of the Tsar and his wife could be seen making their entrance. Sophie looked up, as curious as the rest: she'd never caught even the slightest glimpse of the Imperial family before, beyond the portrait of the children Boris kept hanging in the hallway. Their visits to the capital were increasingly rare, and she saw that they were accompanied by a number of dour-looking guards in military uniforms. It was the children who caught her eye first, all dressed in white: the four girls in matching lace-trimmed frocks, their carefully arranged long hair hanging down over their shoulders. As the audience bowed and curtsied, they took their seats together in a group – and beside them was their little brother Alexei, dressed in a sailor suit, a manservant close by, ready to minister to his every need.

But there was not much time to stare. Almost the moment the Imperial family had taken their seats, the house lights went down, plunging everyone suddenly into darkness. The orchestra began to play a stirring melody, and after a few minutes, a single spotlight appeared in the centre of the ring. Standing within it was a single, splendid figure, dressed in an immaculate tailcoat, spotless white breeches, tall leather boots, and a glossy top hat. Sophie assumed it was a man, but as the figure performed a low bow, she realised that the ring master in the top hat was, in fact, a woman.

'Your Imperial Majesties! My lords, ladies and gentlemen! Welcome to Fanshawe's Circus of Marvels!' she proclaimed, in a ringing voice that seemed to echo out to every corner of the auditorium. 'An evening of spectacle and entertainment lies ahead of you. My name is Freddie Fanshawe, and it is my great pleasure and privilege to welcome you here tonight. For our first act, I am delighted to introduce one of our most remarkable stars: Madame Fleurette, Queen of the Air!'

The spotlight was extinguished, making the elegant figure of Freddie Fanshawe vanish like a blown-out candle flame. A gasp of anticipation ran around the dark auditorium – and then all at once, the lights burst into a blaze of brightness, brilliant scarlet and gold.

'Look!' gasped Luka, and they all looked up, to where a magnificent figure could be seen descending with impossible grace from the rafters of the high ceiling. It was a trapeze artist, dressed in a glittering rainbow of feathered plumes, like an impossibly exotic bird.

She was like the extravagant Rivière's peacock, unfurling its magnificent jewelled tail, Sophie thought. The twinkling music of the orchestra seemed to rise and soar with Madame Fleurette, as she glided high through the air, reminding Sophie of how it had felt to fly through the skies in Nakamura's aeroplane. The audience gasped and applauded at her daring, and up in the Imperial box, the Tsar's children leaned forward in admiration, peering at her through their gilded opera glasses and whispering to one another behind their hands. Madame Fleurette performed one somersault, and then two, somewhere between a bird in flight and a firework, exploding up into the sky. The music reached a crescendo as she performed three magnificent somersaults – before at last she swung down to the ground to a roar of applause and flowers heaped at her feet, as she curtseyed low and blew a kiss to the Imperial box.

But Madame Fleurette was just the first of the evening's delights. Sophie forgot all about the Bureau, and the spyglass, the notebook and even the *Fraternitas*, as she watched in fascination. Next, 'Miss Hercules' appeared in the ring: a young woman not much older than Sophie, dressed like an Ancient Greek in a flowing white tunic, a wreath of laurel leaves about her head. She proceeded to demonstrate the most extraordinary feats of strength: she twisted an iron bar into a spiral; broke a chain with her bare hands; juggled with three enormous cannonballs; and even lifted an immensely tall and strong-looking man from the audience over her head, as though it was perfectly easy, smiling graciously at the audience all the while.

As Miss Hercules left the ring amidst a roar of delighted applause, Freddie Fanshawe returned. 'Our next act is brand-new, designed especially for our tour of Russia. Your Majesties, ladies and gentlemen – may I present to you *The Dance of the Firebird*.'

Almost at once, the music began to rise again, in a delicate crescendo of silvery strings that sent a shiver over Sophie's skin. A circle of dancers appeared, moving in perfect rhythm to the music, rippling out from the wings, or floating down as gracefully as feathers, suspended on invisible wires. Each was clad in a gauzy frock of deep crimson, or rich orange, or gold: it was like watching petals blowing in the wind, or a circle of flames flickering.

'Beautiful!' gasped Vera in awe, as the audience broke out in a spontaneous burst of applause.

A new line of dancers flitted into the ring, leaping and spinning into pirouettes – and now it was Sophie's turn to gasp aloud. But it was not the sparkling golden lights, nor the effortless grace of the twirling dancers, nor their beautiful swirling costumes that had astonished her. It was one of the dancers – the tallest of them all, who had shining dark hair. She wore a deep red ballet frock, which looked as though it was scattered with rubies; there were red and orange feathers in her hair; and her face was concealed by a mask of glittering gold paint. Just the same, Sophie would have recognised her anywhere – and now she leaned forward, clutching the balustrade so hard that her knuckles turned white.

It seemed as astonishing as something out of one of Vera's fairy tales. It couldn't possibly be real, she thought stupidly to herself. And yet Sophie felt absolutely certain that the dancer in the red dress, twirling in the ring below her, was Lil.

CHAPTER NINETEEN

The Ciniselli Circus, St Petersburg

'What do you think you're doing? You can't just go rushing off like this,' hissed Carruthers, as Lil dragged her coat quickly over her ballet dress. They were backstage in one of the big dressing rooms – not far away from them Cecil was zipping one of the acrobats into a skintight costume, whilst a clown sat before a mirror, carefully painting his face. 'The show's still going on! You haven't even taken your make-up off!'

'I have to go!' snapped back Lil at once. 'Look, I said I'd help out when one of the dancers sprained her ankle – and I did. But I'm not here to have a jolly old time at the circus or admire the Tsar. I'm here to look for Sophie, remember?'

'But you won't find her now! It's late – and it's dark – and you look completely ridiculous. You can't run about the city like that. You don't even know where you're going!'

Lil glared at him. 'I have to go. Thanks to *you*, I'm out

of time. The Chief has ordered us back to Hamburg and I've still no idea where Sophie is. I went to half the hotels in the city this afternoon, and none of them were any use.'

'Look, can't you just wait until tomorrow? Our visas won't be ready until the afternoon at the earliest. I could come with you – we'll look for her together.'

'No,' said Lil. She was hanging on to the hope that she'd somehow be able to find out something tonight – anything that might have a chance of leading her to Sophie before Carruthers dragged her away from St Petersburg. 'I'm not hanging around any longer. I won't waste any more time!'

She flung the dressing-room door open. 'I have to look *now* if I'm going to have even the slightest chance of finding –' But then her voice cracked suddenly and broke off. 'SOPHIE?' she gasped, in disbelief.

She couldn't believe what she was seeing. There before her, standing on the threshold, her arm raised as if to knock on the door, was Sophie herself, quite as if she'd been conjured there by the circus magician. She'd done her hair differently, plaited and pinned around her head, but there was no doubt about it – it was her. She didn't look injured or sick, nor like someone who had just escaped from prison or from the clutches of the *Fraternitas* – nor any of the dreadful things that Lil had imagined. She looked simply like herself.

Lil gave a little scream of delight. '*Sophie!*' she cried again, leaping forward.

Sophie felt Lil's arms envelop her and staggered back. It was true: the ballet dancer really was Lil. She made a strange sight, dressed in an ankle-length red ballet frock and red satin ballet slippers, a winter coat thrown roughly over the top, her hair still scraped into a high bun, and her face shining with gold paint – but Sophie's only thought was how marvellous it was to see her.

'Oh, Sophie – you're all right!' she burst out. 'And you're here!'

'Of course I'm all right,' laughed Sophie, almost choked by her enthusiastic embrace. 'But whatever are *you* doing here? What are you doing performing in a circus? Is it part of a new assignment?' Her eyes widened at the sight of Carruthers, gaping at her from just behind Lil. 'Did the Chief send you both?'

'I came here to look for you – to find you and bring you home!' Lil released her at last but kept a tight hold of her hand as though she didn't dare to let go of it. 'I was so worried about you! We all were, when we heard you'd gone missing. I thought you'd been kidnapped by the Count – or caught by the *Fraternitas*. Sophie, what *happened* to you?'

'What do you mean?' asked Sophie, her forehead creasing into a frown. 'Missing? I wasn't *missing*.'

But Lil didn't seem to have heard her. 'I could hardly believe it when the Chief said you'd disappeared in St Petersburg. It was simply *awful* when he said he hadn't heard from you for more than a month. I was imagining the most terrible things.'

'More than a month?' Sophie stared at her, baffled. 'But I've been sending reports to the Bureau ever since I got here. I send one via the British Embassy every week.'

Carruthers intervened hurriedly. 'Er – don't you think we might want to go somewhere a little more *private* for this conversation?' he whispered, gesturing around the dressing room. 'I don't know if you've noticed, but this probably isn't the best place to go shouting about the Bureau and the British Embassy.'

Lil scowled at him, but all the same she dragged Sophie forward – through the hustle and bustle of backstage and then out of a side door that led out on to a deserted street at the side of the circus building. Carruthers hurried behind them.

Once they were safely outside in the cold night air, Lil turned to Sophie at once. 'I don't understand. The Chief said he hadn't heard anything from you for weeks.'

'But that doesn't make sense. I've been writing all the time!'

'Well, none of your messages have reached him – not since you came to St Petersburg,' said Carruthers briskly. 'He thought you'd disappeared.'

'But he sent me a telegram *back* just the other day,' protested Sophie, rummaging in her pocket for it. It had been one of the papers she'd taken with her, in case Viktor returned to do any more snooping in her room.

Now she handed it to Carruthers, who unfolded it and read it aloud: '*ORDER GRANDFATHER'S BIRTHDAY PRESENT AND BRING ASAP – CLARKE.*'

'What does it *mean?*' asked Lil, puzzled.

'It's a reply to the letter I sent him,' said Sophie. 'It's my instructions – they do make sense.'

Carruthers shook his head. 'I don't believe the Chief sent this telegram. Why would he have sent a telegram to you here in St Petersburg, without saying a word about it to me? I always arrange all his telegrams,' he added a little peevishly.

'Perhaps he didn't want you to know about it,' Lil pointed out.

Carruthers looked like he was going to argue, but then Sophie said: '*Shhh!*' Two dark figures had emerged from the circus building, and at once the three of them drew back into the shadows. It was two men – one a large man with square shoulders, the other smaller, wearing a cap. They seemed to be having a furtive conversation in whispered voices.

'I know that man!' murmured Lil in a low voice. 'That's Rogers – he's one of the circus hands. The one with the crate of guns, remember?' she added to Carruthers.

'And that's *Viktor!*' said Sophie, in astonishment. 'He's a student at St Petersburg University and a friend of the family I'm staying with – but he's been snooping about my room and asking questions. What's he doing here, talking to someone who works for the circus?'

At that moment, the two men's conversation seemed to come to an abrupt end. Viktor murmured something to Rogers, who took an object out of his pocket and put it in Viktor's hand. Even in the dark, it was quite clear to see that the object was a revolver.

Sophie and Lil exchanged a quick glance as the two men stalked off in opposite directions – Viktor towards the brightly lit entrance of the circus building and Rogers towards the big gate that led into the yard behind.

'I'm going to follow Viktor,' said Sophie. 'I want to know what he's doing here. I've got a feeling he's up to no good.'

Lil felt a familiar thrill of excitement in her stomach. This was more like it, she thought! She and Sophie were together again, and there was investigating to be done. '*I'm* going to follow Rogers,' she announced.

Sophie nodded at once, as though she'd expected nothing else. 'Right. Let's meet after the show. Come to my lodging house – it's not far away, and we can talk privately there. It's number 3, Ulitsa Zelenaya – the pink house by the canal.'

She grinned at Lil and then disappeared after Viktor, running lightly down the dark street without even looking back. Without another word, Lil darted after Rogers. 'So, I'll come with you, shall I?' muttered Carruthers, making haste to hurry after her. 'Right . . . very good.'

Lil hurried through and into the yard, with Carruthers close behind. She could hardly believe that she'd done it – she'd found Sophie. Or Sophie had found *her*, perhaps – but whichever way round it was, it didn't matter, because now they were together again. How Lil had missed this – working with someone who knew you so well that you both knew exactly what you were going to do, without needing to say a word.

The yard was dark and empty now; the motor-vans and carriages had long since vanished. But there was one vehicle standing waiting in the darkness – a rather dilapidated-looking wooden cart, pulled by a single sturdy carthorse. Rogers was standing beside it speaking to the driver. As she watched, the driver jumped down from his seat and followed Rogers into one of the circus sheds, which adjoined the outbuilding in which Ravi's snakes were kept.

Beckoning to Carruthers to follow her, she crossed the cobbled yard after them. The door of the shed stood open and inside she could hear them talking in Russian. Of course, she couldn't understand a word that they were saying, but she elbowed Carruthers forward, closer to the door. He was already listening intently, a frown on his face – but then Lil pulled him back sharply, inside the doorway of the shed where the snakes were kept. Rogers and the driver were coming out again, this time pushing a trolley upon which was balanced a wooden crate. Lil stared at it, certain it was the same crate they'd seen in the luggage van

– the crate that Hanna had tried to help with – the crate containing the guns!

There was no sound in the yard but the squeak of the trolley wheels, as Rogers steered it towards the cart. The driver helped to manoeuvre it into the back, with much grunting and struggling. Once they had positioned it securely, Rogers said something else to the driver. The fellow looked at him sharply, then nodded and flicked the reins. He gave Rogers a kind of salute, before clip-clopping slowly out of the yard and away into the night. Rogers watched him go – and then, to Lil's surprise, he bolted the two doors that led from the circus building into the stable yard from the outside. Instead of returning inside the building himself, he turned and walked quickly out of the gate and away down the street as if he were in a great hurry.

Lil watched him go, fascinated. What was it Carruthers had said on the train? *Who knows, maybe they have a delightful little sideline in illegal gun-running?* Was that what she had just seen? Was the circus being used as a cover to smuggle guns secretly into St Petersburg – and had Rogers just arranged for them to be delivered, even while the Imperial Gala took place?

Carruthers was staring after Rogers too. 'What did he say?' Lil asked him eagerly.

Carruthers shook his head, as though he was still trying to make sense of what he'd heard. 'He told him where to deliver the crate – and that was strange enough. But that wasn't all. At the end he said something like: *Now, get out of here. You don't want to be anywhere near this place when tonight's performance ends.*'

On the other side of the circus building, Sophie was trailing Viktor back towards the entrance, blazing with electric lights. She stayed well back, keeping to the shadows, grateful for her dark coat and for Vera's blue scarf, which she slipped up to cover her blonde hair so it wouldn't catch the light.

Viktor was making a beeline for a young lady who was leaving the circus performance early and was climbing into a motor-taxi.

'Hotel Europa,' Sophie heard her say to the driver, in a clear, distinctly English voice.

'Miss – excuse me – Miss,' said Viktor. 'Miss – I need to speak with you!' He put out a hand and grabbed hold of her sleeve, and she turned to look at him indignantly. As she did so, Sophie saw it was Miss Russell.

'Let go of me!' Miss Russell declared, shaking his hand away and opening the motor-car door.

'But I must speak with you. I have a message. A most important message!' hissed Viktor.

'A message – for *me*?'

'No,' Viktor said, his voice dropping lower. 'This message is for *Mr Gold*.'

'Mr Gold?' Miss Russell stared at Viktor as if she thought he were mad. 'I don't know what you're talking about. I don't know anyone of that name.'

'But you are the English journalist, are you not? Miss Roberta Russell?'

Miss Russell bristled. 'Yes, that's my name. Look, is this about a story? If you've got something you want to tell me about, you'll have to find me tomorrow. I haven't time now.'

'Of course,' said Viktor, nodding earnestly. 'You must leave at once. I understand that. But this is not a story. It is a confidential message – a most important message for Gold. *I am his man,*' he hissed meaningfully.

'Gold's man?' Miss Russell repeated, obviously baffled. 'I'm afraid I don't know what you mean. Is Gold's another circus troupe? I already told you, I don't have time now. If you've got something to tell me, you'll have to come back tomorrow. I'm writing about the circus, so I'll be here all day – you can find me here, if you must.'

She got briskly into the motor car and drove away. Viktor stared after her for a moment, and then muttered something angrily to himself and walked back into the circus building.

Sophie went inside too. She knew that she should return to her seat, otherwise Vera and the others would wonder what had become of her. A few minutes later, she was back in the gilt and velvet of the circus arena, watching

228

the Fabulous Fanshawes – but although her eyes were fixed on the marvellous horses, her mind was whirring like the intricate workings of a Rivière's music box.

Lil was here in St Petersburg. It was almost too wonderful to be real. And yet the reason she was here was because she had thought Sophie was missing. The Chief hadn't been getting any of her letters. What's more, Carruthers said he didn't believe the Chief had sent her that telegram – but if so, who had? There were only two possible explanations, Sophie thought. The Chief was either keeping her correspondence to himself and concealing it from everyone for some mysterious reason of his own. Or someone had been intercepting Sophie's messages to the Bureau. If this was the case, then they would certainly know she had the notebook – and the spyglass too. A growing sense of dread began to creep over her, and her hand closed tightly around them in her pocket.

Then there was Viktor, sneaking about her room, asking questions about her and the Count – and then turning up here at the Imperial Gala, absolutely the last place she'd expect him to be. What was he doing, slinking about outside in the dark, talking to that fellow that Lil had said was a circus hand – and then taking a gun from him? Why had he been pestering Miss Russell? And who was the *Mr Gold* he kept talking about? Was it possible that he was the mysterious contact Viktor had mentioned at the secret meeting with the other students – the one who had given them their 'orders'. Is that why he'd told Miss Russell that he was *Gold's man*? But why would he think that Miss Russell, an English journalist, had any connection with an underground Russian revolutionary?

There was something else too, something that was bothering her as she stared at the glittering golden chandelier above her – the word *Gold* itself. She knew that Viktor was not the only one who had talked about someone called 'Gold' recently, and now it came to her in a rush. The Count had also used the same name, hadn't he? He'd said it was the code name of the Countess's contact in the *Fraternitas*.

Around her, the audience gasped and cheered, as the horses waltzed in time to the music. Elena's eyes were wide with awe, and Luka had obviously lost his heart completely to the beautiful black horses. Even Nakamura was leaning forward in his seat. But Sophie barely saw any of it. She was still thinking hard about *Mr Gold*, and all at once, she could feel the strands beginning to weave themselves into place, like Vera's nimble fingers, braiding her hair.

If *Mr Gold* was a member of the *Fraternitas*, then could it be possible that Viktor was too? Or more likely still, had Viktor been led to believe that Mr Gold was an important member of the revolutionary movement, and followed his orders accordingly? Had he been tricked and manipulated? Could the *Fraternitas* be using him to stir up the revolutionaries? Were they the ones who had intercepted her messages? All at once, she felt as if the *Fraternitas* were invisibly closing in on her, even as she sat watching the circus. In spite of the warmth of the crowded auditorium, she felt cold inside.

The performance was coming to an end now – the Fabulous Fanshawes had dismounted and were bowing to the crowd, as the other circus performers joined them in the ring. The ballet girls in their scarlet and gold dresses, Madame Fleurette in her magnificent feathers, the snake charmer with his python glistening around his shoulders beside Miss Hercules – and at the centre of it all, Freddie Fanshawe herself, smiling and bowing. The people were cheering and applauding and calling out '*Bravo! Bravo!*'

Across the auditorium, Sophie glimpsed Viktor amongst them. He was back in his seat, applauding politely, but at the same time his eyes were darting around him. He looked over at two people sitting not far away from him and gave them a quick nod – and to Sophie's surprise, she saw they were Mitya and Nikolai.

Luka had seen them too. He pulled at Vera's sleeve. 'Look, *Babushka*! Mitya made it to the circus after all! He didn't miss it!'

Vera looked over in surprise, even as the orchestra struck up 'God Save the Tsar' to conclude the performance, and all around the auditorium people rose from their seats. 'Mitya?' she exclaimed. 'But . . . what is he doing here?'

Luka and Elena grinned and waved across the

auditorium – and Mitya saw them at once, his mouth dropping open in astonishment. But he was not merely surprised, Sophie realised – he was horror-struck. His eyes blazed with sudden panic, like a lightning flash, and in that single, heart-stopping moment, Sophie knew why.

Even as Viktor nodded again to Nikolai, and Nikolai drew a gun from his pocket, she knew what was coming. Students in green caps seemed to have appeared all around the auditorium: many were taking handfuls of leaflets from their pockets, whilst others were producing weapons, and waving them at the Imperial box. This must be the plot she had heard them discussing in the basement: the 'task' they had been given. This was why Rogers had handed Viktor a gun in the alley. They had been planning an attack at the circus – and now it was too late to stop them.

CHAPTER TWENTY

Secret Service Bureau HQ, London

Joe stood in the shade of a tree, across the cobbled square from the Secret Service Bureau. It wasn't the easiest of places to watch and wait unseen – but luckily he'd had plenty of practice at that kind of thing. He'd learned to keep out of the way and out of trouble when he was just a kid on the streets of the East End – and while he'd been sleeping rough, he'd got clever at slipping about, steering clear of the coppers and the Baron's Boys. You learned a fair bit about hiding in plain sight when your neck was on the line.

Now, he'd found the right place for what Billy would call a 'stake-out' – a dark corner by the wall, shaded by a tall tree, where he had a clear view of the entrance. But although he'd been waiting here for over two hours, there hadn't yet been anything to see.

It was a dingy sort of day, and it had begun to drizzle. Joe stifled a yawn and leaned back against the tree. No doubt about it, standing around waiting in the rain was dull.

If Billy had been here, he'd probably have brought something to read, but Joe had never been much of a reader – until a year or two ago, he hadn't known how. Besides, he couldn't afford to be distracted, he reminded himself. You had to keep your wits about you on a job like this.

He'd been pondering what to do ever since Forsyth and Brooks had paid their visit to the Taylor & Rose office that morning. This wasn't much of a plan – but it was better than nothing. There had been something fishy about their visit, and especially the way that fellow, Brooks, had acted. The only thing he could think was that he should watch for him at the Bureau and try and tail him, to see where he went and what he did.

He knew exactly where the Bureau was, of course. He'd been there plenty of times before, driving Sophie or Lil to one of their meetings with the Chief. But he'd never been inside himself. Looking up at the big stone building now, he felt a prickle of discomfort. Places like this made him feel all wrong – they weren't meant for fellows like him, but for chaps like Captain Forsyth. The swaggering sort, who were used to having money in their pocket, and telling people what to do, who'd never even come close to sleeping on the streets or begging for their dinner.

But now, it struck him suddenly that he'd got used to having a bit of money in his pocket too. It was a long time since he'd had to sleep rough. No question about it: his life had changed completely in the last few years. Now, just occasionally, he found himself dreaming of what might come next.

They weren't very grand dreams, but he found them exciting, just the same. Sometimes he'd imagine himself rising through the ranks at Sinclair's, until one day Mr Sinclair would put him in charge of the stables. He'd have dozens of fine horses under his care, and all of the stable lads would look up to him and call him 'sir'. Other times, he'd picture himself having a house of his own – not a big fancy place, but a cosy little house, something like the Lims' place out in Limehouse, or perhaps like the house where Billy lived with his mum on the other side of the river. Sometimes, he'd even wonder what it might be like to leave London altogether and live in the countryside. He had vague pictures in his head of a white-painted farmhouse, surrounded by green meadows full of buttercups, and a pond with ducks in it. There'd be woods, and fields, and a paddock for horses of his own.

Somehow, Lil had a habit of always popping up somewhere in this vision – not doing anything particular, just throwing sticks for Daisy (who, of course, would be there too), or feeding the horses apples and sugar lumps, or keeping him company, wandering through a field of buttercups. Stupid, really, he told himself now. As if a girl like her would ever want to rough it with him, on some country farm. She was made for London and glamour: she ought to always be on the stage, in a fancy frock, with the spotlight shining on her and everyone cheering. He'd always known that she could never really belong with a fellow like him. And yet . . . there'd been a moment on the station platform when they'd said goodbye – a split second, nothing more than that – when he'd almost thought that if he *had* kissed her, she might have kissed him back . . .

It was for Lil, really, that he was here. If there was something funny going on, if that fellow Brooks was up to something, then he needed to make sure she knew about it. He didn't like the idea of her in St Petersburg, alone, with only that fellow Carruthers who he didn't trust.

Just then, he straightened up suddenly, seeing that the door was opening at last. A man was coming briskly down the steps: his face was hidden by a large umbrella but the black raincoat he was wearing looked familiar. Was it Brooks?

Slipping quickly behind the trunk of the tree, Joe watched intently as the man stuck a large envelope inside his jacket, glanced at his watch, and then quickly walked on.

Joe slipped quietly after him, across the yard, under the archway and out into the street beyond. It was simple enough to shadow him through the narrow streets, and out on to the noisy clamour of the Strand. The rain was falling harder now, and no one was paying much attention to anything but getting inside. Joe wondered whether he might be headed to the ABC or one of the other cafés and eating-houses along the Strand – but instead, he cut down a little lane, going in the direction of the river.

Joe followed, careful to keep a good distance between them. A moment or two later, the man went through a gate into a small park, and Joe slipped after him, grateful for the cover of the trees.

The park was quiet after the hubbub of the Strand. There was no sound but the patter of rain on leaves, and almost no one there, besides an old man feeding the pigeons, and a woman pushing a baby in a large black perambulator. The man went briskly onwards, past them, his feet crunching over the gravel, and Joe followed, feeling more and more intrigued. He wished that the fellow would move the umbrella so he could see his face, and know for sure if it was Brooks – but instead, the man stopped abruptly in front of a bronze statue of some old fellow or other – bending down, as though to read the inscription on the plaque beneath it.

Joe stopped too, sheltered by a large evergreen bush. Peering between the wet leaves, he saw to his astonishment that the man was not merely reading the plaque as he had first thought. Instead he seemed to be slipping the large envelope he had been carrying beneath a loose stone at the base of the statue. A moment later, he had straightened up and was walking rapidly away, without looking back.

Joe stared after him, uncertain what to do next. On the one hand, he wanted very much to know what was inside that envelope; on the other, perhaps he ought to keep following. Then again, the man had obviously left that envelope for someone else to collect – and there was something about the way he'd walked so briskly, occasionally looking at his watch, that made Joe guess that he was working to a schedule. If so, if Joe went to look at the envelope now, he might risk being discovered by whoever was coming to pick it up. On the other hand, if he stayed back, watching and waiting, he might just be lucky enough to see whoever was coming to collect it.

Almost the moment that thought had crossed his mind, he heard footsteps approaching, and hurriedly squeezed further inside the evergreen bush, getting very damp in the process. Between the leaves, he saw that a woman was approaching: a rather smart woman in an expensive-looking tailor-made suit, carrying a green silk umbrella. She bent down beside the statue, as if she too was examining the plaque, but from his hiding place Joe could see her gloved fingers quickly lifting the loose stone and whisking out the envelope. She glanced at it quickly, and then dropped it into the handbag she carried, before getting to her feet, brushing off her gloves as though to whisk away even the faintest speck of dirt, and walking swiftly away again.

This time, Joe knew he must follow. Hastily, he squeezed out of the bush, and went after the woman, who was walking out of the park and straight back up towards the Strand. He dodged after her through the crowds, eager not to lose sight of her – pushing his way between the people as they headed along the Strand until they came to Fleet Street.

Here, he saw the woman walk up to a large, impressive red-brick building and go inside. Joe stared after her, in some surprise. He knew the place at once – apart from anything else there were great big gold letters running the length of the building, reading *NORTON NEWSPAPERS* and *THE DAILY PICTURE*. It was a newspaper office.

Joe rubbed his eyes for a moment, trying to make sense of what he'd just seen. Was it his imagination or had the man brought some kind of documents out of the Secret Service Bureau and passed them secretly to a woman who had taken them straight to the offices of one of London's most important newspapers? Could it be part of one of the Bureau's mysterious assignments – or was it possible that Brooks was leaking secret information to the press? Why would he do something like that – and if he was, what possible connection could that have to the peculiar visit he had paid to Taylor & Rose?

Omnibuses and motor-taxis rumbled past, and people pushed by on the pavement, but Joe stood still, eyeing the big building beside him. None of this made the least bit of sense, he thought, but he was becoming more certain by the minute that something very strange was going on at the Bureau. He put his hands in his pockets and walked through the rain back towards Sinclair's, anxious thoughts buzzing in his ears.

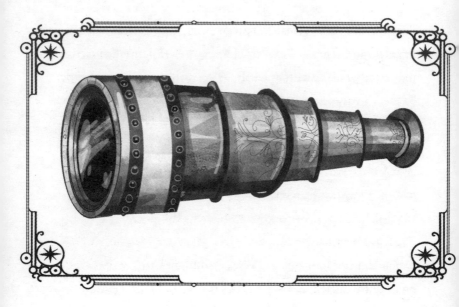

PART V

'Since I last wrote, something terrifying has occurred here in St Petersburg. The Tsar of Russia, Alexander II, has fallen victim to a dreadful assassination plot. It happened like this: on Sunday, as the Tsar was travelling along the Catherine Canal, a member of a revolutionary group threw a bomb under the wheels of his carriage. The explosion killed and wounded several people, but the Tsar himself was safe – until another man threw a second bomb, and then the Tsar was gravely injured. He was carried by sleigh to the Winter Palace, but he died there later that day.

'Since then there have been many police arrests of rebels, and more outbreaks of violence. Our Russian hosts are terribly upset, and I am very glad we were on the other side of the city when the attack took place – for the thought of witnessing such a horrifying spectacle makes me shudder.'

– From the diary of Alice Grayson

CHAPTER TWENTY-ONE

The Ciniselli Circus, St Petersburg

The circus auditorium was plunged into pandemonium. All around were gasps and screams as people realised what was happening. The students scattered around the auditorium were on their feet; a cascade of leaflets were flung into the air; someone yelled out: 'For freedom!' and then there came the crack of a bullet being fired, zipping high over the heads of the crowd.

The uniformed guards had already leaped forwards, screening the Tsar and his family from danger. Behind them, Sophie caught a frenzied glimpse of the girls in their white dresses, clinging to each other in fright, whilst Alexei had already been gathered up in the arms of his enormous manservant. Below them the orchestra kept on playing, as if uncertain what else to do. In the ring, the horses whinnied and reared up, as their riders rushed to grab for their reins.

Horror washed over Sophie. She remembered how the Chief had advised her to *avoid public gatherings*.

She remembered what her mother had written about how Tsar Alexander II had been assassinated out in the street, and she remembered how the Russian minister, Stolypin, had been shot only a short while ago, in the midst of a crowded theatre. But surely Mitya and his friends could not really be planning to assassinate the Tsar . . . could they? She remembered what Mitya had said: *I have no objection to taking action, as long as you are certain that no one will get hurt.*

She found she was on her feet: all around her, the crowd was standing. Men were appearing all over the auditorium – tall, burly men, who just a moment ago had seemed like any other members of the audience, dressed in evening coats and top hats. But now they were grabbing the students, tearing their weapons from their hands, pushing them down to the ground. Sophie realised that this must be the *Okhrana* – the Tsar's secret police.

It was the students who were panicking now. One or two made a dash for the Imperial box, but others were running desperately for the exits, pushing spectators roughly out of the way, doing anything they could to avoid capture. One grabbed a young woman, pushing her in front of him as though to use her as protection from the police, and she let out a shriek of terror. Somewhere below them, another gun went off, to more screams from the crowd.

Across the auditorium, Sophie saw Nikolai being wrestled into submission by two enormous policemen; the gun he was holding ripped from his grasp. Mitya was

244

dashing towards the door, another policeman close on his tail. But Viktor was nowhere to be seen.

She felt frozen to the ground, but she could feel Nakamura's fingers gripping her arm. 'We have to get out of here – it's not safe!'

Turning, she realised he had already scooped up a weeping Elena in his arms; and that Boris had done the same to Luka, who was struggling and demanding, 'Put me down!' though Boris was paying no attention. 'Follow me,' he said gruffly, making for the doors, Nakamura hurrying close behind him. Sophie glanced back for a moment at the chaos unfolding beneath them. Children were crying, people were screaming, the orchestra had abandoned their instruments and were frantically helping the rest of the performers get the frightened animals out of the ring. Everywhere, people were making a run for the exits: there was going to be a stampede.

Vera was still standing stock-still, staring at the place where Mitya and Nikolai had been. 'What was he doing?' she murmured. Sophie took her gently by the arm and pulled her after Nakamura and Boris. 'Don't worry,' she found herself saying, in as soothing a voice as she could manage. 'He ran – I saw him. He got to the door. I'm sure he'll get away.'

But she spoke with more optimism than she felt. There were policemen everywhere: she could scarcely believe there were so many. What chance did

Mitya have of escaping arrest?

Boris and Nakamura led the way through the crowds, going so fast that Sophie had to half run to keep up with them, dragging Vera along beside her as quickly as she could manage. Out in the street there were yells and the shrill of police whistles, and the thrum of heavy boots on cobbles. Motor engines roared, and somewhere, Sophie heard another scream. Where were Lil and Carruthers, she wondered. Were they safe? Should she go back and look for them?

'Hurry!' Nakamura instructed her over his shoulder, and she pulled Vera onwards. Lil and Carruthers were agents of the Secret Service Bureau: they were more than capable of looking after themselves. Her duty was to help the family get to safety.

She was panting with the effort of keeping up with Boris and Nakamura whilst dragging Vera along with her. By the time they at last turned away on to the quieter back streets the sound of engines and voices had faded into the night. Now there was nothing but the gentle plashing of the canal, and their own feet, hurrying in rhythm over the bridge, towards home.

'What happened?' Vera said breathlessly, still dazed.

'Why was Mitya there?' came Luka's voice, thin and small from against Boris's shoulder.

'There was a plan . . .' Sophie tried to explain. She looked from Vera, to Boris, to Nakamura. 'I overheard the students talking. Viktor said he'd received orders from someone important, who'd given them a task to do.'

Vera stared at her, bewildered.

'But Alice . . . why didn't you *say* anything?' asked Boris.

'I don't know,' said Sophie wretchedly. Vera's face was so full of sadness and pain that she could hardly look at her. It was dreadful enough that Vera had already lost a beloved daughter – would she now lose a son too? Mitya might not have been holding a gun himself, only a handful of leaflets, but Sophie knew that simply being there, in a green students' cap alongside the other revolutionaries, would be enough to see him arrested, sent to prison – or worse. Why *hadn't* she spoken up, or tried to stop them? 'I didn't realise – I had no idea it would be something like that . . .' she said.

'How could you possibly have guessed? To attack the Tsar and his family . . . they must be mad,' murmured Nakamura, shaking his head.

'But that's just it. They said they weren't going to hurt anyone. They talked about making people sit up and take notice. But they were quite clear that no one was going to come to any harm.'

Her voice faded away. Her thoughts kept flashing back to the gunshots, the screams, the policemen wrestling students to the ground. It struck her suddenly that it could not have been a coincidence that the audience had been full of policemen, disguised as ordinary guests.

The Tsar's *Okhrana* had been ready to pounce the very second the students had revealed themselves. That could mean only one thing, Sophie realised: they had known the attack was coming.

Someone had tipped off the secret police – and all at once, she felt sure she knew who it was. The student attack; the *Okhrana* in the audience; the chaos and mayhem; the mysterious *Mr Gold* – it was all connected, and the thread that linked it all together was the *Fraternitas Draconum*.

CHAPTER TWENTY-TWO

The House on the Ulitsa Zelenaya, St Petersburg

The second they were inside the house, Boris put Luka down and then turned back towards the door. 'I'm going out again. I have to find him,' he declared.

Sophie saw that his face was grey. He was just as horrified as his wife – perhaps more so, she realised. He had spent his whole life working by appointment to the Tsar: in a flash, she thought of the portrait of the Tsar's children hanging in the hall and then the girls in their white dresses, clutching each other in terror. The same girls for whom he had spent years lovingly crafting perfect music boxes.

'I can't believe that any son of mine would do such a thing,' he choked out.

'He only agreed to the plan because he was told no harm would come to anyone,' Sophie tried to reassure him. 'I heard him say so myself.'

But Boris didn't seem to hear her. He was headed to

the door, but Nakamura stepped quickly in front of him, stopping him short. 'Boris – you mustn't. There will be police everywhere on the streets. They will be rounding up anyone they suspect – you might end up arrested yourself, and then what would Vera do?'

'Besides, if Mitya managed to get away then he might come here, looking for your help,' Sophie added.

'Or the police may come looking for *him*,' went on Nakamura gravely. 'In which case, we will need you here.'

Boris looked from one to another of them, and then sighed, his shoulders slumping. 'Very well. Come, I'll help you take the children up to bed,' he said heavily to Vera. 'I must keep myself busy somehow.'

Together, they hustled Luka and Elena upstairs, and Nakamura and Sophie were left alone. Suddenly the house felt very quiet. The clock on the mantelpiece showed that it was almost midnight. The Count and Alina must have long since retired to bed and now silence lay heavy over the house, as thick as a feather eiderdown.

Sophie peered out of the window at the dark and empty street. There was nothing to be seen: only the smallest ripples disturbed the waters of the canal, and ink-dark shadows were broken by the faint light of a single street lamp, hazy with mist.

Nakamura came to stand beside her, and as he did so, the thoughts she'd been turning over in her mind ever since they'd been watching the circus seemed to unravel themselves. 'What if it was all a set-up?' she said. 'What if Viktor was tricked into planning the attack – by an agent of the *Fraternitas?*'

Nakamura looked astonished, and rather confused. 'But . . . how could that be?'

Sophie quickly explained what she'd heard Viktor say to Miss Russell, and his mention of *Mr Gold*. 'The Count said that "Gold" was the code name for someone important in the *Fraternitas*. What if it's the same person, and he was the one who gave Viktor his instructions?'

'But why would the *Fraternitas* want the students to attack the Tsar?' asked Nakamura, puzzled. 'From all you've told me about the society, their principles hardly match with the students' ideas of freedom and revolution and democracy.'

Sophie shook her head. 'It's not as simple as that. The *Fraternitas* are agents of chaos. It's more about causing trouble than anything else. Suppose they tricked Viktor into organising the plot at the circus – then tipped off the Tsar's secret police, knowing how harshly they'd punish the revolutionaries?'

Nakamura was frowning. 'In order to stir up both sides against each other, you mean? And to make trouble flare up in St Petersburg?'

'Exactly,' said Sophie. It might sound like a wild idea, but the more she thought about it, the more it made sense. It would even explain what Viktor had been doing in her room – she'd assumed he was looking for something to steal, but perhaps *Mr Gold* had given him the task of hunting for the notebook and spyglass?

'But *why?*' asked Nakamura again. 'How could trouble in St Petersburg possibly benefit the *Fraternitas?*'

Sophie thought for a moment. 'Because Russia is an important ally of Britain and France. If there was trouble here – violence, assassinations, even a revolution – Russia would no longer be able to help their allies if there was a war. They'd be too busy dealing with their own problems. That would leave Britain and France weakened. It's like the Count said about the secret weapon, the one the notebook talks about. The *Fraternitas* are doing whatever they can to upset the balance of power in Europe – and in doing so, to help spark off war.'

She shook her head. For as long as she'd known of the existence of the *Fraternitas*, they'd been working secretly, pulling the strings to try and engineer war in Europe. She knew that they believed they could benefit financially from a war, making money by manufacturing and selling weapons. Everything they did seemed to lead back to that single terrible goal.

Nakamura gazed out of the window too, his face grave as though he was thinking very hard about what Sophie had said – and the quiet house seemed even heavier with silence than before. Then Sophie went on: 'The part I still don't understand is why Viktor was trying to talk to *Roberta*

Russell, of all people. Especially when she obviously didn't understand a word he was saying.'

'Could he have mistaken her for someone else?' suggested Nakamura.

'Yes, perhaps. But he knew her name – and he knew she was a journalist. He really seemed to believe that she knew *Mr Gold* and would be able to pass his message on . . .' She drew back from the window, seeing several figures crossing the bridge over the canal. 'Look – someone's coming!'

But as they came closer, she realised that they were neither members of the secret police hunting for Mitya, nor escaping students seeking refuge. She hurried to open the front door. Coming up the steps were Lil, Carruthers, and two other people – a tall, fair girl who towered over even Lil by several inches, and a slim, dark-haired boy who had something long and sinuous draped over his shoulders, which Sophie realised – rather to her surprise – was a large snake.

Carruthers was the first through the door. 'For heaven's sake, let me in quickly,' he said without ceremony. 'That *thing* won't stop hissing at me.'

'Oh, Sophie! I'm so glad you're safe!' said Lil, running up the steps after him. 'I'm sorry we're so late – the circus was in chaos. But we're here now. This is Hanna and this is Ravi – we brought them too. I hope that's all right – they're awfully good sorts, and we've told them who we are and what we do.'

'*Some* of what we do,' added Carruthers, in a warning tone.

'Hanna, Ravi, this is my dearest friend Sophie. She was at the circus tonight, in the audience.'

'Hello!' said Hanna, looking around the cosy dark little hall. She looked rather familiar, and Lil explained. 'You might have seen her in the ring – she's Miss Hercules.'

Ravi bowed low, and Sophie recognised him too – although he looked quite different without his grand snake-charmer costume. 'I hope you don't object to my snake,' he said, in a very polite voice. 'This is Shesha, my python. He was excited after tonight's performance and did not wish to be left behind.'

'We've got a terrific lot of things to tell you,' Lil ran on.

'Come this way – into the parlour. We can talk there.' Sophie hustled them through as quickly as she could and closed the door behind them. Nakamura was putting more wood on the fire, and if he was surprised to see four strange people coming into the room – one of them wearing a python as though it was a scarf – he didn't show it.

'You must be Captain Nakamura,' said Lil, rushing over to him at once. 'You won't remember me, but I was on the airfield in Paris. I'm Lilian Rose – and this is Captain Carruthers.'

'You're Sophie's colleagues,' said Nakamura, shaking their hands and then bowing. 'It's a pleasure to make your acquaintance.'

'These are our friends from the Circus of Marvels,' Lil went on. 'Hanna – and Ravi.'

'I saw you both performing this evening,' said Nakamura. 'Truly, a spectacular entertainment. It is only a pity that it ended in such a terrible way.'

'It was awful!' exclaimed Hanna. 'We could see it all happening above us. And the animals went wild of course. We had quite a job to calm them down.'

'Was anyone hurt?' asked Nakamura.

'Not badly – not as far as we know. There were a few injuries – people who fell trying to escape. And one policeman was shot in the hand. It was lucky the police were there! They must have had a tip-off that something might happen. Fanshawe was furious with them. She said they should have told us so that we could cancel the show and people wouldn't have been in danger.'

Nakamura looked like he was going to ask another question, but Carruthers interrupted, looking impatient. 'Er – don't you think we should talk about all this *in private?*' he said in a meaningful voice, looking at Sophie.

Sophie frowned at him. 'If you're talking about Captain Nakamura, then he isn't going anywhere,' she said with determination. 'He's been my only ally here in St Petersburg, and he's just as involved in all this as anyone else.'

'Very well,' said Carruthers, flinging himself down into an armchair, as if to suggest there was no sense trying to reason with anyone. 'What's important is that we get to the

255

bottom of what's going on here.'

'We think Rogers – that fellow we saw – was involved in the attack tonight,' began Lil, as she took a seat beside Sophie. 'He *knew* it was going to happen. And he smuggled a whole crate full of guns into the city, on the circus train – rifles, revolvers, ammunition. When we first saw them we thought they must be circus props for a Wild West act, or something of that kind.'

'But there *is* no act like that at the Circus of Marvels,' said Hanna, looking mystified. 'There would be no reason at all to have a box of guns on our train.'

'None,' agreed Ravi, while the python twisted itself along one of his arms, hissing to itself. Carruthers inched a little further away from him with a shudder, whilst Nakamura watched, fascinated.

'The guns must have been for the students,' said Sophie. 'That was how they got their weapons past the checks on the door – they were *inside* the circus already. I suppose that's what Rogers was talking to Viktor about.'

'Who's Viktor?' asked Carruthers at once.

'He's a student at St Petersburg University and he's part of the revolutionary group who staged the attack at the circus tonight – in fact, he's the ringleader. But I think it was a set-up. I think Viktor was tricked into organising the attack and the police were tipped off on purpose.'

'Gosh!' exclaimed Lil at once. 'So who was really behind it?'

Sophie smiled in spite of everything. It felt so unlikely and yet so wonderfully *comfortable* to have Lil here beside her, in Vera's parlour. 'I believe it was a man known as *Mr Gold*,' she explained. 'And I'm fairly certain he's a member of the *Fraternitas Draconum*.'

'*What?*' exclaimed Carruthers.

'Wait – this fellow, Viktor – does he live here, in this house?' asked Lil suddenly.

'No,' said Sophie, rather surprised by the unexpected question. 'This house belongs to Vera and Boris Orlov. They live here with their grandchildren and their son, Mitya, who was at the circus tonight too. He's part of Viktor's group, and one of the students who was tricked into taking part in the plot tonight.'

'Perhaps that makes more sense of it, then,' said Lil, looking at Carruthers. 'Just *listen to this*. We followed Rogers into the yard behind the circus building. There was a funny old cart waiting for him there in the dark. While everyone else was inside watching the show, he loaded it up with a big crate – a crate which I happen to know contained guns.'

'Rogers must have already given some of them to the students – but there were still plenty in the box,' Carruthers interjected. 'It was obviously heavy.'

'But *this* is the strangest part. Rogers gave the driver an address – presumably, the place he should deliver the crate.'

'It was *this address*,' said Carruthers. 'The address

you'd just given us – for this exact house. *Number 3 Ulitsa Zelenaya.*'

Sophie and Nakamura stared. 'Are you sure?' asked Sophie, astonished.

'Absolutely,' said Carruthers.

'That's why I wanted to know if Viktor lived here,' added Lil.

'But why would Viktor have guns sent *here*?' Sophie wondered.

'To hide them away from the authorities?' suggested Nakamura. 'For all we know, tonight was not the only attack that has been planned. There may be more to come.'

Ravi had been frowning deeply through this, obviously trying to follow their conversation. Now, he spoke up. 'But are we not missing something important? If the driver was supposed to deliver this crate of guns here, several hours ago, then where is it now?' He gazed around the parlour, his arms stretched out, as though to indicate that there was clearly no big crate of guns anywhere to be seen.

Nakamura got to his feet. 'He's right. But if this crate really did turn up here while we were out at the circus, Herr Schmidt might know about it,' he said to Sophie. 'I'm going to go and wake him up.'

He hurried upstairs. Carruthers got to his feet too, looking impatient. 'Look – this is all very well,' he said bossily. 'But you still haven't explained what the *Fraternitas* have to do with any of this. What's the connection?'

'I heard Viktor say he worked for a man he called *Gold*, which I found out is a code name for someone high up in the *Fraternitas*. But then there's also this,' Sophie announced, feeling in her pocket for the notebook and holding it out. 'I caught Viktor snooping about in my room earlier today. I think he might have been looking for it.'

Carruthers' face lit up with an uncharacteristic flash of excitement. 'Is that what I think it is? The stolen notebook?'

'Yes – and that's not all. The notebook contains the instructions for making a spyglass, like this one,' she explained, producing the velvet box and opening it. 'If you look through it, it allows you to see the clues hidden in the dragon paintings.'

'Good heavens!' exclaimed Carruthers, gazing at the glittering spyglass lying inside. 'How did you get this?'

'That's what the telegram was all about,' Sophie went on. 'The telegram I *thought* was from the Chief. I wrote and asked whether I should bring the notebook straight back to the Bureau or have the spyglass constructed first. He told me to go ahead and have the spyglass made – so that's exactly what I did.'

'Except that the telegram wasn't from him,' objected Carruthers. 'I'm sure of it.'

'I don't see how you can possibly be so certain,' argued Lil.

'You don't understand,' said Carruthers. 'The Chief doesn't hide anything from me – he couldn't. I see everything that goes in and out of that office. Really, the only way I could have missed this was if the telegram hadn't been sent until after we'd already left to go to Hamburg.'

'And it couldn't have been,' said Lil promptly. 'It was dated the day before we left.'

'But if the Chief didn't send the telegram, then surely it's obvious who did . . .' said Sophie.

'*The Fraternitas*,' breathed Lil.

There was silence for a moment. Hanna and Ravi were looking around in confusion, obviously without the first idea what they were talking about. But Sophie knew that Lil too had already pieced it together in her mind. It was quite clever when you thought about it. The *Fraternitas* had found a way to intercept her messages to the Chief – whether here in St Petersburg, or back in London. They knew where she was and what she was doing. They'd let her go to all the trouble of persuading the Count to give up the notebook, and having the spyglass made. Now, presumably, it was part of Viktor's job to steal them both from her before she took them back to the Bureau. Goodness knows what they had told him about her, or about why the spyglass was so important to them.

Carruthers snapped the velvet box shut. 'We've got to get this and the notebook out of St Petersburg and back to the Bureau immediately. We cannot possibly risk either of them falling into the hands of the *Fraternitas*.' He looked at Sophie and Lil. 'We'll set off first thing tomorrow.'

'But we can't just *leave!*' Lil protested at once. 'The attack at the circus – the students – Rogers' gun-smuggling – the *Fraternitas* being mixed up in it all. What if Captain Nakamura is right, and this attack was just the beginning?'

'This could all be part of an even bigger plot to stir up trouble in St Petersburg,' said Sophie. 'If they succeed, who knows what the consequences might be?'

'We'll notify the Russian authorities. They can deal with it,' said Carruthers promptly. He looked up and saw Hanna's bewildered expression. 'I'm sorry, but this has to be our priority – it's a matter of British security. It's more important than anything else.'

Sophie frowned. It was true that the notebook was all she'd thought about for months – but now she was here, in Vera's parlour in the middle of the night, in the light of the glowing fire, she was suddenly no longer so sure she agreed with him.

'No. We aren't leaving,' she insisted. Apart from anything else, she couldn't just desert Vera and Boris. They had generously taken her in and given her a home in St Petersburg. Now they were heartbroken – and who knew what might happen to Mitya? She couldn't possibly abandon them now.

Carruthers looked from Sophie to Lil rather scornfully. 'Well, even if neither of you can see sense, I can,' he declared, snatching the notebook out of Sophie's hand. 'I'm taking this and the spyglass too – and I'm getting them out of here. You can do whatever you want, but I'm taking these to the Bureau.'

Sophie leaped to her feet, snatching the notebook back at once. 'You can't do that!' she protested.

'Why not?' insisted Carruthers, putting out a hand to grab it back again, but Sophie stepped backwards.

'Because I gave my word that I would give this only to someone I trust absolutely. I promised I would see the weapon destroyed and I don't break my promises.'

'Oh, so now you're saying you don't trust me?' said Carruthers angrily.

'Well, at the moment I must say that *I* don't trust you very much either,' said Lil, coming to stand beside Sophie. 'How can you even think of leaving everyone in the lurch like this? Just because you want to rush off to the Chief and get all the credit for Sophie's hard work!'

'That's not it at all!' said Carruthers pompously. 'It's quite obviously the only sensible thing to do.'

Lil stared at him for a long moment, as though she had suddenly been struck by something. 'Sophie's letters have been going astray. We know *someone* has been sending messages back to her, pretending to be the Chief. Someone has been intercepting them, someone who works for the *Fraternitas* . . . And you said it yourself, a dozen times. Everything that goes in or out of the Bureau goes through your hands.'

'What are you babbling about now?' muttered

Carruthers crossly.

Lil glared at him, her hands on her hips. 'What if it's *you*? What if you're the one secretly working for the *Fraternitas* – spying and sneaking, and passing information back to them?'

Carruthers gave a derisive laugh. 'Don't be so ridiculous!'

'*Am* I being ridiculous? I saw your secret spy hole with my own eyes!'

'It's not a *spy hole*! You don't know what you're talking about!'

'No wonder you're so keen to go off with the notebook and the spyglass by yourself. You're probably planning to hand them straight over to your real bosses!'

Carruthers stared at her, speechless. 'Is that really what you think of me?' he demanded.

The parlour door creaked open. Nakamura was on the threshold, and just behind him – wearing a rather moth-eaten velvet dressing gown and an old-fashioned nightcap with a tassel on it – was the Count.

'It's true,' said Nakamura breathlessly. 'A big crate was delivered here – about ten o'clock this evening. They took it down to the cellar.'

'I supposed it must be for you,' said the Count to Nakamura, looking dazed and still half asleep. 'Aeroplane parts, or something of that sort. Did I do something wrong?'

But just then, the front door banged open and someone

else came running into the room. Sophie jumped to her feet. '*Mitya!*' she exclaimed.

He was wild-eyed and gasping for breath 'Where are Mama and Papa? The police were after me, but I managed to get away. I know I shouldn't have come here but I had to tell them the truth! None of that was supposed to happen! No one was supposed to get hurt! I had no idea there would be so many guns – there would only be one or two, Viktor said, in order to take a few pot-shots at the flags and the Imperial Eagle. We were just going to shout some slogans, throw our leaflets into the air and shake everyone up a bit, you know? And then we were going to make a run for it and scatter before they could catch us. It had all been arranged. But then there were so many guns – and the police turned up – and it all went wrong. It was a trap! They made it look like we'd set out to assassinate the Tsar, and harm his family – but we'd never have done that!'

'I know,' said Sophie, trying to reassure him. 'I think it was a set-up. I think Viktor –'

But before she could say anything else, there was a sudden roar of a motor-car engine, loud in the silent street. Feet were pounding up the steps outside; someone was hammering hard on the front door.

'Police!' yelled a voice. 'Open up at once!'

CHAPTER TWENTY-THREE

London and St Petersburg

On Fleet Street, the shops were closing. The chemist was putting up his shutters for the night; beneath the red and white striped awning of a café, a waitress in a frilly white apron was turning the 'Open' sign to 'Closed'. Clerks were streaming out of offices, hurrying towards the omnibus or the underground train; and a boy selling newspapers yelled out headlines from the evening edition.

Not far away from him, Joe was standing close to the offices of *The Daily Picture*. He'd talked over what he'd seen with Billy, and they both felt sure that more investigating must be done. Billy had taken himself off to the public library. 'I want to look through some back issues of *The Daily Picture*,' he told Joe excitedly. 'If Brooks really is leaking information from the Secret Service Bureau, then maybe there'll be some hints of it I can find.'

But the library wasn't Joe's kind of place. He'd decided to stick with what he was good at. He'd wondered about going back to the Bureau to watch for Brooks again, but in the end, he'd found himself drawn back to the offices of *The Daily Picture*. Somehow he felt sure that they were important. Now, as he watched, he caught sight of the woman he'd seen the previous day, coming out of the building along with half a dozen other people – newspaper reporters, filing clerks, typewriter girls, all finishing their work for the day.

She was dressed just as smartly as before, in the same trim tailor-made suit, with a neat hat perched on her head at a stylish angle. She wore the same white gloves and carried the same expensive-looking handbag. She walked straight past him, past the paperboy on the corner; and Joe followed at once – dodging between the bowler hats and boaters. Was there any chance she was going to the park, to pick up another hidden message from Brooks he wondered. But no – she couldn't be. She was going the other way along Fleet Street, walking purposefully. Joe could just see the top of her hat, bobbing gently above the crowds.

A little way along the street, she flagged down an omnibus and climbed aboard. Joe had to run to catch up, but managed to clamber on too, before the bus pulled away again. He hadn't expected her to get on a bus at all – she looked more like the kind of woman who'd take a motor-taxi, or at least the underground. He wiped his forehead, catching his breath and fishing in his pocket for some change for the ticket. He hadn't even had time to see which bus it was, so he just said: 'All the way please,' to the conductor.

The woman had taken a seat on the top deck, quite near the front, her white-gloved hands folded neatly in her lap, her handbag placed on the seat beside her. Joe settled himself down several rows behind, wondering where she was going. He watched her carefully but she didn't move, only stared ahead as the omnibus swept forward in the throng of cars and carriages, heading east along Fleet Street, towards the old City.

'Police! Open up!' yelled the voice again. The hammering on the door grew louder. From upstairs came the sound of anxious exclamations and Mitya looked desperately around him.

There were feet on the stairs, and then Vera came rushing in, with Boris close behind her. 'Mitya!' she cried out.

'Get upstairs, quickly,' said Boris, grabbing his son's arm, and dragging him towards the staircase. 'We have to hide you!'

'Oh golly,' breathed Lil, realising what was happening. 'They had that crate of guns sent here on purpose, didn't they? Now the police are here, and if they find the weapons . . .'

'Then Mitya and his family – or any of us – could

be blamed for plotting to assassinate the Tsar,' finished Nakamura.

'Goodness! What should we do?' asked Hanna.

'We have to try and stall them while we find the crate,' said Sophie at once. If you could be imprisoned on the basis of a policeman's suspicion that you might be a revolutionary, she didn't dare to imagine what they might do if they found a whole crate of smuggled guns secretly hidden in a cellar. If they found Mitya he would certainly be arrested – and they might arrest Vera and Boris too. Her breath caught in her throat as she realised the house was full of strangers in St Petersburg – as British citizens she and Lil and Carruthers might be all right – but what about the others? 'We have to get those guns out of the cellar before the police find them.'

Boris and Mitya had already disappeared upstairs, and now, gathering herself, Vera stormed towards the front door and flung it open: 'What do you think you are doing, banging on people's doors in the middle of the night?' she demanded bravely.

But her voice was hardly heard. A horde of policemen, huge and intimidating, in their red and silver uniforms, were surging into the house. 'Vera Ivanovna Orlov?' demanded one, obviously their Chief. 'I am Officer Morozov of His Imperial Majesty the Tsar's *Okhrana*. We are here for your son, Dmitri Borisovich Orlov. We have information that he was the leader of the dangerous revolutionary group who attacked His Imperial Majesty, the Tsar and his family, tonight.' He turned to several of his men. 'Search this house!' he ordered them. 'Look for the guns!'

'What are you talking about?' demanded Vera. 'Our son is not involved in any such plot!'

'What's happening?' Lil whispered in Sophie's ear, not understanding the Russian speech.

'They're here to arrest Mitya – and to look for *guns*,' Sophie whispered back.

Nakamura had already taken advantage of the hubbub to slip down the stairs to the cellar, closely followed by the Count. 'I'll go with them,' whispered Hanna. 'I might be able to help.'

Lil nodded and turned to Ravi. 'I think it's time for a diversion. Can you help me – and Shesha too?'

Ravi beamed. 'Of course. Shesha will be delighted to be of assistance,' he declared, lifting the enormous snake from around his shoulders.

Sophie understood at once what Lil was planning. She gave her a quick nod, and then darted forward to where Vera was still trying to argue with Officer Morozov, as his men pushed roughly into the house. She saw them shove their way into the dining room and into Vera's kitchen, pushing books off shelves, opening cupboards, and sweeping dishes off tables, letting them shatter on to the floor.

'You've got this all wrong!' Vera was pleading.

'Out of my way, old woman,' said Morozov, pushing her

away from him. 'Or I'll see you and your husband arrested and thrown into prison. Where is your son?'

He made for the stairs, but before he could take another step, Sophie called out in French: 'Take care! Watch out! There's a poisonous snake loose in this house!'

Morozov turned to stare at her. 'A *snake?*' he repeated, in scornful disbelief.

'Some of the performers from the Circus of Marvels are lodging here,' she explained rapidly. 'One of them is the snake charmer – but his snake has escaped. He says it is very dangerous! Please, you must tell your men to beware or they may be bitten!'

Lil darted forward too. 'There it is – I see it!' she shrieked, pointing and screaming as if absolutely terrified. She spoke in English but her meaning was quite clear – Morozov and several of his men drew back, glimpsing the sinuous form of a simply enormous snake, slithering rapidly towards the stairs.

Ravi came chasing after it, playing his part to perfection. 'Oh, come back at once, you *naughty snake!*' he cried, though Sophie could see his eyes twinkling. Shesha turned his head, quite as if he understood what he was supposed to do, hissing loudly and dramatically in Morozov's direction.

'You say this snake is dangerous?' said Morozov to Sophie.

'Oh yes, terribly dangerous. It is one of the most poisonous snakes in the world.'

'It's a *Black Death Python*,' invented Lil readily, still speaking in English but making a fearsome face to illustrate this description.

Morozov looked alarmed. 'Men, be careful!' he yelled out. 'There is a venomous snake loose in this house!'

Lil and Ravi continued after Shesha, who was performing magnificently – first blocking the policemen who were trying to surge up the stairs, then weaving himself through Morozov's legs, making him yell out in horror, then slithering back down to the hall, where he tripped up several more of his men. Lil and Ravi capered after him, with shrieks and entreaties.

Amongst the chaos, Sophie darted down the narrow stairs that led to the cellar. Seeing that the key was in the door, she grabbed it and locked the door behind her. That should keep the police out for a little while at least, she thought grimly.

In Nakamura's cellar room, she found the Count, Hanna and Nakamura himself, standing around a large wooden crate.

'This is it,' the Count was saying, still looking very perplexed by what was happening and how he had found himself in the cellar in his dressing gown and nightcap. 'This is the box they delivered.'

'Your friend was right,' said Nakamura to Sophie, as he peered under the lid. 'It's full of guns – dozens of them. If the police find this here, Mitya will certainly be locked up for the rest of his life.'

'Surely there must be something we can do?' said Sophie, looking desperately around the room. But there was no way out except for the window, high up in the wall.

Nakamura followed her gaze. 'It's big enough to fit through, but the question is how we get it up there. It's so heavy.'

But the Count's eyes lit up suddenly. 'Look – there's a hook up there on the ceiling,' he said, pointing upwards. Sure enough, high above her head, Sophie saw that a large metal hook had been screwed into a big wooden beam beside the window. 'If we can find some rope, we could make a kind of pulley,' he suggested.

'There's some rope over here!' said Hanna, quickly unearthing a coil of it from a pile of old rubbish in the corner.

Nakamura seemed to know what to do straight away. 'Tie this end to the box, as securely as you can,' he told the Count. 'We need to get the other end up and over the hook.' He stared at the high ceiling speculatively. 'Sophie – perhaps if you were to stand on my shoulders?'

At one time, Sophie might have hesitated. But she was quite a different person now to the girl who'd once been so frightened of heights she'd hung on to Joe for dear life as they'd escaped over East End rooftops. She'd travelled hundreds of miles across Europe in an aeroplane: this was nothing. She'd kicked off her shoes before Nakamura had even finished the sentence and had the end of the rope wrapped securely around her wrist.

'Wait,' said Hanna. 'Stand on my shoulders. I'm taller – and besides I know how to do it. I do this every day in my act.'

Quickly, she bent her knees and held out her hands, palms upwards. 'Now, you stand to face me,' she told Sophie. 'Put your right foot on to my right thigh – here – and then put your hands in mine.'

Sophie put out a foot tentatively. Hanna's leg felt very strong and solid. 'Now, swing your leg around and put your left foot on my left shoulder. Good.' She sounded completely calm, as though there were not twenty policemen stampeding above them, ransacking Vera's parlour. 'I'm going to push you upwards . . . Put your other foot on my right shoulder, now get your balance . . . That's it. Now I'm going to stand up.'

Sophie felt Hanna moving smoothly upright, tightly holding on to Sophie's ankles. She felt herself rising upwards, wobbling precariously. For a moment she thought she was going to lose her balance but she managed to fling out a hand and grab on to the metal hook in the ceiling, steadying herself. Her feet slipped a little on Hanna's shoulders but Hanna held her firm.

'There you go,' said Hanna. 'Now the rope.'

As quickly as she could, her fingers shaking, Sophie unwrapped the end of the rope from her wrist and fed it through the hook. Somewhere above, she heard a policeman yell: 'This way – down to the cellar!'

'Is that right?' she called down to Nakamura, who was busy helping the Count secure the other end of the long rope around the big box, looping it several times.

'Yes – and now we have to open the window. There's a pole around here somewhere, I know, but do you think you can reach it?'

'I think so!' The window catch was stiff, and it took her some effort to open it and fling the window open. Frosty air rushed into the room.

'It's done!' she called out, wobbling even more precariously, as the police began to hammer on the cellar door:

'Who's down there? This is the police!'

'Let go!' said Hanna at once. 'I'll catch you!'

Against all her instincts, Sophie did as she was told; for a moment she fell, but to her astonishment, Hanna caught her neatly, and set her on her feet as though at the end of an acrobatic performance.

Nakamura and the Count were already heaving on the rope, trying to lift the box. But even with the pulley, they weren't strong enough to raise it more than a few feet. Sophie and Hanna darted at once to join them, and hauled on the rope too – and with the help of Hanna's enormous strength, the box began to move jerkily upwards towards the open window.

'How are we going to get it out?' asked Hanna.

'We'll have to swing it,' said Nakamura breathlessly. 'Pull the rope to the right – that's it – now left. Let it swing – let it gather momentum.'

'We must judge it just right!' exclaimed the Count. 'We must let go as soon as it is through the window – quickly before they see anything – and it will fall down into the canal!'

Above them, the box began to sway to and fro. The rope strained under the weight of the box and Sophie began to fear it would snap in two. But by some miracle it didn't; instead, the box began to swing more strongly, and then it had swung right out of the open window, above the canal.

'Let go!' yelled Nakamura.

They released the end of the rope, and with a rattle and a crash, the box went spinning down, down, down into the canal with an enormous splash. Just at that moment, the police broke down the door and came swarming into the cellar.

'What is going on down here? Arrest these people at once!' yelled Morozov. To her horror, Sophie saw that two strong policemen had already seized Nakamura, who was struggling in their grasp; while another was making straight for the Count, who had backed towards the corner, whimpering in terror. Hanna threw Sophie a horrified glance, as two more policemen ran through the door in her direction.

But worse was to come. Creeping into the room behind the policemen, unnoticed by anyone, came Viktor, a determined look on his face. He looked straight at Sophie and then made a dash towards her.

Dodging a policeman, Sophie ran. There was nothing she could do to help Nakamura and the others at that moment – but she would not let Viktor take the notebook and spyglass for the *Fraternitas*. She raced quickly up the narrow stairs, dashing through the hall, where Vera now stood weeping as two policemen dragged Mitya out to their waiting motor car.

There were people on the stairs – she couldn't go that way, so she spun swiftly in a different direction. Everything Ada Pickering had ever taught her was flashing into her mind. Viktor might be bigger and stronger than she was, but she was small and quick and she could use that to her advantage. She wove left and right around more policemen, and then darted into Vera's kitchen, hoping to barricade the door behind her. But Viktor was still there, forcing his way in. He made a grab for her, but she was too fast – twisting out of his reach and running through into the little pantry beyond.

All right: she needed a weapon. The pantry might not be the most obvious place to find one but Miss Pickering had taught her that there was always something, if you knew how to look for it. She spotted a broom leaning against the wall and seized it, spinning the handle around and slamming it back against Viktor's legs, making him cry out in pain.

Still holding the broom, she dashed forward, through the door that led out into the yard. Outside, her feet slipped on the frosty cobbles, but she kept going. She heard the tabby cat yowl, somewhere in the dark.

Somehow Viktor was beside her again: he was faster than she'd given him credit for. She hit out sharply with the broom handle, but he dodged her blow.

'Give them to me. The notebook and the spyglass!' he demanded wildly.

'A notebook? A . . . spyglass? I don't know what you're talking about!' she bluffed at once.

'Yes – yes you do! And you *will* give them to me,' he declared, pulling the revolver from his pocket and pointing it straight at her.

CHAPTER TWENTY-FOUR

London and St Petersburg

The omnibus rattled onwards, carrying them through the old City, past the great dome of St Paul's. Joe watched as trees and buildings flashed past, certain that the woman from *The Daily Picture* would soon get off the bus – but she kept on sitting quite still in her seat, looking straight ahead of her.

In spite of himself, Joe found his heartbeat quickening. They were on the edge of the City now, and the omnibus was carrying them closer and closer to the streets of the East End where he'd grown up. But the once-familiar landmarks now seemed haunted by the ghosts of the past. It was easy to imagine Jem, leering out of the dark, whispering 'Hello, Joey Boy' – or Red Hands Randall, reaching out a hand in a red leather glove. And then the Baron himself like a shadow – the phantom of childhood stories, the villain from his nightmares. He tried to shake them away. Jem and Randall were locked up in prison; and the Baron was dead and gone, he reminded himself. These streets did not belong to him anymore.

At long last the woman from *The Daily Picture* made ready to get off the bus. Perhaps she was catching a train from Liverpool Street station, Joe thought, as he slipped off the omnibus after her.

But instead of turning towards the station, the woman kept on walking at the same measured pace. Night was beginning to fall now, and Joe felt as twitchy as a nervous cat, as he followed her past dirty little shops and down-at-heel inns. She looked completely out of place here in her trim suit and neat hat, her handbag over her arm. Where on earth could she be going? Joe wondered.

She turned off the main street, down a narrow, disreputable-looking alley – past some barefoot kids playing with a grizzled old dog, past a couple of fellows sitting on a doorstep, swigging from a beer bottle. Joe followed at a careful distance, keeping his pace brisk. He didn't like the way those two fellows were staring at him. He'd got too used to Piccadilly Circus and the West End: this side of town was different. In the distance, he could hear footsteps coming along the alley behind him, and he sped up again, catching a flashing glimpse of the bow on the back of the woman's hat, as she turned left, and then right, and then left again, and then –

Joe was all alone, at the end of an alley. Nothing lay ahead of him but a blank brick wall. The woman had gone, as though she had vanished into the air. There was nothing left but a skinny cat, nosing around an old dustbin. It was a dead end.

Footsteps were coming towards him, faster and faster. His heart beating more rapidly now, he spun round, to see a figure coming towards him down the alley – blocking his way out.

He'd been a fool, he realised – a wave of horror breaking over him. The whole thing had been a trick: the woman must have known he was following her all along. She'd led him here deliberately, to these back streets of the East End – and now he was cornered and alone.

He took a step back. It was growing dark now, but even in the dim light, he could see the glint of something. He knew at once it was a revolver.

Sophie thought fast as Viktor waved the revolver closer towards her, in a shaking hand. 'Give them to me – now,' he said again, a sharp note of desperation sounding in his voice.

He didn't really know what he was doing, she realised. 'What are you playing at?' she demanded sharply, trying to take control of the situation. 'Who's put you up to this? Don't you see that they've tricked you?'

But Viktor only came closer, still waving the revolver. 'I know what you're trying to do – but you won't succeed! Your underhand spy tricks won't work on me!'

Spy tricks? Sophie stared at him in surprise as he went on: 'I know who you are. I know you're in St Petersburg undercover – and that *Alice Grayson* is not your real name. I know you're a spy, working for the British government. I know that the British are in league with the Tsar and his men – and I know that Orlovs are helping you with your schemes! Gold has told me everything. I know you're planning to seize the secret weapon and hand it over to the authorities, so they can use it against the masses. To crush the workers, and keep them down!'

So *that* was what the *Fraternitas* had told him to convince him to come after her. 'Viktor, this is all wrong –' she began, but his speech seemed to have given him new confidence, and he pointed the revolver at her more steadily now.

'Be quiet!' he hissed. 'Not another word! Give them to me – or I will shoot you right this minute!'

But there was no way she would give the notebook and spyglass up to the *Fraternitas*. And there was nowhere else she could run. She would have to knock the revolver out of his hand, she decided, gripping the broom handle more tightly and making ready to spring.

But all at once, she heard footsteps on the cobbles, and a voice yelling out her name: Lil's voice. Viktor glanced over his shoulder in surprise, and seizing her moment, Sophie struck out hard with the broom handle. He gave an agonised yelp, the revolver slipping from his fingers and skidding across the yard. Almost at the same moment,

Lil was on him, kicking out at his knee, bringing him crashing down on to the cold, frosty ground.

Carruthers appeared in the pantry doorway, a dark silhouette, a gleam of light catching on his horn-rimmed spectacles. 'What's going on?' he demanded sharply.

'He was trying to shoot Sophie!' Lil panted, still grappling with Viktor. 'He's the one working for the *Fraternitas!*'

Carruthers looked at her, and then at the revolver. Sophie had already started out towards it, but it was closer to Carruthers, and now she felt a sudden chill of fear. If Lil was right in her suspicions, would Carruthers side with Viktor and turn the revolver against them? She stared at him and for a moment, he stared back. Then, all at once, he dived forward – ignoring the gun, and instead helping Lil to wrestle Viktor to his feet.

Viktor was shouting angrily about *traitors* and *spies* as together, Lil and Carruthers pinned his arms behind his back, and frogmarched him towards the house. Sophie grabbed the revolver and followed them, her hand still clenched tightly around the notebook and spyglass in her pocket.

They found the hallway empty and the front door wide open. Morozov stood outside the house, supervising his men as they dragged Nakamura, Hanna and the Count outside after Mitya. Lights were coming on in nearby houses, and neighbours had gathered to whisper in shocked voices at their doors.

'Let go of him, you brutes!' Sophie heard Vera screaming, chasing after the two officers holding Mitya, as Boris tried to pull her back.

Carruthers surveyed the scene for a moment, and then took a deep breath. 'Right then,' he muttered to himself. 'Time to make the old man proud.'

Puffing out his chest, he declared in a loud and extremely English voice. 'Officer Morozov? Are you the fellow in charge here? I am Captain Samuel Carruthers of the British Army – here in St Petersburg on government business.'

Morozov turned and stared at him in surprise. Carruthers might not be wearing a uniform, but at that moment, there was no mistaking him as anything but a British Army officer – especially when he reached into his pocket and presented Morozov with an identity badge. Carruthers repeated his remarks in crisp, efficient Russian, so that everyone present could understand them, before he went on: 'I'm afraid there's been a misunderstanding. These people you are arresting are innocent!'

'But Captain,' said Officer Morozov, looking very confused as to where this commanding British gentleman had suddenly appeared from. 'They are anarchists – revolutionaries! They are the ones behind the plot to assassinate His Imperial Majesty, the Tsar. We have information that it was planned in this very house – and that they are storing illegally smuggled guns here.'

'*Guns?*' repeated Carruthers. 'No, I'm afraid that cannot be possible. You have been misinformed. There are no guns in this house. Your men have not found any evidence of them, have they?'

Morozov looked embarrassed. 'Well . . . er . . . no,' he admitted. 'But –'

Carruthers interrupted before he could say any more. 'However *I* have found a gun,' he said, taking Viktor's pistol swiftly from Sophie. 'Just now I removed *this* unpleasant weapon from this young man – who I'm sorry to say was using it to threaten this young lady. Now, I'm not sure how things are done here, but I must say that in *England* we would not stand by and let ruffians menace *innocent, defenceless* young ladies with a gun.'

Morozov gaped like a surprised fish. 'I can assure you, sir, in Russia such a thing would never be permitted,' he began – but Carruthers had not finished yet. 'It is quite clear that this house is anything but a hotbed of revolutionary activity!' he swept on. 'I can see that you are a sensible man, Officer – surely it must be clear to *you* at any rate, that this is a perfectly ordinary lodging house, and nothing more. Look – up there on the wall behind you – a picture of the Tsar's children! Now, tell me, is that what you would expect to find in the headquarters of a revolutionary cell?'

'But we have information!' exclaimed Morozov. He pointed to Mitya. 'This man was seen at the circus tonight. He was part of the plot against His Imperial Majesty!'

'This young man *may* have been at the circus tonight,' said Carruthers. 'Several of us were. I was there myself, as a matter of fact. But he did not shoot anyone, nor was he in possession of a weapon. And simply *being present* does not necessarily make him a part of the plot against the Tsar, does it? Not unless you plan to arrest half of St Petersburg society, that is.'

'But he ran!' protested Morozov. 'When my men went to arrest him – he fled! And we found books in his room, here in this house. Books containing dangerous and subversive ideas!'

Carruthers gave a wonderfully dismissive snort. 'Books! Of course you found books. This man is a student at St Petersburg University – a most promising young fellow. Of course he must educate himself by reading all kinds of literature. As for the rest of these people your men are arresting, they are nothing whatsoever to do with any plot. They are performers from the Circus of Marvels. May I remind you that the circus is here on His Imperial Majesty's own personal invitation? Think of the embarrassment that would be caused if he were to discover that you had mistakenly locked up several of the star performers, especially after the ordeal they have already faced tonight?'

'He's right!' Sophie heard one of the policemen whisper to another in a doubtful voice. 'That's Miss Hercules – I know it! I saw her in the ring. Surely we can't really be going to arrest *her*?'

'Furthermore,' Carruthers concluded. 'As a representative of the British government, I will vouch for each of these individuals *personally*. If they are arrested without due cause, I'm afraid I shall have no choice but to go straight to the British Embassy to raise the matter with Sir George Buchanan himself.'

At the name of the British Ambassador, Officer Morozov turned a little pale. 'There's no need to do that, Captain,' he murmured at once. 'We understand that a terrible mistake has been made.'

Behind him, his men were already letting go of Hanna, Nakamura, the Count and Mitya, murmuring uncertainly to each other. Vera darted towards Mitya and flung her arms around him.

'Thank you, Officer,' said Carruthers, with a respectful and approving bow. 'I could see you were a man of sense and honour. I would suggest that in their place, you arrest this violent and dangerous young man, before he can cause any further harm to this lady.'

'Quite right, sir,' said Morozov hurriedly, summoning two men who at once stepped forward and grabbed the furious Viktor, marching him away towards their waiting motor car.

'I beg your pardon most humbly, *madame*,' said Officer Morozov to Vera, performing a low bow. 'On behalf of my men, we extend to you our deepest regrets about this evening's . . . er . . . activities.'

He ordered his men away, leaving Hanna, Nakamura and the Count standing beside Vera and Boris, with Mitya between them. Sophie's knees were weak with relief.

'I don't know who you are – but I thank you from the bottom of my heart,' said Vera, surging towards Carruthers and kissing him firmly on both cheeks. 'You have saved our family.'

Carruthers looked pink, embarrassed – and a little uncertain. 'Well, I'm not sure it was strictly speaking the proper thing to do,' he admitted, speaking in his usual voice. 'Forgive me, but you *were* part of that plot at the circus, weren't you?' he said to Mitya.

'Yes. But it wasn't what it looked like. There was no intention to hurt anyone. You know I would never agree to a plan to assassinate the Tsar – or to harm his family, or anyone else,' Mitya said soberly, looking at his father and mother.

'Viktor pushed Mitya and the others into this,' Sophie explained. 'He was the one who changed the plans and arranged for all the guns. Then he had the crate sent here, so that Mitya would be framed for organising the crime!'

'But Viktor wasn't really the one behind it all,' Nakamura reminded her.

'No. I think he was instructed by Mr Gold – his contact, who he believed to be an important revolutionary leader. *He* was really the one responsible. He manipulated the students, supplied the guns – and then tipped off the secret police!'

'And now Viktor and Nikolai and many of the others are behind bars,' said Mitya anxiously.

'I would have thought prison was the best place for that Viktor,' snorted Lil. 'Waving a revolver at Sophie like that! It serves him jolly well right, if you ask me.'

'Well, it wasn't entirely his fault,' said Sophie. 'He'd been told all kinds of things about me by Gold . . . that I was a British spy scheming with the Russian authorities, and that you were all helping me,' she explained, nodding around to Mitya and the rest. 'Which explains why he helped frame you. He obviously thought you were a traitor to the revolutionary cause.'

Mitya was frowning. 'There's much to be done,' he said, drawing himself up, looking suddenly less scruffy and more purposeful. 'I'll arrange a meeting of our group. We must try and help the students who have been arrested and do what we can to secure their release. I'll set Viktor right about me, and about this *Mr Gold* too. I have heard stories of these kinds of agitators, stirring up trouble amongst the revolutionary groups, whilst all the time they are really working with the police.'

Sophie nodded. 'And perhaps then you can set the students on the right path – and make some real change,' she said.

Mitya smiled at her gratefully and Vera put an arm around Sophie's shoulders, giving her a little squeeze.

'What I'd like to know is how you managed to get rid of

the weapons,' said Lil, as Ravi scooped up Shesha who had come slithering back to him, his evening's performances now complete. 'Where's the crate now?'

'With any luck, at the bottom of the canal,' said Nakamura, who was looking very relieved to be a free man once more. 'Which in my opinion is the best place for it!'

'Yes – no one will be able to use those guns now,' agreed Sophie, with satisfaction.

'Which means we don't have to worry about them. We can go back home,' said Lil.

Home. Not long ago Sophie had been staring down the barrel of Viktor's gun; but now all that was over. Whatever else the *Fraternitas* might have in store, she'd have Lil and Carruthers by her side on the journey home – and before long, she'd be back in London. She felt once again for the now-familiar shape of the spyglass and notebook in her pocket, and smiled with satisfaction and relief.

Home. In London, Joe was back on home turf – but it didn't feel like home to him any longer. Now shadows loomed and stretched out in the alley, as the dark figure moved closer towards him.

He had to move – he had to do something. There was nowhere to go or to hide, but he kicked out at the dustbin beside him, sending it spinning forward and taking the opportunity to dart past and away down the alley, back the way he had come.

It had begun to rain, running down the collar of his jacket, but he kept on running, splashing blindly through the puddles, through a nightmare labyrinth of twisting alleys. Behind him, he could hear the thud of footsteps, coming after him.

It all felt so familiar. He'd run down these streets many times before. He'd run from Jem and the Baron's Boys, the knife wound on his arm throbbing in pain. He'd run down streets like these in Limehouse with Lil and Sophie, his heart thumping. Now he was running for his life once more. It was because he knew something, he realised. Whatever he'd stumbled on, whatever the connection was between the Bureau and Norton Newspapers, it was important. So important that they would shoot him to keep him quiet.

He'd been lucky so many times before. He seemed to have been born lucky, he thought – thinking in a flash of everything that had happened to him. He'd have to count on that luck to hold out now. Speeding up, he ducked around a corner, dived around another alley. He'd lost his bearings, but he knew he had to keep on running. It was his only chance.

He turned another corner, but then stopped short.

All at once, his luck had run out.

The alley stopped abruptly – a derelict old house stood at the end, the windows boarded up. He ran towards the door, tugging desperately at the handle, but there was no time to break it open or pick the lock. He could already hear the footsteps, moving towards him.

He turned, shivering in the rain, to face the dark figure. The blood was pounding in his ears as he realised, with a sudden shock, who it was.

'You don't have to do this,' he said in a shaking voice, but it was no good. He cast one last desperate look around for a way out – but there was nothing. No one to rescue him now. He knew that it was too late.

Perhaps it had been too late for a long time, he thought. Perhaps he'd been on borrowed time ever since that night he'd run away from the East End.

The dark figure took another step forward and stretched out an arm. He heard the revolver click.

Joe squeezed his eyes tightly shut. He thought of anywhere but here, anywhere but the dark East End alley, rain on his face and mud beneath his feet. Instead, he thought of the familiar smell of Sinclair's stables, the way the horses whickered gently to each other, their warm breath and the fragrance of hay. He thought of sitting in the Taylor & Rose office with Billy, eating jam tarts with the fire going, and Daisy lying at his feet.

He thought of fields of buttercups, and Lil when she smiled. He thought of her looking up at him on the station platform, with that look in her eyes that said maybe – just maybe – he had a chance with her after all.

It was the last thought in his mind before the gun went off.

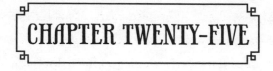

CHAPTER TWENTY-FIVE

The Way Back Home

In the pale morning sunlight outside the Ciniselli Circus, Lil and Carruthers were saying their goodbyes.

'You really cannot stay – not even one day longer?' said Ravi, looking disappointed.

'I'm afraid not,' said Lil, with a smile.

'We have orders,' added Carruthers. 'And *this time*, we're going to follow them,' he told Lil. She shrugged and grinned back.

'I'm still awfully disappointed that you weren't hiding on our train because you were eloping,' said Hanna with a sigh. 'It was such a wonderful, romantic story!'

Lil giggled. 'We were definitely *not* eloping,' she said.

'Most certainly not!' exclaimed Carruthers, with a revolted shudder. But just the same, he wasn't such a bad sort after all, Lil reflected. Perhaps one of these days, she'd even manage to call him 'Sam'.

A little distance away, Sophie had her own farewells

to say. She'd said goodbye to Vera, Boris, Mitya and the children that morning. 'We shall never forget you,' Vera had said, her eyes bright with tears. 'You have been like another daughter to us, *lapochka*. And we thank you from the bottom of our hearts for all you have done for us.'

That had been hard enough – but now she must say goodbye to the Count and Nakamura, who had insisted on accompanying her as far as the Ciniselli Circus.

'What will you do now?' she asked them, a little sadly. 'Will you stay on with Vera and Boris?'

But Nakamura shook his head. 'No. I think it is time to say farewell to St Petersburg. We had a narrow escape, and I don't believe either of us wish to end our days in prison. I am going to head home – and I've invited Herr Schmidt to come with me.'

'Really?' asked Sophie, surprised and pleased by this development. In spite of everything he had done, she'd developed an odd fondness for the Count.

The Count looked pleased too. 'Captain Nakamura tells me that my knowledge of military matters and aviation will be useful,' he explained proudly. 'He has kindly offered me the chance to travel to Japan with him, and when we arrive, I will be given the position of military advisor.'

So in a way, the Count was to turn spy himself, passing his specialist knowledge of European politics and military matters to the Japanese, Sophie thought with a grin. It seemed strangely appropriate. Ever since she'd arrived in St Petersburg, there seemed to have been double agents on all sides: Viktor, who believed he was working for the revolutionary cause although he was really doing the bidding of the *Fraternitas*; Carruthers, who Lil had suspected of being a *Fraternitas* man, but was actually nothing of the kind; the mysterious Mr Gold; and even herself, she realised. For in some ways, Viktor had been right. She *was* an undercover spy, posing as Alice Grayson – and even briefly as a *Fraternitas* agent – whilst really working for the British government. She thought again of how he had accused her of being on the side of the authorities, who planned to use the weapon against the people, and all at once she felt again that chilly, uncomfortable sensation sweep over her. What did the Chief plan to do with the weapon exactly?

'Well, you couldn't get much further from Arnovia and the *Fraternitas* than Japan,' she said to the Count now. 'How will you travel there? Will you fly?'

'We've been offered the chance to travel with the circus on their train,' explained Nakamura. 'I've been to see Miss Fanshawe this morning, and it's all been agreed. Their train is easily large enough to transport our aeroplanes – and Miss Fanshawe is most interested in our expertise in aviation.'

'We may even be able to help design a new flying act for the circus,' added the Count, looking enthusiastic at the prospect.

'And it sounds like they will be happy to have us, now that your friends are departing,' said Nakamura, nodding to Lil and Carruthers who were strolling over to join them. 'After all, we both know a little Russian so we may be able to make ourselves useful.'

'It sounds like a wonderful plan,' said Sophie. 'Write to me from Japan, won't you? Let me know about the rest of the journey – and that you made it home safely.'

Nakamura didn't hug her goodbye, but instead he bowed very low. 'Of course: it would be my pleasure. *Taylor & Rose Detective Agency, Sinclair's Department Store, London* – that is the right address, isn't it? I have no doubt we shall meet again someday, Sophie. It has been a great pleasure to travel alongside you.'

The Count was looking at Lil uncertainly. 'I wonder . . . I know I don't deserve it – but might I ask you to do me a small favour?' He produced a slightly crumpled envelope from his pocket and held it out to her. 'I've written this to Anna and Alex. It isn't much, but I wanted them to know how sorry I am for everything that happened – for my part in the kidnap plot against them, and er . . . well, you know . . .'

Lil nodded. 'I'll give it to them,' she promised, taking the envelope and putting it carefully into her pocket.

'And tell me, are they well?'

'Very well,' said Lil, with a small smile. 'And Würstchen, their dog too.'

The Count nodded gratefully and stepped away. 'Goodbye and thank you,' he said formally, shaking hands with all three of them.

Lil took one final look at the proud façade of the Ciniselli Circus. 'Well, I suppose we'd better be on our way. Time to say goodbye to the Circus of Marvels and St Petersburg.'

'*Do svidaniya!*' whispered Sophie, under her breath – pausing to wave one last time to Nakamura and the Count, who were now standing beside Ravi and Hanna on the steps.

As they turned away, suitcases in hand, Miss Roberta Russell was getting out of a motor-taxi, accompanied by Walters, the photographer.

'I must say, it's really *too* disappointing,' she was saying to him. 'Here I was, wishing the boss would send me to cover a *real* news story – instead of an air race or a circus performance – and then the Tsar of Russia is nearly assassinated, right here in this very building, and I miss the whole thing! Just think – if I'd only stayed until the end of the show, my exclusive report could have been on the front page of newspapers all over the world. But *no*, the boss insisted that I had to get my story wired over by midnight, so I rushed back to the hotel to write it up.'

Walters shrugged. 'I'd say we were better out of the way. I'd never have been able to get a good shot in all that scrum. Besides, we were still the first British journalists on the scene – and we can do follow-up interviews with the circus performers today, can't we? Get their take on it – that's a good angle.'

'And I suppose I don't necessarily have to *say* that I wasn't there . . .' mused Miss Russell thoughtfully.

'I'd like to get some more portrait shots done too,' the photographer went on. 'I still need one of Madame Fleurette – and just look at that kid with the snake, over there. I must get some pictures of him.'

But Miss Russell was not looking at the young snake charmer. Instead, she was staring at two young women and a young man, who were walking together away from the circus building, each carrying a small suitcase. There was a rather puzzled expression on her face.

'Do you know, I could swear that young woman is Sophie Taylor. One of those lady detectives from the agency in London. She was mixed up in the air race in Paris.' But then she laughed. 'I'm seeing things – it can't possibly be her,' she said to Walters, who wasn't really listening, already hurrying ahead of her into the circus building, thinking of the pictures he would take that day. 'I mean, what on earth would *she* be doing in St Petersburg?'

Along the street, Lil, Sophie and Carruthers were deep in conversation.

'What did they say at the Embassy?' Sophie asked Carruthers. He'd been to the British Embassy that morning to pick up travel visas for himself and Lil, but also to ask some important questions about Sophie's letters to the Chief.

'The fellows I spoke to confirmed the letters had been received, and had gone into the diplomatic bag,' Carruthers reported. 'They showed me the paperwork to prove it. Which I suppose means that whoever has been intercepting your letters has been working from London.'

Sophie and Lil exchanged glances. 'Could someone have intercepted them on their way to London, before they reached the Bureau?' asked Lil.

'By opening a secure diplomatic bag? I don't really see how, not without it being noticed,' said Carruthers. 'Which can only mean that they've been taken *at the Bureau itself*.' He shook his head, as if he could scarcely believe such a thing could be possible.

'So, there's someone at the Bureau we can't trust,' said Sophie, the very thought of it sent a cold shiver running down her spine. 'Someone *on the inside* is working for the *Fraternitas*. We've got a double agent of our own.'

'That's the first thing we need to get to work on when we're back home,' said Lil, with a decisive nod.

'And until then, we must remember that we can't trust *anyone*,' said Sophie. 'Except each other, of course.'

Carruthers' face broke into a crooked smile. 'Oh, so you *do* trust me now, then, do you? You don't think I'm the double agent any more?'

Lil's face turned red. 'Of course not. I knew I was wrong the second you helped me with Viktor. I'm awfully sorry I accused you like that. But you know, you can't really blame me. Not when you think about that spy hole of yours – and the way you wanted to go haring off with the spyglass.'

'Maybe not,' said Carruthers with a shrug, then a little sigh. 'Look – there's something I should probably tell you. I've been keeping it a secret, but it might help to explain why I would never do anything to betray the Chief, or the Bureau – and maybe why I have sometimes seemed a little . . . well . . . *wound up* about this assignment.' He paused for a moment. 'The Chief – well, he's not *just* a Chief to me. He's also my grandfather.'

For a moment there was a surprised silence, and then Sophie gave a delighted laugh. 'Of course! C for *Carruthers*. We guessed so many different things that C might stand for but we never once thought of that!'

'He has a tendency to think of me as simply his grandson,' Carruthers went on, looking a little shame-faced. 'As though I'm still just a schoolboy in short trousers. He can be rather protective and he likes to keep me out of harm's way. I've been asking to be sent on a field assignment for months, and with this mission, I wanted to show him I could be trusted just like all the other agents. I'm afraid it made me rather particular about getting everything right.'

'So *that* was what you meant last night when you said *time to make the old man proud*,' said Lil. 'Gosh – and he would have been proud, you know. I don't think he could have done it better himself! And just think of all the other things you've done – stowing away on a train, going undercover in the circus, not to mention stopping Mitya and the others from being arrested. I'd say you've proved yourself, all right!'

'We couldn't have done it without you,' Sophie agreed.

'I mean, Sophie and I are pretty good at *some* things. You know, for *innocent*, *defenceless* young ladies,' said Lil with a wink. 'I mean, flying across Europe in aeroplanes, and tailing wanted men, and getting hold of top-secret notebooks for one thing,' she added, grinning at Sophie.

'Not to mention performing in the circus, and organising diversions with snakes, and taking down unpleasant chaps with guns,' said Sophie, grinning back.

'But do you know, when it came to telling off that *Okhrana* fellow in such a marvellously pompous way – I don't think *either* of us could have done that.'

Carruthers made a noise that was somewhere between an indignant snort and a laugh. 'I'm happy to have been of service.' He paused. 'Well . . . I suppose I'd better say goodbye here, if I'm to head to the railway station.'

They'd agreed that Carruthers would catch the train to Virballen, and from there to Hamburg, where he would collect the report from the Bureau's agent. Meanwhile, Sophie and Lil would travel directly home to London, to deliver the notebook and spyglass to the Chief as soon as possible. They'd worked out that it would be quicker for them to travel home by sea, taking the steamer across the Baltic.

'Take care,' said Lil. 'Remember, the double agent could be *anyone*. Be on your guard, won't you?'

Carruthers tipped his hat to them. 'I'll see you back at the Bureau. Good luck with the journey back to London.'

'And good luck with Hamburg,' said Sophie.

'After everything you've done here, collecting a report is going to be a breeze,' Lil added.

He smiled at them both. 'Good hunting,' he said quietly, as he went on his way – for a moment sounding so much like the Chief that Lil wondered that she'd never made the connection before.

She slipped her arm through Sophie's, and the two of them walked on together. But Sophie was frowning to herself. 'Do you think we really should just hand over the notebook and the spyglass to the Chief?' she asked, voicing the question that had been on her mind ever since her conversation with Nakamura. 'I know those are our orders – but is it really the right thing to do? After all, we don't know for sure what he's planning to do with it. What if he's going to find this weapon and hand it straight over to the Army, for *them* to use for goodness knows what.'

Lil shook her head at once. 'Oh no. There's absolutely no way we're going to let him do a thing like that. *We* rescued the first two paintings and I've been tracking down more of them, while you've been here. *You* travelled all the way across Europe to get that notebook and spyglass, and nearly got yourself shot in the process. We've done the hard work – and I've had more than enough of the Chief keeping us in the dark. So when we get back to London, things are going to change. He can't walk all over us any longer. We're going to insist on knowing *exactly* what is going on. If we're going to keep working for the Bureau, he can't go on treating us like a couple of little girls who don't matter. I've had quite enough of that.'

Two hours later they were standing side by side on the deck of the St Catherine steamer, chugging slowly out into the Gulf of Finland, watching St Petersburg slip away behind them across the water. Seagulls swooped overhead, and the sun caught the blue-grey waves and tipped them gold. Lil felt a joyful bubble rise up inside her, as the glittering spray flew upwards. She'd done exactly what she had intended – and Sophie was with her again, just as she was supposed to be, and now they were heading for home together.

Beside her, Sophie was gazing back at St Petersburg, watching the vanishing city, reflected in the water. The birthday-cake palaces were growing smaller and smaller, becoming merely doll's houses. Bridges and towers retreated; the twinkling golden spires dwindled, until they seemed as small as a Rivière's jewel, lying against the satin of the sky.

'It's awfully strange to think I'll probably never see it again,' she said, pushing back the strands of hair the wind was blowing across her face.

'Never say never,' said Lil. 'After all, in our line of work, who knows where we might end up next? Perhaps we'll come back to St Petersburg again some day.'

'Perhaps we will,' said Sophie. 'It's not a place I ever thought I'd visit – but I must say, I'm awfully glad I did.'

'It's all been rather unexpected, hasn't it?' Lil agreed. 'I mean, who'd have thought I'd travel across Europe with Carruthers – or especially that we'd both end up joining the circus!'

Sophie laughed. 'But now the adventure is over and we can go home.'

'Oh, I'm not sure the adventure is ever *really* over,' said Lil. 'But yes – home. Just think of all the things we can do. Sleep in our own beds! Eat a jolly good dinner!'

'Go to Lyons Corner House for tea and buns.'

'Well, of course. That goes without saying.'

'But first we'll go to the Bureau. We've got work to do.'

'We need to tell the Chief what's what – and use the spyglass to examine those paintings – but what's more, we need to find out the truth about the double agent at the Bureau, who's working for the *Fraternitas*.'

'I'll tell you what else,' said Sophie. 'I want to investigate *Mr Gold*. Do you really think there's any way he could have a connection to Roberta Russell?'

But Lil didn't answer. Watching the swirling water had suddenly reminded her of standing on the deck of the boat to Ostend – and what she'd been thinking about then – and her mouth curved into a smile. 'Of course, before we go to the Bureau, we should go to Taylor & Rose and see the others,' she added more slowly. 'Everyone will be awfully glad to see you home safe, Sophie. And it will be so wonderful to see them too.'

Sophie looked at her sharply. Lil's face had taken on an uncharacteristically dreamy look – and could that be a faint blush on her cheeks? 'Anyone in particular that it will be *so wonderful* to see?' she asked archly, raising her eyebrows.

Lil blushed harder. 'Oh no,' she said, with a little laugh. 'You know, just everyone.'

'Everyone. Ah yes, I see,' said Sophie, with a smile.

The two friends stood in silence after that, feeling the wind against their cheeks. Here, the water was as smooth as glass, mirroring the sky arching overhead. It was hard to tell where the water ended and where the sky began, thought Sophie, staring out across the pale blue, back towards the city which was now little more than a shimmer of pink and turquoise and gold on the horizon. Together, they stood and watched as St Petersburg vanished away from them, twinkling in the mist like something from an already half-forgotten dream.

THE DAILY PICTURE

SHOCKING EVENTS IN ST PETERSBURG!

KILLER PERFORMANCE AT IMPERIAL GALA

Eyewitness account: Our reporter Miss R Russell is on the scene of a terrifying assassination attempt against the Tsar of Russia and his family. She relates first-hand the petrifying events that took place at the Imperial Gala performance of the Circus of Marvels (p. 2)

RUSSIAN POLICE FOIL PLOT

The Russian police have made a number of arrests in St Petersburg following the attack on the Tsar and his family. The plot is believed to have originated with a violent revolutionary group, who may also have been behind the assassination of Premier Stolypin in September. There is speculation that (continued p.4)

Portrait of Tsar Nicholas II with family. Photography Giuseppe Moforne

INTERNATIONAL NEWS

Bomb strikes in Libya: Italy drops bombs from aeroplane in world's first aerial bombing attack. More information follows on p 21

London Metropolitan Police report 'troubling' increase in gun violence in the East End's slums - p.29

FIRST MOVING STAIRCASE

The motion staircase on the London Underground to open at Earl's Court (p.13)

AUTHOR'S NOTE

Whilst this story and its characters are fictional, like the others in the *Sinclair's Mysteries* and *Taylor & Rose Secret Agents* series, this book takes some inspiration from real-life history.

For example, although the attack at the circus which appears in the story is fictional, the assassination of Russian politician Pytor Stolypin in a Kiev theatre at the start of the book was a real historical event. You may also spot some real historical figures in this story – from daring French pilot Elise Deroche, to British ambassador Sir George Buchanan – and of course Tsar Nicholas II and his family who, just six years after this book is set, met a sad end during the Russian Revolution.

Riviere's, the elegant jewellers, is inspired by the real-life Fabergé, founded by master jeweller Peter Carl Fabergé and best known for its famous Fabergé eggs. Today St Petersburg is home to the Fabergé Museum where you can see many of the wonderful treasures that Fabergé's jewellers made for the Tsar and the Imperial Court.

Although there was no real-life Circus of Marvels, circuses were popular entertainment in the late 19th and early 20th centuries. Large circuses such as the Barnum & Bailey Circus really did go all over the world on their 'grand tours', very often travelling by train. It was common for circuses to feature performing wild animals at this time, when attitudes to animal welfare were very different to ours today. At the time of writing, the use of wild animals in travelling circuses is banned in many countries, though not yet in the UK.

The Secret Service Bureau which appears in this story is (very) loosely inspired by the real Secret Service Bureau, which was set up by the British government in 1909. Initially very small, it soon grew and was divided into two divisions – one to deal with counter-espionage at home in Britain, and another focused on gathering intelligence abroad. Today we know these as 'MI5' and 'MI6'.

ACKNOWLEDGEMENTS

Huge thanks to brilliant Ali Dougal and the fantastic team at Egmont for all their support and enthusiasm for Sophie and Lil's latest exploits. In particular, special thanks to Sarah Levison and Sara Marchington, and to the absolute dream team of illustrator Karl James Mountford and designer Laura Bird for the stunning design.

Researching this book was quite a task, and although there are far too many to name here, I would like to acknowledge my debt to the writers and historians who have written about pre-revolutionary Russia. Thank you also to all those who kindly shared their stories and advice on visiting St Petersburg with me – in particular Katherine Rundell, Hazel Wigginton and Donald Lamont.

As always, enormous thanks go to my parents for all their support, and to my friends – especially Nina Douglas, who patiently helped me unravel a sticky problem involving crates and cellar windows. Thank you also to my husband Duncan, who for this book put up with a lot of long conversations about the intricacies of early 20th century Russian politics.

Spies in St Petersburg is dedicated to my wonderful agent and friend Louise Lamont, who went above and beyond the call of duty for this book, joining me on a research trip to Russia. As well as boldly leading the way around St Petersburg, walking over 60 miles in six days, and selflessly helping me taste all the Russian delicacies we could find, she even taught herself Russian for the occasion. Without her this book would certainly not be what it is (and I would quite possibly still be wandering St Petersburg in confusion, failing to decipher Cyrillic street signs and unsuccessfully trying to order cakes). Luckily I did managed to learn one very appropriate Russian word: Спасибо – thank you.

Finally, a very special thanks to all the booksellers, librarians, teachers and readers (of all ages) who have so enthusiastically embraced Taylor & Rose Secret Agents and this new phase of Sophie and Lil's adventures.